# Novus Intelligens
## Science Agents #2

Pierre V. Comtois

ISBN: 978-1-62420-494-4

## Credits

Cover Artist: Designs by Ms G
Edited by Sherry Derr-Wille

# Acknowledgement

Thanks go out to Gregorio Montejo for ideas and tech support.

# Prologue

Commissioned in 2267, the *St. Sebastian* was not exactly an old ship.

At twenty-two years, and kept in good maintenance, the battleship was in as solid a shape as it was the day it came off the slipways at the Proxima yards. Oh, it had seen her share of action against the Coalition but suffered no damage in those encounters. For those reasons, Captain Cameron Hendry was proud of her, irrespective of the fact the ship was his first command.

So, it was not without a certain sense of satisfaction that he roamed the corridors of the ship on his weekly inspection tour. He came fro m the aft weapons room where he'd found everything ship shape, cut through officer country, and was about to make an unexpected appearance in the mess room. On paper, he was due to inspect the ward room next, but he always considered it good policy to keep the crew guessing. He smiled. Cookie wouldn't like it. Even though little was actually cooked aboard ship with concentrates and meals ready to eat being standard fare, ovens were kept somewhat busy with fresher meals served in the officers' mess. Hendry shrugged. The benefits of rank. Besides, he figured he could use a cup of Cookie's synth coffee.

"Ten, hut," called an over eager ensign as he caught sight of the Captain stepping through the mess hatch. Instantly, a half dozen crewmen in their starched overalls stood to attention. "At ease, men," said Hendry, sketching a salute.

As the scattered men retook their seats at various tables, Cookie poked his head from the galley area.

"Wuzzat?" he said, bewilderedly before spotting Hendry. Instantly, he perked up, saluted. "Sorry, sir. Didn't expect you in till oh-nine-hundred."

"So, you're not ready for inspection yet, is that it?" asked Hendry, hands behind his back and leaning in to take a closer look at the steelite countertop.

"No, sir," replied Cookie, stepping more fully out from the galley. "We're always ready for inspection."

Without appearing to look around, Hendry was aware of the handful of orderlies in the kitchen and standing nervously about the mostly empty tables.

Hendry made a show of running a finger along the counter then pushing through the partition into the galley area itself. There, everything looked ship shape as he'd expected. He knew how proud Cookie was of his domain.

"My compliments, Chief," said Hendry at last. "But where do you keep the coffee?"

"Right here, sir," said Cookie, breaking into a smile.

A moment later, Hendry was sipping from the nipple of a vacuum container when he was interrupted by the ship's warning klaxon.

"Damn. Now what?"

As if in reply, the voice of his XO sounded over the ship's annunciators.

"Will the captain come to the command deck, please."

Hendry admired Lemire's ability to keep any emotion out of his voice when all he likely wanted to do was to shout excitedly for the commander.

Quickly, Hendry stepped through the mess hatch into the relative privacy of the outside corridor calling for the ship's computer to switch the annunciator to the captain's channel only.

"Talk to me, Lemire," he said, as he made his way to the command deck.

"Long range scanners picked up something, sir. Sparks is trying to raise it but so far there's no reply."

"Tell Sparks to keep on it," ordered Hendry as he stepped into the forward up capsule. A few seconds later, he was on the command deck and taking his chair amid the various tech stations. "Kill the klaxon, XO."

Lemire did so.

"Any reply from the target?" Hendry asked.

"Not a peep, sir," said the XO. "No call signs either. Looks like this might be it."

Hendry said nothing, thinking.

The *St. Sebastian* was ordered to the region of Eta Cassiopeia to investigate the disappearance of two Terran spacecraft in the remote system. When the first ship disappeared, a freighter hauling ore from M-12, a planetoid dragged in the wake of Eta Cassiopeia as it orbited around its weaker partner, it was a tragedy, but nothing more was suspected than some rare, though not impossible, natural catastrophe or technical malfunction. A search of the area yielded no clues. Piracy was considered but dismissed. Although there had been cases of space piracy in the past, they were strictly small time, local affairs. Anything of the sort taking place over nineteen million light years from Earth was simply not cost effective. A search in the region failed to find any sign of the missing freighter. After that, a second ship also failed to report in and tragedy became an emergency. The odds mounted astronomically indicating the disappearances were not natural or accidental. A more intensive search was required and that's where the *St. Sebastian* came in.

"Still no reply, Sparks?" asked Hendry.

"Nothing, sir."

"Battle stations!"

"Battle stations," repeated Lemire, his orders being conducted throughout the ship via annunciator. "This is not a drill. Repeat. This is not a drill. Battle stations!"

"Secure for silent running," ordered Hendry.

Under silent running, the ship's electronic signature on most wavebands would shrink to almost nothing rendering the *St. Sebastian* virtually invisible to ordinary sensor arrays. Special planes and flanges deployed around the outside of the hull would soften its configuration, changing the ship's outline, making it more difficult for standard wave lengths to find it.

As his crew took battle stations, Hendry considered the nature of the unidentified ship. At a final briefing held at Naval Command, it was suggested that if the missing freighters had been victims of hostile action rather than accident, it could be the Coalition.

Despite the recently signed treaty between the Terran Consortium and the Outer Arm Coalition that ended a decades old war, the two sides had not become friendly but simply retreated to their respective corners. On the surface, the peace held, but there was still much distrust by Terrans of the former enemy. Also, it was not unreasonable to suspect the Zhapoologani were behind the missing freighters either officially or via a renegade element who refused to acknowledge the war had ended.

Of course, there was also the other possibility.

A frisson of anticipation ran down Hendry's spine.

This could be a first contact situation. It was true the only aliens the Consortium encountered in the years since extra solar colonization was made possible had been the Zhapoologani and their associated races but that did not preclude others being out there beyond Terran space. Naval officers were trained in first contact protocol as well as technique against the possibility after all and Eta Cassiopeia did represent the limits of territory claimed by Earth.

"Has the target made any threatening moves?" asked Hendry.

"None, sir," replied Lemire. "We picked it up at the limit of our sensor range just holding its position."

"Has it tried to make contact?"

"No, sir."

"Then let's break the ice. Open formal communications with the target."

"Open formal communications, Sparks," ordered the XO. "Standard pulse."

"Aye, sir."

The comm shack directed a signal to the unknown vessel by way of letting it know there was no doubt the *St. Sebastian* was aware of its presence.

There was no reply.

"Not very friendly, are they, sir?" said Lemire.

"Let's see what we're dealing with," suggested Hendry.

Immediately, an image of the unknown vessel appeared on a number of screens around the command deck including the captain's own.

"I don't recognize the design," said the XO. "Doesn't match any

Coalition battlewagon I've ever seen."

Hendry agreed. The shadowy mass that confronted them a few thousand standard miles ahead bore no resemblance to any ship he'd ever seen. It seemed to be composed of a dark, light absorbing material that was all flat planes and obtuse angles.

"What do sensors make of it EO?" he asked.

"Not enough data to draw any conclusions, sir," reported the engineering officer from his console.

"Hm. What are you getting from the target, Sparks?" asked Hendry. "Anything at all?"

"No, sir. It's like they're on shutdown."

"Data feed?"

"Standard digitization signals, sir. Nothing else."

"That definitely eliminates a Coalition ship," concluded Lemire. "We'd recognize their signature."

"All stop," ordered Hendry.

"All stop," repeated the XO as engineering brought the slowly drifting *St. Sebastian* to a halt.

The two ships now hung motionless in space each waiting for the other to make a move. At least, that was how Hendry imagined it. Who really knew what his counterpart was thinking?

"Maybe their comm equipment is down," mused Hendry. "Engineering, try blinking our exterior lights. Standard SOS. Remember that one?"

"Seems I do from my old Trail Life days, sir," smiled the EO. "Here goes."

From an angle given him by optics outside the ship, Hendry saw the running lights dim then go on again several times.

There was no similar reaction from the opposing vessel.

"Well, they couldn't have missed that," declared the EO.

Just then, there was a flash from the target with beam of light striking toward the ship's aft spaces.

Hendry felt nothing but a premonition told him the beam hadn't missed its target.

Then the engineering officer's board lit up with a dozen emergency lights.

"Sir! Engineering is reporting our sub-photon engines are off line. We've been hulled!"

"Damage report," ordered Hendry. "Weapons hot!"

"Weapons hot," shouted the XO to the annunciator. Instantly, weapons ports opened around the hull of the ship and units were powered up.

"Sir. The engines are completely down. That particle beam pierced the ship like we weren't even there. Went right through the sub-photon matrix chamber and continued right on through to the other side."

"Through a triple layer of military grade tintinabulum?" said Lemire. "Impossible!"

"It's possible, all right," replied the EO. "Because someone just did it!"

"Well then, that's no Coalition ship!"

"Can the damage be repaired?" asked Hendry, ignoring Lemire but knowing the answer to his question even before he had the EO's reply.

"No way, sir. We can't repair damage like that on our own. We'll have to wait for help from Rigel base at least."

"That means we're dead in space," mumbled an ensign from where he was monitoring ship's life support.

"Belay that," ordered Hendry.

The young man was right, but it was the job of the captain to keep his crew focused in a battle situation, otherwise he risked panic and destruction of the ship at the hands of the enemy.

Less than a minute passed since the particle beam strike and with weapons on line, Hendry ordered an immediate strike back.

In response, a triple spread of Mark IX photon pulse cannon fire leapt from the *St. Sebastian* in the direction of the opposing vessel. Everyone on the command deck waited in tense silence as thrusters on the opposite side of the ship fired to counteract the force of the broadside and keep the battleship from drifting out of position.

"A hit!" shouted the weapons officer.

Immediately, there was a cheer from the command deck crew that Hendry quickly killed.

"WO, report!"

"All three volleys hit the target," said the weapons officer as he studied his instruments. "Can't tell if there was any damage…no, wait. Optics are showing extensive damage to the target's hull. Three holes in its starboard side."

Hendry finally allowed himself a smile.

"Hold it, sir. Sir, I don't know if my instruments are reading this right but…it looks as though the enemy is repairing the damage…fast! I can actually see the holes we made closing up!" Then, with rising panic in his voice, "Fire the cannons, sir! Fire again!"

"Fire at will," ordered Hendry.

"Fire at will," relayed the XO.

Immediately, a full barrage of pulse cannons let go in the direction of the opposing vessel even as Hendry ordered a real time view of the target. The image appeared in time for him to see multiple hits on the enemy craft knocking it off its beam.

Cheering broke out again around him but even as he watched the image, the stricken spacecraft righted itself with the massive damage inflicted by the pulse cannons being visibly repaired. Seeing that, Hendry's heart sank. The enemy withstood the *St. Sebastian*'s most deadly attack and was no doubt preparing for a counter strike. In addition, the *St. Sebastian* had no motive power and stabilizers were not powerful enough to offer defensive maneuverability.

*A sitting duck*, thought Hendry, before driving the thought from his mind.

Outside, now showing no damage, the still unidentified enemy ship began to close in on the *St. Sebastian*.

"Continue firing at will," ordered Hendry and as the cannons opened fire sending shudders through the ship, he swung to Sparks. "Send a hyper-bandwave pulse of all ship's activity to date to headquarters."

"Aye, sir," replied Sparks with no hint he knew what sending such a message meant.

The hyper-bandwave pulse would send every last byte of data from the *St. Sebastian* of all its day to day activities, internal communications, and soft/hardware status to Naval Command. Also included would be its meeting and final confrontation with the unidentified vessel including everything it discovered about its capabilities.

*At least headquarters will know what they'll be up against*, thought Hendry as the enemy ship continued to advance through the hail of cannon fire taking damage no ship had a right to expect and survive.

But this one did.

Finally, as the enemy vessel grew so large as to fill the forward view screens, it let loose with its own weaponry.

As it turned out, the hyper-bandwave message sent by the *St. Sebastian* was the last anyone ever heard of the veteran battleship.

# Chapter One
## *Science Agents*

Victor Conroi.

He repeated the name to himself.

Victor Conroi.

*It was still hard to get used to* thought Jules as he watched his wife swimming in the lagoon, her long, languid strokes barely disturbing the water's surface as if she was moving in slow motion like one of those old time flicks they'd seen at one of the resort's theaters.

Come to think of it, it was hard even to get used to the idea he and Mooney were married.

He sighed and closed his eyes against the artificial illumination ringing the duraglass dome enclosing Artemis Colony. The illumination could be adjusted to simulate a daytime cycle. Right now, it was simulating an early afternoon on Earth. However, the colony wasn't on Earth, it was on one of Jupiter's four major moons. In this case, Callisto. He and Mooney occupied one of its posh honeymoon suites complete with multi-level bungalow snuggled in an artificial jungle setting that included the lagoon Mooney was just now crossing.

The honeymoon suite was Mooney's idea from the start. Ever since passing through the Callistan resort shortly before they were wed, she talked of returning for something other than business. At the time, they'd traveled there on a case for Military Intelligence, tracking down Georg Heintzel, a renegade scientist who planned to exploit forbidden black hole technology ostensibly to give the Terran Consortium the edge in its long running war with the Outer Arm Coalition. Although his intentions were noble, the technology had been banned for a reason. Use of it had the very real potential to unleash forces that could threaten the entire galaxy. For that reason, science agent Jules Santros was assigned to put a stop to the mad plan.

Jules Santros.

It used to be his name before the black hole mission.

Now he was Victor Conroi.

It had been months since he acquired the new identity of Victor Conroi; a physicist who'd graduated from the Institute of Advanced Metaphysics and had been working in pure research for Military Intelligence Science Division which conveniently accounted for there being no history of his comings and goings since graduation. Still, changing one's identity wasn't like changing into a new 'suit of clothes. How could a man throw off his identity so easily? On the other hand, what was in a name after all? He was still Jules Santros inside, wasn't he? It was what he kept telling himself but couldn't help feeling his identity was tied up in his name. Without it, was he still the same Jules? Sure, his mind was the same, his body was the same but did he keep his own soul? Or was it split between himself and the other Jules? Did he even have one? But as he'd learned, it didn't pay to think too deeply about such things because he suspected that someday it might compel him to do something desperate. As he'd done before, Jules made a conscious decision to find something else to think about.

The name change was made necessary due to how the black hole mission had concluded, he reminded himself. Something he couldn't really complain about as it was indirectly his fault and he'd wound up with Mooney as his wife.

Jules opened his eyes to watch Mooney's slim form slice through the temperature controlled water. She'd chosen to go swimming *sans habillier* as the French might say, and he was again reminded he ought to have had no regrets at the way things turned out.

But he did.

Regrets and a lingering feeling of guilt continued to nag at the edges of his conscience because in marrying Mooney, he'd left behind another woman, Joan, whom he'd loved dearly in another life.

Closing his eyes again, Jules thought back to that day aboard the *Constitution*. He and Mooney had been aboard, having finally run down

Heintzel at PER-734, a collapsed star where the renegade intended to prove his theory regarding black hole technology. Luckily, that plan was foiled by Henitzel himself who fired a pulse-pistol at the radical cube he believed could contain the energies generated by the artificial black hole he created. Unfortunately, the structure wasn't as firm as he believed, and a rupture resulted.

By all rights, Jules should have died there as the ship that housed the experiment began to collapse around him, but a last minute save by one of Heintzel's colleagues reversed time placing Jules back aboard the *Constitution* and safe from the eventual disaster. The only drawback was that in being saved, Jules had actually been duplicated. There was now the Jules that existed before the rewind and the Jules that was plucked from that first run through.

After consideration, Jules decided not to let the other Jules know of his existence. That Jules was every bit as genuine as he was and looked forward to returning to Joan just as he did. To avoid complications, Jules chose to deny himself that satisfaction and let the other Jules and Joan go on with their lives. He would follow a different path with a new identity. A path, he had to admit, made easier by the presence of Mooney.

Mooney, 'Manda Mooney, had been an agent for the Consortium's Exterior Ministry assigned to keep tabs on him as he hunted Heintzel. At one point, she'd saved his life and was forced to reveal herself. After that, they decided to join forces. Along the way, Jules' feelings for her developed from a purely professional attitude to a more caring one, so by the time the Heintzel situation was over, he'd definitely felt conflicted over his affections for her and those for Joan. Still, it would've been no contest if he'd had to choose between the two. Fortunately, and to this day, he still wasn't sure if that was the right word, the dilemma was solved when he found himself one of two Jules.

The sudden sound of a splash roused him and when he opened his eyes again, he saw the spreading ripples where Mooney had dived to the bottom of the lagoon. The water was clear as glass and where the light was right, he caught glimpses of her body as it undulated among the rocks.

As much as he understood the necessity of his action in letting the other Jules go to Joan, he continued to harbor feelings of guilt for what his mind told him was an abandonment of his wife. Feelings he hadn't hesitated in confiding to Mooney who sympathized and worked patiently with him to see through the problem and rationalize his actions. As a result, feelings of guilt greatly subsided allowing he and Mooney to be wed, but he wondered if they would ever completely disappear. Was his still thinking of her as "Mooney" in his mind instead of 'Manda a result of that guilt? He didn't know. He referred to her as Mooney when they first partnered and kept calling her that after they became more than professional colleagues, turning it into a pet name.

"C'mon in, the water's fine," called Mooney, temporarily breaking the surface of the lagoon.

"Not right now," replied Jules from his somno-recliner.

Mooney shrugged and dove beneath the surface again.

*In some ways, Mooney is actually a better fit for me as a partner than Joan was.* The biggest difference being that Mooney wanted and expected a family some day. Something Joan refused to talk about and Jules quietly disagreed with.

He'd resigned from his position with the Military Intelligence Science Division in order to spend more time with her in the field as a xeno-archeologist. He supposed in the back of his mind, his real purpose was to somehow move her in a more domestic direction. There was no way of telling at this late date if spending more time with each other would have succeeded in moving the needle, so it was useless to speculate. With Mooney, at least, there was no need for such speculation. Sure, he was still connected with the Science Division having returned after successfully concluding the Heintzel mission while she'd since managed a transfer from the Exterior Ministry to the Division, but those associations were definitely tenuous at the moment. Neither of them were on the clock and since their marriage some months ago, hadn't heard from Henri Leclerc, director of MI.

Which was fine with Jules.

It was Leclerc who came up with the Victor Conroi sobriquet.

Besides not being used to the name, Jules wasn't even sure he liked it. It sounded too much like the standard cover name it really was. But Mooney got a kick out of it, something she often teased him about. She seemed to take particular delight in using it in public places, putting an inflection in her voice, making it sound lascivious. They'd received more than one disapproving glance from eavesdroppers as a result, something that pleased Mooney no end.

Jules couldn't help smiling at that.

Another difference with Joan. His former wife could be playful but it'd been a learned response over years of marriage. It came naturally to Mooney who'd taken to him quickly during the Heintzel affair and made their professional partnership a natural precursor to a more intimate one.

Another splash and laughter from Mooney shook him from his mood. Or was it the effect of the somno-recliner? Whatever its origin, he determined to throw it off with quick action.

Leaping to his feet, he shucked off the bathrobe he'd been wearing and joined Mooney in the lagoon by way of a clean dive that knifed through the cool water leaving barely a ripple behind. Arcing his body, he opened his eyes and the clarity of the water allowed him to spot his wife right off. Being red haired, her skin was naturally pale, appearing milky white against the formacrete bottom of the lagoon. At the moment, his decision to enter the water took her by surprise and so his approach from beneath her was still unexpected.

Jules took a moment to admire Mooney's shapely form as her legs scissored the water and her long hair floated in a red halo around her head. In a flash of memory, he recalled their first visit to Callisto, an outer moon of Jupiter that was about the size of Mercury. Actually, Artemis Colony, located on its crater scarred surface. The colony was notorious, depending on your point of view, throughout the Consortium as a honeymooners' paradise. With its series of streams fed from an underground ocean and warmed by the reflected light of nearby Jupiter, it was theoretically possible to swim your way through the whole colony, moving from one pool to another all protected under the largest free-standing dome in the Consortium. Altogether, the Artemis Colony covered over a hundred square miles of the moon's surface, but within the dome, made of the strongest polymers in the duraglass family, visitors could enjoy every kind of entertainment, a list that Mooney fully covered in her sales pitch to Jules.

"Callisto isn't just any old resort getaway," she'd insisted. "Ever hear of the jungle pool complex? For the right price, you can spend a week in there without ever meeting another human being. Just swimming and lounging under the foliage with that big colorful planet hanging over you like a huge balloon. And then there's the nightclubs, the restaurants, casinos, theaters, tours of the inner moons, the fast 'cars and slow dancing at the famous Jovian Lounge. And I won't even mention the fully equipped honeymoon suites where I'm told some couples stay and don't come out for weeks."

"Okay, okay. I'm sold!" Jules replied but hadn't needed the hard sell.

Mooney herself would make even the icy barrenness of Pluto a fun place to be. A fact he was quickly reminded of as he reached out to a slim ankle, the one with the little gold chain around it, and gave it a playful tug.

Instantly, Mooney spun around, doubled over, and sped downward, her hands reaching out for him.

Jules pulled back, tried to turn, but he wasn't fast enough.

Mooney took him by the shoulders and, forcing him down, nimbly climbed upward until she could place her feet atop his shoulders, and used them to thrust herself to the surface.

Floundering amid a school of silvery fish that scattered at his desperate movements to regain his equilibrium, Jules found the bottom of the lagoon and sprung upward, rocketing after Mooney and catching her on the surface. They breeched, laughing, Mooney's arms pinned in Jules' embrace. There was silence then as Jules pressed his lips against his wife's, stifling her laughter. For the next few seconds, they hung there in the tropical waters, as if it was the first night of their honeymoon and not the third week.

"You call this a romantic embrace?" asked Mooney at last, her arms still held helplessly at her sides.

"It's the only way I could be sure of holding on to you," smiled Jules. "You're as slippery as an eel."

"Oh, I haven't been as difficult to catch as all that these past few weeks, have I?"

Jules had to admit that she hadn't.

Taking advantage of his distraction, Mooney squirmed free and ducked beneath the surface. Jules followed and for the next few minutes played underwater tag with Mooney's white form always tantalizingly out of reach.

Finally, they mutually agreed to call it quits and head for shore.

"You really put me through my paces that time," said Jules, still out of breath.

"You want some of this, you've got to earn it," laughed Mooney, completely unselfconscious in her nakedness. "Otherwise, you wouldn't appreciate it as much."

"I appreciate it, I appreciate it!" laughed Jules, stripping off his trunks and shrugging back into his robe.

"You still object to taking one of these fully equipped honeymoon suites?" asked Mooney, picking up a comb and running it through her hair.

"Well, I was right about it being expensive..."

"MI picked up the tab so you have nothing to complain about. Now, was I right or was I right?"

Jules admitted it was a good idea. Looking around, he admired the enormous expense the investors in the Artemis Colony put into it. The enormous dome placed over a series of million-year-old impact craters was only the most obvious element of the resort. There was also the massive landscaping work that had to be done once the dome was in place; reshaping the craters to conform to architects' plans, tapping into the subterranean oceans for use in filling the series of artificial lakes in the common areas and pools in the private suites, pumping out the native carbon dioxide that made up the moon's atmosphere and replacing it with oxygen, importing hundreds of plant species from all over the Consortium to create an incredible jungle environment dotted with hotels, casinos, entertainment complexes all connected with white ribbons of smartways where self-driving vehicles whisked guests from point to point.

Three weeks before, he and Mooney, under the names Victor and 'Manda Conroi, registered at the resort's main desk and been shown to their private suite: a quiet lagoon surrounded by impenetrable jungle foliage overlooked by a shaped formacrete "lovers' bungalow" that climbed up the side of a rocky cliff. The bedroom unit was placed such that if they wanted to, the honeymooners could step out the sliding auto doors and dive into the lagoon, a benefit that Mooney often took advantage of.

"Now, what about tonight?" asked Mooney, finishing with her hair and sitting down to examine a ding in her toenail.

"Well, I thought we could stay in and relax…"

"At Artemis Colony?" demanded Mooney. "Haven't you heard this is the colony that never sleeps?"

"Seems I've been told that before."

Mooney stood up and came over to him, draping her arms around his neck. "I've got an idea."

"Yes?"

"How would you like to go on a little EVA later on?"

"An EVA? I thought we were on a honeymoon, not at work."

"It's not what you think," said Mooney.

"Since when is anything to do with wearing a spacesuit not a bother?"

"When it involves Lover's Ledge," replied Mooney as if she'd succeeding in trapping him into something.

"Huh?"

"C'mon! Don't play coy with me. You must have gone through the resort info-pads we've got lying around the suite."

"Well, no," admitted Jules, resting his forearms on Mooney's hips. "As a matter of fact, I've been letting you handle the activity schedule for this trip."

"Hmph. Well, Lover's Ledge is only one of the most beautiful experiences the solar system has to offer anywhere…"

"Now you're sounding like one of those tour guide come ons at the main desk."

Mooney pushed herself out of his arms. "You're not being serious."

"Just joking! What's on your mind?"

"There's an EVA walk scheduled for tonight to go out to Lover's Ledge where there's a spectacular view of Jupiter as it comes up over the horizon."

"That does sound interesting." Jules had to admit.

"Good. We'll go to dinner at the Starlight first, and then…"

"Uh, mind if we just have dinner here for tonight? I'd just like to relax before going on an EVA."

Mooney softened and smiled. "Sure, honey. Didn't know I was wearing you down."

"Wearing me down, huh?" Jules reached for his wife but she dodged just out of his reach leading him on a chase that wound about the deck furniture, up to the second level of the cottage, and somehow into the bedroom.

# Chapter Two
*Lover's Ledge*

Sometime later, Jules dabbed at the corners of his mouth with a napkin and leaned back in his chair.

"Good dinner," he said, satisfied.

They'd just finished a meal consisting of leek gratin, topped with mozzarella, and fried eggs with mustardy bread crumbs. Dessert had been tiramisu made with ladyfingers and mascarpone cheese.

Jules reached over for the wine, a vintage 2008 Dos Cabezas Toscano red blend from old Sonoita, Arizona, and refilled Mooney's glass before doing the same for his own.

"One thing I have to say for these resorts," said Jules, setting down the bottle. "They don't stint on the extras."

"We're definitely getting our money's worth," agreed Mooney, sipping contentedly at her wine. "Or should I say, MI is?"

They both laughed at the little joke.

The meal had been prepared in one of Artemis Colony's many real kitchens where food was made ready using real meat and real vegetables cooked by real chefs. Sure, home made food from 'wave dispensers was good and could hardly be told apart from the genuine article even by connoisseurs, but tasting and knowing were two completely different things.

Tonight, Mooney chose their meal from the menu available at Chez Denis, one of the colony's several French restaurants. Delivery was made about an hour later using the restaurant's door to door service with a maître d' setting the table and arranging the meal in accordance with French table manners. In light of Mooney's preference on not getting dressed before they were due to leave for the pre-EVA tutorial, Jules decided to spare the maître d' embarrassment by dismissing him with a generous tip.

At the moment, Mooney sat in her robe, her legs curled up in such a way that the fleecy cloth fell away displaying what seemed to Jules to be an endless expanse of white thighs. Inwardly, he felt vast relief at his decision to get rid of the maître d'.

"It's hard to imagine this wine was bottled in 2008, shipped across three hundred-sixty-five million miles between Earth and Jupiter, only to wind up here and now for the two of us to enjoy," remarked Mooney, swirling the red liquid around in her cup and watching its film drain back down only a little more slowly than it would have back on Earth.

"I never thought of it that way before," mused Jules, himself lounging in shirt and shorts.

"Penny for your thoughts, as the saying goes," said Mooney after a short silence.

"Was just thinking how much of a near thing it was that a simple moment like this, drinking this wine, the complicated series of events both historical and technological, needed to arrive at this point, almost didn't happen. It could have all ended with that last mission."

Wary when her new husband's thoughts veered in the direction of that crisis moment, Mooney sought to defuse the situation.

"But the crisis was averted," she said, very deliberately wriggling her toes. "You saved us. Not only from possible cosmic catastrophe in a black hole event, but from defeat in the war with the Coalition."

"Those are good things, I suppose," he said.

"Darling," said Mooney, "there's no 'suppose.' It's the truth. You should be exultant...I am. We saved the Coalition, the entire human race. You've got to stop dwelling on might have beens and concentrate on what is." She threw her feet down and came around the table to his side, placed her arms around his neck and kissed him. "And what is, is me. I love you, isn't that enough?"

"Plenty," said Jules, pulling her around onto his lap. "More than the Consortium, more than the whole human race, more than...well, more than anything, none of it would've mattered if it weren't for you."

She hugged him close then, burying her face in his neck. She knew what he was thinking. Of Joan, of his "other" wife, of whether walking away from her had been the right thing to do. The question would always remain between them, but it was one Mooney was certain would grow less important over time. There was nothing inappropriate in the situation. There were two Jules now, both totally equal and the same. Only one could have returned to Joan. The only problem to be reconciled was that her Jules still felt like he was the "original" Jules who abandoned his duty to his wife. But he wasn't. He was his own person now, just as if he'd been widowered. It was something they'd discussed often in the past, before and after their marriage and something, Mooney was sure, they would continue to revisit in the future. It was her fervent hope however, as time passed, Jules would see the logic of his decision and the need for him to have forged ahead with a new chapter in his life.

"So, isn't it about time we got ready for the EVA?" he asked, nose still buried in Mooney's silky hair. "Wouldn't want to miss Jupiter rise, now would we?"

"Nope," said Mooney, slipping from his lap and modestly arranging her robe. "Be ready in a snap." Pausing only to drain the wine from her cup, she skipped off back into the cottage.

With less time needed to prepare, Jules took a few minutes to savor the rest of his wine before following at a more leisurely pace.

It was about an hour later when they exited the cottage, walking arm in arm along the flowered path leading around to the stall where they kept their assigned speedcar. Somewhere behind the dense foliage across the smartway lay another private suite occupied by newlyweds, Mag and Toma Tristom, a couple they met at the resort's orientation session and had a few double dates with since.

"I called Toma to find out if she and Mag were game for EVA," informed Mooney. "Seems they weren't busy tonight."

"Surprising," grinned Jules, who received an elbow in the side for his trouble.

"Here they come now," said Mooney, waving to the couple as they emerged from among the foliage across the way. "Hey, Toma!"

The couple crossed the smartway with Toma nodding in the direction of their speedcar. "You guys driving tonight?"

"Only right since you drove the last couple times."

"Hop in," said Jules, ordering the 'car's lift top doors to rise.

"The north hatch," prompted Mooney when they were all settled.

Immediately, the 'car slid smoothly from the stall and unhesitatingly onto the empty smartway, moving north on the white ribbon of hidden electronics as it wound through the pseudo-jungle.

"This place never ceases to amaze me," remarked Mooney, looking out at the passing foliage. "That they could carve out a paradise like this out of such an inhospitable environment."

"It's easy when you have the right tools," replied Toma. "As well as proper planning."

"Terra forming and manipulating alien environments is becoming the norm in Consortium space," added Mag. "It means the pressure to keep expanding to more systems will ease. The need to find planets that can sustain human life won't be so important."

"The less friction we have with people like the Zhapoologani, the better, I say," said Jules.

"And how," agreed Mag. "I was on SR-22 when one of their battle groups struck the colony. It was a close call until some of our ships managed to run them off."

"You were on SR-22?" asked Mooney, interested. "That's in the Sirius system, isn't it?"

"Yeah. Was there as a consulting agronomist. Atmosphere had just reached optimum and they were ready to introduce some of the hardier grains. In fact, that was where I met Toma."

"Really?" said Mooney, playful suspicion in the tone of her voice. "Pretty remote out there, isn't it?"

Toma laughed. "We weren't exactly stuck on a desert planetoid or anything. I was there doing essentially the same thing Mag was, consulting. Only I was a landscape engineer and was working with the colonial admin on what trees and grasses and such like would work on SR-22. Sirius A is a much stronger sun than Sol, so it's important to get the plantings right."

"Is that how you got the job here at Artemis?"

"Um hm. My work on SR-22 helped," said Toma modestly. "But this was a plum assignment."

"Worth it too," said Mag. "They included a free suite in her contract."

"Could never afford it on a landscaper's salary."

"Nor an agronomist's," agreed Mag. "But then, Toma's reputation preceded her."

"Is that why you married her?" joked Jules. "Because she could save you a bundle on a honeymoon?"

"It helped," smiled Mag, looking over to his wife, a tall, athletic looking brunette.

By then, the speedcar took them from the pseudo-jungle to the peripheries of the colony where admin buildings, environmental control apparatus, maintenance garages, and public speedcar lots dominated the view. The 'car slowed and took a few turns before coming to a halt before a non-descript 'crete structure built right up against the side of the dome's foundation. A sign reading EVA Tours was placed over the door.

"Well, this is where we get out," said Mag.

The men exited the 'car on either side before helping the ladies out. Jules ordered the vehicle to place itself in standby mode and watched it slide over to the nearest lot to wait for their return. Inside the building, it was cool and bright. A small knot of tourist types stood waiting by the information desk.

"Guess we weren't the only ones with this idea," Jules whispered in Mooney's ear.

As they joined the group, they caught the youthful tour guide's introductory remarks as he outlined the night's event.

"Good evening," said the man in typical upbeat tour guide fashion. "My name's Todd and tonight, you're all in for a real treat. Something you can't catch anywhere else in Consortium space. You can travel all the way to Procyon or Proxima Centauri, or even Sirius but you won't find a sight as spectacular as Jupiter rise right here in the good old Sol system. Which, I'm assuming, is what you're all here for?" Pause for chuckles at his little joke. "Jupiter rise is due in about," he paused again to check his chronometer, "two hours Terran time. It'll take you about that long to walk over to the overlook at the Marinaris Escarpment, what we at Artemis Colony prefer to call Lover's Ledge, where you'll get the best view. So, let's not waste any more time and get down to basics. Anyone here *not* familiar with EVA routine? The electro-polerization process or what we call

PE for short? Or 'suit safety, etcetera?"

As usual in such situations, people began looking around to make sure they wouldn't be the first to raise their hands but eventually they came up and as it turned out, most present had not had any such experience.

"Well then, it's a good thing I set aside enough time for a tutorial before we open the hatch," said the tour guide. "Although there really is nothing to it, hardly more than the routine safety instructions you all received on the rocket to Callisto, there are still a few things that it won't do any harm to review including the fact that our 'suits are equipped with the latest electro-polarization technology for your convenience. Might I ask those of you with experience in EVA help me out a little? The sooner we get everyone up to speed, the sooner we get you out the hatch."

The guide's spiel was a little too bright and peppy for Jules' tastes, but he and Mooney complied with his request for help. The guide was right in how simple and safe use of EVA equipment had become, so there were very little excursionists needed to hear beyond assurances that it was all perfectly safe and that it was virtually impossible for anything to go wrong with their 'suits. A good time and a spectacular view of one of the seventeen wonders of the Consortium was guaranteed for all.

Finally, everyone agreed they were comfortable with the resort issued EVA 'suits and were sufficiently aware of their operation.

"All right then, let's don our helmets and make sure they're secured to the neck ring. Remember, we'll be using the buddy system so make sure your partner double checks your 'suit before we exit the dome."

Jules went over Mooney's 'suit and found nothing to concern him then she did the same for him. The final step was activating the PE function that immediately stiffened the fabric, creating a bulky EVA unit from what looked like a baggy, ill fitting 'suit. Since everyone was already separated into twosomes, there was no odd man out.

"No problems? Fine. Step over to the air lock now." Todd waved the half dozen or so couples over to a big hatch that opened with an audible hiss. "That's it. File in one by one. Watch your step there."

Once inside the crowded space of the lock, the guide moved to the back and closed the inner hatch. "Now if everyone will turn in this direction, I'll open the outer door."

There was a slow shuffle of bodies as everyone turned and when the outer hatch opened, Jules heard a collective gasp come over the 'comm link in his helmet. The reaction was understandable. Their first view of the surface of Callisto was impressive. Constructed within an ancient impact crater, Artemis Colony lay among a riot of jumbled stones and rocky outcrops through which a path had been blasted by engineers leading to the crater wall. There, in the near distance, Jules could see the ribbon of the path as it zig zagged up the side of the crater to the rim where the glow of a soon to rise Jupiter spilled over the edge. Overhead, the stars were already being dimmed by the reflected light of the solar system's largest planet.

"Just imagine what Jupiter rise itself will look like," the tour guide was saying. "Now, again, just watch your step getting out of the air lock. Very good. Wait for me a moment while I close the hatch. All right now, as I told you earlier, follow me, single file. We'll be going along this path and up the side of the crater. And don't be deceived by the height. Remember, Callisto isn't quite as large as Earth so gravity is a bit lighter. We'll be up to the top before you know it."

As the group began to walk, their 'suits, that felt bulky and cumbersome inside the dome, now seemed easier to move around in, comfortable even.

"How you doing Vic?" asked Mooney, using Jules' assumed name while in public.

"Not bad. Hardly what I'd call romantic though."

"Just wait till we get to the overlook," promised Mooney over their private comm channel.

"Not much chance of a little togetherness with a helmet on," said Jules, a smile in his voice.

"Then enjoy the experience as a matter of scientific curiosity," replied Mooney, gripping the handrail that ran along the trail up the side of the crater. The walk up the steep trail was nowhere as difficult as it looked. True to the guide's word, Callisto's lighter gravity made the climb a snap and in a remarkably short time, Jules was topping the ridge. There, the glow of the approaching planet was more obvious than ever. It seemed ready to break over the horizon any minute.

"Don't worry folks," assured the guide as if reading Jules' mind, "we have plenty of time to reach Lover's Ledge before Jupiter rise. Remember, Jupiter has two and half times the mass of all the other planets in the solar system combined. It's a gas giant so most of it's composed of hydrogen and helium with only a relatively small rocky core. As it rises over the horizon, you'll get a good look at the famous red spot, a massive storm scientists believe has been raging for at least four hundred years."

By that point, Jules wasn't really listening. Instead, he was looking around, admiring the view. Callisto's surface was beautiful in a shattered, blasted way. Behind him, sunk within the crater, nestled the curving dome of Artemis Colony, its contents only vaguely discernible through its duraglass surface. In the opposite direction, down slope from the crater's rim, a narrow road threaded its way among the rocks toward a distant vehicle park where a score of tractors and other maintenance equipment sat in the freezing cold of Callisto's poisonous atmosphere.

"How much of the sky will Jupiter fill when it's fully risen?" someone was asking over the public comm channel.

"Not too long ago, Callisto's rotation was tidally locked to its orbit around Jupiter, so that the same hemisphere always faced inward," explained the guide as the group continued its way across the rocky surface. "But about a hundred years ago, there was a change that still puzzles cosmologists, resulting in Callisto's being able to rotate on its axis. That little stellar mystery may be the bane of scientists, but it's been a benefit to everyone else because it means we have the unique phenomenon of Jupiter rise over Callisto to enjoy. Oh, and when fully risen, Jupiter will fill approximately ninety percent of the visible sky."

There were excited mumbles from the various couples all around including Mooney.

"Hear that, Vic?" she asked, picking up her step.

"Can't wait to see it," admitted Jules.

The rest of the walk passed uneventfully as the group made its way up to the Marinaris Escarpment and finally reached the overlook called Lover's Ledge. There, an area among the rocks had been cleared with stones arranged around about for use as places to sit. Jules and Mooney joined the other couples in finding a spot where they could sit side by side facing the horizon where the faintest hint of brighter light was just peeking above a line of distant hills.

Looking around, Jules noticed their guide retreated to a discreet distance so as not to intrude on whatever romantic moments might transpire among his charges as a result of seeing the seventeenth wonder of the Consortium.

Soon, the suggestion of light grew in intensity until it could definitely be identified as a large stellar object rising from behind Callisto. There were murmurings from among the crowd as Jules listened over the public comm channel in his 'suit. He couldn't blame them. The slow reveal was dramatic and even suspenseful.

"I think this is going to be more interesting than I thought," he said to Mooney, captured in the circle of his arm as she reclined next to him.

"So, you changed your mind about coming out here?"

"I never said I didn't want to come."

"But you were pretty unenthusiastic about it."

"I was not," insisted Jules, giving Mooney a little shake.

"Where's Mag and Toma?" asked Mooney, moving her head about inside her helmet.

Jules looked around then identified the couple by the big red numerals placed on the backs of their 'suits. "Over there, on the right."

"They look like they're more into each other than Jupiter rise," observed Mooney.

"I guess they fell for this Lover's Ledge business."

"Not like us, we're too sophisticated."

"Okay, okay. I admit to feeling a twinge of something. But it sure is frustrating when the most we can do is click our helmets together."

Mooney smiled alluringly from the safety of her 'suit. "Think you can hold that feeling for a few hours till we get back to the suite?"

Before Jules could answer, there was a collective gasp from the public comm channel as the others reacted to their first good look at Jupiter as it continued to rise over Callisto. There were now recognizable striations visible running diagonally across the emerging face of the planet. And here at this distance, the colors were far richer, far more vivid than could ever be seen in static photos, digital imagery, or even real time video.

"Wow," was all Jules could muster as the full size of the emerging planet began to make itself evident.

Rising faster than an earthly sunrise, the Jovian world quickly grew to dominate the night sky and soon, the famous red spot came into view.

"This is amazing," declared Jules, awed as they were bathed in the reflected light of Jupiter. "This was so worth it!"

So impressive was the sight, even Mooney had nothing to say as she clung to his arm in silent wonder.

Elsewhere about them, others could not sit still and rose to their feet, craning their necks inside their helmets to take in the entire sight.

Finally, after a half hour of communal silence, the entire disk of Jupiter was visible above Callisto's horizon and hung impossibly huge before them, movement within the red spot actually noticeable at that close proximity.

Just then, the sound of the guide clearing his throat came over the public comm channel.

"I'm sure you folks will agree Jupiter rise is everything our publicity department claims," he said, approaching the group from where he'd sat not far away. "But now I think we'd better head back before our 'suits' oxygen supply runs out."

With obvious reluctance, the sightseers began to cluster toward the head of the trail with here and there, men giving their spouses' a helping hand up. As they made their way single file back along the path, many could not resist looking back for last looks at the impressive sight. By the time they reached the foot of the escarpment, Jupiter was directly overhead and moving rapidly to its setting position on the opposite side of Callisto.

"Wasn't that fantastic?" asked Mooney over the private channel. "I'd heard how incredible it was but never dreamed it would be so impressive."

"Have to agree with you," said Jules, watching his feet as he began negotiating the down slope into the impact crater. "I've seen some impressive sights around the Consortium and beyond, but it's pretty nice to know you don't have to travel very far from Earth to see one of the most amazing of all."

As a matter of habit, Jules checked his 'suits' oxygen gauge to make sure nothing was amiss and figured the guide planned the excursion just right. They ought to reach the dome's outer hatch with about five minutes to spare.

"He must have done this plenty of times before," said Mooney, noting Jules' concern.

"Just a walk in the park," replied Jules.

Presently, the group was gathered before the big hatch doorway where the guide was using his laser key to get in. There was something wrong with the key apparently because the guide decided to put it away and flipped the lid off a manual finger pad affixed to the side of the dome's foundation instead. He punched in the code that would open the way to the inner air lock, but his bulky glove was making it difficult. He shook his hand and punched in the code a second time. Now his body language indicated he was losing patience. He tried it a third time but the hatch remained closed.

"Any problem, Todd?" asked Jules over the public comm channel.

"Neither my laser key nor the entry code seem to be working," said the guide. "Must be a glitch some place."

Jules heard him asking his 'suit comp to connect him with entry control inside the dome. A pause. He asked again.

"I'm not getting through," said the guide, not without some concern in his voice.

"Let me try," said Jules, switching from the public channel to dome communications. "Connect me with entry control."

Jules listened a moment but there was only dead air. He made the request again. Nothing.

"How do you access the 'suit comp's meta-functions?" he asked the guide.

"I'm doing that now," the guide said. "I...I don't like this."

"What?" asked Jules, aware that the rest of the group was growing restless with the exchange.

"The HUD is showing no connection with entry control," said the clearly worried guide. "The entire comm 'net's dead."

"Try the other channels. Security, garage, maintenance, robot control..."

"Nothing!" shouted the guide, in desperation turning to try

punching in the digital entry code again.

"What's wrong?" asked someone over the public channel. "Why doesn't the hatch open?"

Jules checked his oxygen supply again. Only a few minutes left.

"Vic?" asked Mooney, moving closer to Jules.

Jules, tight lipped, shook his head.

"We're locked out!"

# Chapter Three
*Breathless*

Jules had to hand it to Mooney. No panic. No hysteria. No pleas that he must be wrong. She just checked her own gauge to verify how much oxygen she had left.

"Three and half minutes left," she reported. "With another ten minutes emergency supply."

"Not enough. If we can't get in through this hatch, it's a long walk to the east or west hatches."

"Maybe we can start and eventually come into local receiving range of the east or west comm channels? This might just be a satcom dead zone."

"No go. It's not a matter of not getting a signal. The dome comm units in these 'suits are dead."

"Then what?"

Before Jules could answer, panic set in among their fellow excursionists. The public comm channel was filled with excited voices, each trying to be heard over the others. Among them was the voice of the guide as he pleaded for understanding. It wasn't his fault that the hatch didn't open.

Jules put a stop to it by the simple expedient of sending a static charge through the public comm channel that crackled painfully in everyone's ears.

"Quiet down, everyone," he said when the hubbub had subsided. "We're not going to get anywhere if we panic."

"So what do you suggest we do?" someone asked, not unreasonably.

"Maybe if we bang on the hatch with a tool or something, someone inside will hear it," suggested another.

"You might try that," soothed Jules. "But I doubt it could be heard through the air lock."

30

"What then?"

Jules thought for a moment. "Todd. What about an emergency oxygen outlet?"

The guide shook his head. "There isn't any. The dome was built before the new safety regs were adopted."

Jules raised his hands, forestalling a new round of anxious protests.

"There's only one other thing we can do," he said. "But it'll be a near run thing."

"It's not like we have much choice," someone observed.

"Right. Okay. Over the rim up there," Jules pointed back up the trail leading out of the crater. "There's a vehicle park with a dozen heavy tractors and a couple crew haulers. If we can reach those, we can seal ourselves in the crew haulers and use their life support systems to fill them with oxygen. Once we do that, we'll be able to breathe for hours at least and use the vehicles' comm equipment to contact security within the dome."

"That's a great idea," said someone. "What are we waiting for?"

"Everyone check your oxygen gauges," advised Jules. "We'll all likely need to switch over to our emergency supplies right about now. Do it."

As the group did as he asked, Mooney switched to the private comm channel. "Do you think we can make it to the park?"

"It'll be close," Jules admitted. "Real close. I'll be counting on you help me keep everyone moving. Keep their spirits up. Even in this lighter gravity, they'll be exerting themselves. It'll mean heavier breathing. Using up more oxygen."

Mooney nodded.

Switching back to the public comm channel, Jules said, "Is everyone switched over?" There was a chorus of affirmative replies. "Good. Now listen carefully. Every 'suit has a Y valve attached to the oxygen supply. Couples stay together. If either one of you runs out of oxygen before the other, the one with the remaining oxygen will have to share. You do that by accessing the auxiliary tube from your equipment pouch..." he showed them where it was located on his own 'suit, "...attaching it to your own Y valve and then to your partner's. Flip the directional switch here. It'll reroute your oxygen supply allowing you to share. Hopefully, though, that won't be necessary, but we have to keep it in mind. If Todd runs out of oxygen, a couple who isn't sharing yet will have to help him out." Jules didn't ask for volunteers, but the guide looked relieved. "Okay. We have about two miles to go. Half of that distance up the side of the crater so let's get started."

Going first, Jules led the way up the incline, setting a brisk but steady pace that was intended to keep breathing from becoming too labored. He'd had plenty of experience in EVA before but realized most if not all those behind him would have had only recreational experience at best. In fact, he wasn't even sure how much experience his own wife had.

"'Manda, we've been married for a few weeks now but you know, I have no idea if you've ever space walked before," he said.

"A fine time to ask me!" Mooney replied. "But it so happens I was trained in EVA technique when I was with the Exterior Ministry. Never used it under conditions like this before though."

"Always a first time. Want to bring up the rear? Make sure everyone keeps moving?"

"Sure."

Mooney was fading back when Jules added, "You might talk to Mag and Toma. They can help you with keeping people moving."

"I will."

After that, Jules concentrated on getting up the trail. He reached the first turn in the zig zagging path and took the opportunity to look back. Behind him, the group followed, couples sticking close together, helping each other as they went. Mooney last with the guide. Already, the north hatch looked small against the side of the huge dome. Putting his head down and gripping the metal railing that girded the trail, he forged ahead, trying to pick up the pace without added exertion.

He was encouraged when he reached the top of the ridge. Only a minute or so of oxygen was used. Overhead, the disk of Jupiter was still gigantic and filled the starless sky. It was definitely past the halfway point by then, but its intense luminosity lit up the rocky landscape like daylight on Earth. All around was the evidence of Callisto's violent past with impact craters both small and large everywhere. In the distance, where an area was cleared of rubble, Jules could see the vehicle park that meant survival to him, Mooney, and the rest of the group which now was relying on his leadership to keep them alive.

Surveying the ground before him, he figured it would take a lot more time to negotiate the side of the crater to the ribbon of roadway winding toward the park. From the ridge where he stood, the crater's side fell away steeply and was strewn with loose soil and rocks, some the size of boulders.

Not waiting for the others behind him to gather before starting off, Jules plunged immediately over the ridge and began making his way downward. Trusting to Mooney to keep the others moving, he didn't look back but blazed a trail he hoped would allow the group to follow as quickly as possible.

"'Manda," he called over the private comm channel. "You still with me?"

"We're keeping up. Don't worry."

Jules continued, slipping in the loose, crumbly amalgam that passed for Callisto's soil, stuff as dead and lifeless as anything could be. There was little dust as the composition of the surface tended more toward gravel than actual soil. Once, throwing his falling weight against a boulder, the moon's lighter gravity allowed him to shove it loose and send it tumbling down hill. He hadn't expected that. He took a moment to catch his balance and watch the rock slowly fall away coming to a rest finally in a shadowed hollow. Starting off again, he reached the bottom of the grade without further mishap. Only a few hundred more feet remained to the unpaved road used as access for maintenance vehicles. He didn't bother to look back, preferring to complete this second stretch to the park by reaching the road.

With exactly five minutes of oxygen left, he stepped on the smooth, graded surface of the road and took a moment to look behind him. He was gratified to see the others were keeping up with him with Mooney still bringing up the rear.

"We're making good time," he said over the public comm channel by way of encouragement. They'd need it as by his calculations it would be a close call reaching the parked vehicles before their oxygen ran out.

"But we still need to hurry."

He waved them on past him in the direction of the park until Mooney caught up to him.

"How you doing?" he asked over the private channel.

"So far, so good," said Mooney, nodding for the tour guide to move on ahead of her.

"Your oxygen holding up?" asked Jules as they walked on together following the string of white suited figures as they lumbered down the road.

"Half my emergency supply is gone but only just."

"We'll make it," said Jules, trying to put as much confidence in his voice as possible. "Only about a mile left to go."

"Vic," said Mooney after a bit. "What do you think about all this? Was it deliberate?"

Jules didn't have to ask her what she meant.

"The hatch locking systems not working is one thing," said Mooney. "Those things happen. It *is* funny though that the dome comm channel in every 'suit also failed to work. Coincidence?"

"You have a suspicious mind."

"No more than yours."

Jules sighed. "It does seem strange. Is it because of our line of work something that might be just a coincidence can appear to be something more ominous?"

"Do you believe that?"

"No."

"Glad we've got that settled. Now then, who do you know wants you dead?"

"No one I can think of," said Jules. "That last case was all wrapped up nice and neat. No loose ends. And before that, as you know, I wasn't even working for MI. I was with the Interplanetary Geological Survey."

"Then what?"

Jules shrugged as best he could inside the bulky 'suit. "What about you? Any jealous boyfriends?"

Mooney laughed. "Not that kind." More seriously. "But we can't ignore this. Someone is out to get you or me or both of us."

"One thing you're not considering," said Jules. "Someone might be trying to kill one of our fellow excursionists. Just an ordinary, garden variety murder attempt."

Mooney laughed. "Didn't think of that! Pretty egotistical of me, huh?"

"Only natural. Just the same, soon as we get back, we'll get in touch with Leclerc at Military Intelligence."

"If we get back!"

"Don't be such a defeatist. I'm going up ahead."

So, saying, Jules used Callisto's low gravity to skip quickly to the head of the line, using the public comm channel to prompt the group to move faster. By then, their oxygen supply was well past the half way point and soon some would be compelled to share what they had left.

Ahead, in the lengthening shadows of Jupiter set, the vehicle park continued to come closer. Jules could now make out the individual vehicles, quickly picking out the crew haulers which could each hold up to a half dozen space suited men comfortably. It would be tight for the eight plus one tour guide in their group but that could certainly be put up with once they had the atmospherics working inside their cabins.

Suddenly, he noticed his breathing had become more labored. Knowing what it meant, he confirmed his suspicions by checking the Head Up Display in his 'suit. Less than a minute left. Over the public comm channel, the others began to notice as well and instinctively picked up the pace. Even so, the crew haulers looked farther away than ever.

"Don't hurry," advised Jules. "Keep a regular pace. Try to breath in shallow, short breaths. Remember, those of you with more oxygen, share with your spouses."

Immediately, he saw a few couples halting to attach the auxiliary tubes to Y valves in a selfless display of caring for each other. But then, wasn't that what marriage was all about? Well, this is where each couple will prove how seriously they took those vows taken only days or weeks before when everything seemed so easy, the future so safe and certain.

Turning and walking backward, Jules looked for Mooney at the end of the line and saw with some concern she was sharing her oxygen too, helping to keep the tour guide alive. His gait was uncertain and it was only Mooney's arm under his that kept him moving. They were falling back even as he watched.

With growing anxiety, he forced himself to turn away, not needing to check his own gauge to know he only had seconds left in his own oxygen supply. But now the crew haulers bulked large before him. On either side, other vehicles, tractors and graders scarred by Callisto's stubborn soil, stood silent and heavy. He stumbled against one but managed to stay on his feet. The next thing he knew, he'd banged into the side of something and as his vision cleared, he realized it was the hatch for one of the crew haulers. Realizing he'd forgotten to ask the guide if any code was needed to access them, he reached up blindly to where a handle should have been if no code was needed. He found it and pulled. He didn't hear it, but instead thought he saw a puff of ice crystals spurt from the opening hatch. With infinite relief, he used the last of his strength to signal with his fingers how many of the group should enter the open hauler. He gave a similar signal for the remainder and pointed to the second hauler stationed nearby.

It was all he was able to do before consciousness left him completely.

# Chapter Four
*The Hunted*

"Vic!"

Jules thought he heard someone groan.

"Vic! Wake up!"

Someone slapped his face…hard.

"What?"

It was more of a croak than a spoken word but apparently, he'd made himself understood because suddenly he felt arms around him and a familiar aroma he immediately identified with the brand of shampoo Mooney used.

"What?" he asked again. "Who's Vic?"

Mooney's arms around his neck tightened and her lips covered his preventing him from saying any more. The kiss was a long and lingering one but wasn't inspired by passion, not this time. There was a more practical reason as Jules now discovered.

"Quiet," whispered Mooney, her lips moving against his. "You're supposed to be Victor Conroi, remember?"

Now his eyes opened more fully and he was able to focus on the face swimming before him. It was white and framed with long, red hair. Green eyes stared into his, trying to read whether or not he understood what she was telling him.

"Victor?" He managed as the features of Mooney's face sharpened. "Yeah, yeah. That's me. Victor Conroi."

He felt Mooney's muscles relax as she pressed against him, the tension flowing from her with the realization her husband was safe. His brain hadn't been irreparably damaged by the lack of oxygen.

Her arms remained around him however as she continued to stare into his eyes, searching to make sure he was in his proper senses. Satisfied, she pulled back, smiling.

"You really had me worried there for a minute," said Mooney, brushing a stray lock from her eyes.

"How long was I out? Where are we...?" he began, propping himself on an elbow to look around.

He was on the unyielding deck of a crew hauler. The arrangements of seating and overhead storage bins told him that much.

"We're in one of the crew haulers," confirmed Mooney. "We just made it, thanks to you."

"Everybody?"

Mooney nodded, taking hold of one of his arms and helping him to one of the seats. He still wore his spacesuit but his helmet had been removed. The air in the cabin was stale but smelled sweet to Jules as he took some deep breaths. It felt good to fill his lungs and with each breath, his mind grew clearer.

"I remember now. I fell against the side of the hauler. If we needed a code to get in, we were sunk..."

"There was an access handle," said Mooney. "Just had to twist and pull. When the hatch opened, you fell inside, unconscious. We dragged you the rest of the way in. I wasn't about to get into the other hauler with you over here, maybe dead."

"How long was I out?"

"About a half hour. Time enough to get the atmospherics working pumping oxygen into the compartment and get our helmets off. You took so long to recover...Vic, I was so worried." She threw herself onto him again, arms around his neck, a sob in her throat.

Jules realized then the ordeal she'd been through. Maybe she could handle herself as an agent of the Exterior Ministry and now of Military Intelligence, but she was still a woman. Her feelings were always close to the surface, and she had no problem expressing them when the mood struck her. When such times occurred, all Jules could do was hold her and wait till her concerns were assuaged.

A few minutes later, she was wiping her tears and getting back to business.

"Todd tried the hauler's comm channel and it worked," she said.

"Maintenance is sending us a couple drivers who'll take the haulers back to the north hatch."

"The north hatch?" questioned Jules.

Mooney nodded. "Seems it's back on line."

She didn't say anything else, the cabin being as crowded as it was, but their eyes met and they understood each other.

"Funny," was all Jules could say.

"Yeah."

"No explanation?"

"None. Todd told them about the problem but when it was double checked, maintenance found the lock worked just fine and nothing in the data record to show a short in the system or a glitch in the data feed."

"Just one of those things, I guess."

Mooney shrugged and rolled her eyes so only Jules saw the look. There was more going on here than a simple glitch, a lot more. Or maybe it was just his suspicious nature? After all, things like this did happen on occasion with no explanation or simple coincidence. The nature of their professions, however, made them suspicious of glitches that were too convenient, especially glitches that could have killed them.

Jules craned his neck to take in the rest of the hauler's cabin. It was crowded with fellow honeymooners including their tour guide. All still wore their EVA 'suits but had doffed their helmets, their heads looking too small for their bodies poking out of the enlarged collar rings. There was talking but it was subdued; everyone still being somewhat shell shocked from their near fatal experience.

"How are they doing?" asked Jules, nodding in the direction of the others.

"Not bad, considering," replied Mooney, looking over her shoulder. "No fatalities. Everyone made it into the haulers. You were actually the worst off. Everyone else managed to share their remaining supplies of oxygen."

"Saw you sharing yours with Todd…"

"I did. He returned the favor by helping me haul you aboard. Remind me to put you on a diet."

Just then, there was a crackle over the hauler's comm channel. The tour guide took it.

"I'm your driver," said a voice over the speaker. "I'm at the hatch. Everyone replace your helmets while I come aboard."

Everyone heard and began doing as they were asked. When they were ready, the guide gave the driver permission to enter.

There was a silent movement, and the hatch popped open. The bulky figure of a man clumped silently onto the deck, turned to pull the door shut again, and waited for the atmospherics to make the interior breathable again.

Minutes later, helmets were removed once more and the driver took his position behind the steering column. After a few checks, the passengers were relieved to hear the sound of the hauler's electric motor come to life. A sudden lurch and they were moving. A small cheer went up among the former sightseers. They would soon be back to safety and the comforts of their suites and hotel rooms. In a few hours, their ordeal would be forgotten but not for Jules. The concerns raised by the incident would not disappear so easily and he had every intention of contacting MI to look into the matter.

Meanwhile, the heavy vehicle rumbled down the access road where not so long before, Jules led a desperate group of honeymooners seeking safety, a road that at the time seemed much longer. It took a few minutes more to negotiate the steeper incline into the crater, but they reached the north hatch without incident. There, they were instructed to replace their helmets one last time. One by one, they exited the hauler through the open door. Jumping lightly to the ground, Jules followed the others to the main hatch leading back inside Artemis Colony.

There was a moment of suspense as the group waited for the main hatch to open, but it did and they all trooped inside the lock.

Mooney breathed a sigh of relief once they returned to the orientation room and removed her helmet for the last time.

"I'm sure glad that's over," she said, depolarizing the 'suit and allowing it to fall away in a heap at her feet.

Attendants helped the others and soon had the 'suits back in storage ready for the next excursion. Jules hoped maintenance would make damn sure there was nothing wrong with the hatch or the 'suit comm channels before they let anyone else step outside the dome.

"Everyone, could I have your attention, please?" asked the tour guide, raising his voice so it could be heard above the general hubbub. "Simply as a matter of precaution and because our insurance provider insists after incidents like this, will you all take a few minutes to be checked by our doctor? Although you might feel perfectly fine, there's no telling what even the slightest bit of oxygen deprivation could do to the brain. It'll only take a few minutes, I promise. In addition, the management of Artemis Colony, by way of apologizing for your inconvenience, has made your stay at the resort completely complimentary with anything you've already paid for your stay to be reimbursed to your credit line."

There was a fresh burst of talk then, this time more definitely upbeat in response to the guide's good news.

Meanwhile, there were plenty of questions to be answered about the whole unfortunate incident, and the answers might not have been long in coming as the tour guide, still somewhat shaken from his own experience, came up to where Jules and Mooney were standing.

"Mr. and Mrs. Conroi?" he began. "I know you really want to get back to your suite, but I was wondering if you could come with me to my supervisor's office after you've seen the doctor? I told him if it wasn't for you, we would've all been dead for sure. He wants to find out exactly what happened and, well, I figured you might know more about it than I do. I only conduct tours. I'm not a technical expert. Do you mind?"

"Not at all," said Jules. "As a matter of fact, we have some questions about the incident too."

The guide obviously wasn't sure how to take Jules' reply but managed a thank you anyway.

"Vic," said Mooney, not forgetting to use Jules' official name in front of the guide. "The line for the doctor is over here."

"You know, 'Manda, I don't think I need to..."

When he saw the look in Mooney's eyes, he knew she was serious about a check up. As she should have been. He *had* lost consciousness after all.

"You're right. No sense taking chances on our health." He draped his arm across her shoulders and let her lead the way to where a white overalled medic and some nurses were busy checking over their fellow excursionists, waving instruments over their bodies and checking holo-readouts of brain scans.

A half hour later, after both receiving a clean bill of health from the medic, Jules and Mooney rejoined the tour guide who was waiting to escort them to an official dome speedcar for the drive to the supervisor's office.

"Let me tell Mag and Toma where we're off to," said Mooney. "Just leaving without any word to them would seem rude."

"If you don't mind my saying," said the guide looking after Mooney. "Your wife is a pretty impressive woman. She saved my life for sure tonight."

Jules nodded. "Don't mind at all. I agree with you. She *is* impressive."

"I was out of oxygen," continued the guide. "I mean *out!* I didn't have a partner like you and the couples, so I really was thinking I was going to have to die. My responsibility to the people I was in charge of you know."

Jules nodded.

"But she didn't hesitate at all in sharing her oxygen with me. Insisted on it as a matter of fact even though she had to be running out same as some of the others. Well, I'm impressed. She was just so cool through the whole thing. And then, when you'd gotten the door of the hauler open and fallen unconscious, she never gave a second thought to her own safety but began dragging you in. Practically did it all by herself. When I turned to see if she was coming in after me, I saw her with you and it was only then that I got to help. And she must have been just about out of air by that time."

"Thanks for sharing that with me, Todd," said Jules, impressed all over again with Mooney's dedication. "I'm pretty lucky, I guess."

Just then, Mooney rejoined them.

"What?" she asked, having noticed something in their looks.

"Nothing," said Jules quickly, before the guide could say something that would merely embarrass Mooney.

"Let's see this supervisor," said Mooney, leading the way to where speedcars were already lining up to whisk everyone away to their respective suites and hotels. "Nothing I want more than to get back to the lagoon and indulge in a nice, long swim."

The drive to the supervisor's office didn't take very long what with the priority code the guide gave the 'car's computer. While Jules and Mooney chatted with the guide on inconsequentials such as how long he'd been on the job, his training, and his long range career intentions, the 'car wove in and out of traffic at speeds not allowed those being used by guests. The number of 'cars picked up the closer they approached the visitor center near the east hatchway that led to the rocket port outside the dome. The low lying administration building, located alongside the visitor center, was on the dividing line between isolated honeymoon suites to the north and the more cosmopolitan complex of hotels, casinos, nightclubs, and promenades on the south.

"This is where we get out," said the guide, unnecessarily.

They exited the 'car among a throng of passerbys no doubt headed for the numerous supper clubs lining the colony's main promenade not far away. Jules admired the liberal use of fountains and artificial streams transforming the dome into an arboretum filled with the soothing sounds of running water. Everywhere there were plants of all sizes, heights, and colors from every planet in the Consortium. The admin building itself was nestled amid a plethora of Altairan ferns that nearly hid its rounded outlines from view.

The tour guide seemed to know the way, leading them down a set of 'crete steps and through a bank of clear plas doors that fronted the entire structure. Inside was a beehive of activity with clerks and uniformed maintenance, security, and convenience personnel moving about, intent on whatever business maintenance, security, and convenience personnel did. After signing in and receiving small identification badges that clung to their clothing, Jules and Mooney were shown to a down capsule that delivered them to the fifth lower level with nary an indication of movement.

"My supervisor's office is right down here," the guide was saying, extending an arm in the vague direction of a clear plas doorway, one of many that lined the roomy corridor ahead of them.

The doors swished aside at their approach and a girl sitting at a workstation greeted them.

"Hi, Todd," she chirped.

"Miss Reynolds," replied the guide, trying to keep a serious tone in his voice. He didn't fool anyone though. It was immediately obvious the two knew each other in something other than their professional c apacities. "This is Mr. and Mrs. Conroi. We're here to see Mr. Tenot at his request."

"Of course. He's expecting you."

The girl must have signaled Mr. Tenot in some way because no sooner had she mentioned his name, then the room's inner door slid open and the gentleman himself welcomed them into his office, shaking hands with Jules and Mooney in turn as he did so.

"Please sit down," he said, motioning to some pneuma-chairs ranged around his own workstation.

As Jules took one of the chairs, he noticed Tenot had not been alone. There were others in the room with him.

"I'm glad you could come along with Todd here."

"No problem," said Jules. "We understand your situation. What happened at the north hatch was serious."

"Very," agreed Tenot. "And let me introduce the others. This is Jeth Saki, our maintenance manager, and Lorko Mune, our security manager."

Jules nodded in their direction. The two stood to one side of the workstation, neither looking too pleased.

"According to young Todd here, your group was unable to access the north hatch upon your return from, uh, Lover's Ledge?" opened Tenot.

Jules nodded again. "That's right. It might have been simply accidental that the laser key didn't work. Maybe even the manual entry code system too. But what made the whole thing very strange was that none of the comm channels in any of the guests' EVA units worked either. One or two in a group that size, maybe, but not all of them at once."

"Are you suggesting they were tampered with in some way?" asked Mune.

"I'm saying the odds that they were are mighty damn high."

Just then, Tenot cleared his throat. "Why don't we get young Todd's version of events first?"

Unaccustomed to being among some of the colony's most senior staff, the tour guide was understandably nervous as he recalled the events leading up to the lock out, including his introductory routine and making sure the guests were familiarized with use of the EVA equipment.

"Were the comm channels checked prior to the tour?" asked Mune.

The tour guide nodded. "Absolutely. I didn't check them myself but the tech staff did and they didn't report anything unusual."

Tenot turned to Saki, the maintenance manager. "Is that right?"

Saki nodded. "I spoke to the crew at the north hatch and they confirmed all the comm channels were open during pre-EVA checks. For that matter, the hatch keypad was sound as well."

"Is that right, Todd?" asked Tenot.

"Yes, sir. Everything checked out as usual. In fact, there were no problems with the private or public comm channels the entire time we were outside. It was the north and then the east or west dome comm channels that didn't work. We only found that out when we returned to the hatch and couldn't get in."

"The keypad was unresponsive?"

"Yes, sir."

"And the laser key?" asked Jules. "That operates on an independent wave source."

"It worked fine when we tested it after the group got back inside," reported Saki.

"You don't find that strange?"

Saki shrugged. "It happens. Never at Artemis Colony mind you, but it can happen."

"Could that suggest direct tampering?"

"Not likely. It could be shut down indirectly. Its functions are linked to the cloud."

"But it wouldn't be easy."

Saki shook his head. "No way. It would take a pretty savvy customer to find their way through the cloud and then past redundant security codes and passwords to alter its programming."

There was silence for a moment then before Mune suggested perhaps the young tour guide could return to his duties.

Catching the security manager's meaning, Tenot agreed, thanked the guide for his cooperation and level headedness under the stress of an emergency, and dismissed him.

Looking relieved, the guide stood but before leaving, bent toward

Mooney. "I'll get your speedcar from the north hatch parking area and return it to your suite," he said.

Mooney flashed him a smile. "That's very nice of you, Todd. Thank you."

"I think he has a crush on you," said Jules after the guide left.

"Jealous?" replied Mooney, a twinkle in her eye.

Before Jules could say anything more, he was interrupted by Mune.

"We can talk more freely now, I think," said the security manager.

Jules raised a questioning eyebrow.

Mune saw it and took Jules by surprise with his next words.

"After hearing our guide talk about you and your wife's resourcefulness during the emergency, I took the opportunity to do some checking," explained Mune. "Frankly, I was a little taken aback when I discovered the two of you are with Military Intelligence."

"How did you find that out?" Jules asked.

"I used to be with the Off-Planet Police and still have some connections."

Jules let it go at that.

Seeing neither Jules nor Mooney was going to volunteer anything further, Mune continued. "I don't see any reason to beat around the bush. Are you two here in an official capacity? Are you supposed to be undercover or something? You can speak freely. These offices are secure."

"No," replied Jules. "We're not here on business."

"So why are you here?"

"We're on our honeymoon, why else should we be here if not on business?" returned Mooney, indignantly.

"I'm sorry," mitigated Mune. "It's just that your presence on Callisto in conjunction with this serious failure in colony security seemed like it might be more than coincidental to me."

"All right then," said Mooney, mollified. "So, what about the others in our excursion group? Have you checked them out as well?"

"As best we can but as far as can be learned, there's nothing out of the ordinary about any of them. Just your average honeymooners: a couple speedcar programmers, secretaries, a mechanic, an accountant, a flyer jockey, landscaper, even a baker. No criminal records. No one who would likely have the kind of enemy who'd want them killed. Or any enemy for that matter."

"Certainly not anyone with the technical sophistication to get past the colony's redundant systems and cut off key pad access to a hatch or selective interference with EVA 'suit comm channels," added Saki.

"True," agreed Jules. "It'd have to be someone who was not only expert in redundant systems but with the single minded determination to take the time to get past them. Whoever that was, they'd have to have a real mad on to bother."

"Not to mention be willing to kill a dozen other people along with the primary victim," pointed out Mooney.

"I didn't consider that," mused Tenot, obviously chilled by the thought.

"Could it be one of those mass murderers?" asked Saki.

"I'm not ruling anything out," said Mune.

"What are you doing to trace the tampering?" asked Jules of Saki.

"Everything we can," the maintenance manager replied. "We have some good people on the payroll and they've all been rerouted from other jobs to work on this one. No luck so far though. No shorts, no surges, no glitches of any kind."

"So, it looks like you can rule out accidental failure then," Jules said.

Saki nodded.

"What about natural phenomena? Does Jupiter's proximity or any of its moons have any kind of effect on local electronics and data systems? What about the red spot? Storm systems on earth sometimes interfere with communications."

"We've long since compensated for magnetic and tidal effects," said Saki. "And whatever effects the red spot might promote are purely local."

"Then that leaves us with human interference," concluded Mooney.

"Right, and that's going to be a bit harder to pin down. Right now, we're trying to narrow down likely nodes where physical access can be had by visitors or employees but it's like looking for that proverbial needle in a haystack."

"How many nodes are we talking about?" asked Jules.

"Thousands."

"I was afraid of that."

"Whoever this person was, they were good," said Mooney. "Will you lock down the resort?"

"Heavens, no!" blurted Tenot. "That would be a nightmare of logistics. Imagine all the reservations that would have to be canceled. The arrangements that would need to be made for guests who would have to remain until the investigation is over."

"Closure does seem like overkill," admitted Mooney, rubbing her chin. "You think whoever did it will run?"

Jules shook his head. "Not sure. Depends how safe from discovery they think they are."

"With thousands of nodes to check and with no guarantee even if the right one is found it'll yield any more information, I'm guessing they already feel pretty darn safe."

"We're using standard security profiling software on anyone who's checked out after the incident," said Mune. "If we get any matches with criminal records or psychological screenings, we intend to detain them for questioning."

"That's something," said Jules.

"We're also double checking the guest list for anyone who's staying here unaccompanied," added Mune. "It's not unusual but Artemis Colony *is* known primarily as a honeymoon destination. Of course, nothing says it couldn't be a couple we're looking for or someone who arrived with someone else as cover."

"It gets more complicated the longer we talk about it," sighed Mooney.

"Which is why we're asking you to help us in any way you can," said Tenot. "Being with Military Intelligence, any advice you can give us will be gratefully accepted."

"I appreciate your confidence in us," said Jules, rising. "If we think of anything you haven't covered, we'll certainly let you know. For now, though, I think Mr. Mune is doing all he can under the circumstances."

Jules took Mooney's hand as she rose from her chair then shook hands all around.

They waited until they were outside the admin building, waiting for a public speedcar, to talk again.

"What do you think?" asked Mooney.

"I think they haven't a prayer of finding who did it," said Jules, truthfully.

"Those thousands of contact points where someone could access the colony's computer system?"

"Right. This took some expertise and the fact that whoever it was, was willing to kill a dozen people to get the one person they wanted tells me we're dealing with something other than a personal vendetta."

"Then you think we were the actual targets?"

"Something like this just doesn't happen every day," figured Jules. "It's the unusual nature of it all that bothers me."

"You don't go for the mass murderer theory?"

Jules shook his head. "That particular psychosis ended a hundred years ago. The last known case was way back in the 2170's. Society has moved on."

"Okay, let's say it was us. Maybe it's best we approach it that way if only to keep on our guard."

An empty speedcar pulled up to the edge of the plaza and as the door lifted up, Jules helped Mooney in saying, "Suite 106."

"You're right," agreed Jules, throwing himself down beside his wife. "We can't leave anything to chance. Which begs the next question…"

The door fell silently closed and the 'car glided smoothly onto the smartway, following the outbound traffic lanes north to where the private suites were located.

"…whether we were both the targets or just one of us," finished Jules.

"Seriously, do you have any enemies out there that are unaccounted for?"

"None that I know of," said Jules, thinking. "It's just not that kind of business."

"Someone working for the Coalition?" asked Mooney, watching the developed portion of the resort outside the 'car give way to forest green.

"They might be holding a grudge against you for denying them that black hole tech. It might have cost them the war."

"Too outlandish. I mean, blaming one person for something as vast as all that. If they've got a mad on, it's for the whole human race, not just me."

"Okay then. We're back to square one. Someone might be out to kill the both of us or either one. What to do about it?"

"The next step is obvious, I think."

"Contact the Director."

"Right."

Just then, the speedcar glided to a halt where a simple placard stated "Suite 106."

The 'car door lifted and its two passengers stepped out. Nearby, an access to the smartway indicated where the stall for their own 'car was located, nearly hidden among the plant life. Arm in arm, Jules and Mooney strolled over to where a path led into the concealing jungle and eventually to their bungalow.

Mooney peeked through the foliage to check the stall.

"It's there," she reported. "Todd brought the 'car back from the north hatch."

"We'll have to remember him when we leave," said Jules. "Give him a good tip."

"He's a dear," said Mooney, giving Jules' arm a squeeze.

Overhead, the duraglass dome was clear enough to be invisible. Outside, stars could be seen but faded when they came within the nimbus of Io, one of Jupiter's four largest moons, whose reflected light shone down on their jungled surroundings and illuminated the path as it wound among trees and shrubs from a dozen different worlds. Here and there, night blooming flowers stared silently in the pale moonlight.

"Feeling okay?" asked Jules, patting her hand.

"Um hm. Just glad to be here with you, my husband. I like the sound of that."

"Hope you still feel that way after we talk to Leclerc. Nothing like a business discussion with the head of MI to shatter the mood."

"Well, I think we have the remedy for that..." Mooney began to say when she stopped suddenly.

"What…" Jules began to say when he saw what it was that Mooney had seen.

They'd just rounded one of the turns in the pathway when a dark form blocked their way.

"It looks like a body," said Mooney, releasing Jules' arm.

"Yeah," agreed Jules, suddenly alert.

He was still standing there, looking around for any sign of danger, when Mooney rolled the body over to see who it was.

"Not good," she reported. "It's Todd."

"The tour guide?" asked Jules unnecessarily. He crouched beside Mooney to look for himself. She was right. "Killed by a pulse pistol."

"And with a full charge," observed Mooney, indicating the large hole punched in the center of the young man's chest. The edges of the wound were charred. "I don't get this."

"Must have been a case of mistaken identity," guessed Jules. "He pulled up in the stall with our 'car and in the dark, whoever killed him, assumed it was one of us. Me, most likely."

"Then what happened at the north hatch wasn't an accident," concluded Mooney. "Someone is out to get us."

"Or just me," corrected Jules. "Todd wasn't as good looking as you."

"In the dark, who could tell?" countered Mooney. "They could've been after me or the both of us for all we know."

"Maybe. Right now, there's no reason to believe whoever did this isn't still around. Most likely waiting up at the bungalow to ambush you if they still think Todd was me."

"In that case, wouldn't they have tried to hide the body?"

Jules shrugged. "No sense taking chances. Look, there's a fork in the path just up ahead. You take the one that leads away from the suite. Find your way back to the stall. Use the 'car's comm to call the admin building for help. I'll stay here and make sure whoever's out there doesn't get away."

"Now wait a minute…"

"No time for debate. Go."

Realizing it wasn't the time or place for an argument, Mooney rose to her feet and, crouching low, followed Jules up the pathway. There was no sign of danger by the time they reached the fork and after a quick kiss, she vanished amid the surrounding foliage.

Relieved Mooney was gone, Jules proceeded with increased caution, hugging the near edge of the trail where overhanging fronds and branches allowed him some cover. Somewhere, a few hundred yards around the next bend lay the bungalow, dark and quiet as it snuggled in its man made forest.

Thoughts of the bungalow, however, gave Jules an idea. Assuming the killer to be waiting up ahead, if he could get around and take him from the rear, he might be able seize the element of surprise. The suite itself was bounded on three sides by the stream that fed all of the colony's pool system including their own private lagoon. If he could find the access that allowed circulation of water from the stream to the lagoon, he could use its thrust to hurry him underwater before his breath gave out. Emerging in the lagoon, he might be able to catch the killer while he watched the head of the pathway leading to the bungalow from the opposite direction.

So thinking, he left the pathway, carefully cutting through the local jungle in the direction of the stream. He moved slowly so as to make as little sound as possible as well as trying not to disturb any of the fronds and leaves that lay at every hand. The slightest movement among the plants would stand out easily in the bright moonlight.

He arrived at the edge of the stream without incident and stripping to his shorts, slipped into the rushing water. It was cool but not cold as he pushed himself off, using a slow breast stroke to keep from making any noise or ruffling the surface of the water. Slowly, the stream straightened out and as it angled off to the north and east, he came within distant sight of the bungalow silhouetted against the starry Callistan sky. It was all dark and from the looks of it, undisturbed, but looks, as he well knew, were deceiving. A Terran night bird chirped hollowly from somewhere in the forest and was answered by something else that was assuredly not of Earthly origin. But Jules had no time to wonder about that as he felt the water grow warmer about him.

Dimly, the moonlight reflecting on the surface of the water showed movement indicating the presence of the submerged access chute leading to the lagoon. Somewhere a few feet down, heating elements warmed the water of the lagoon to tropical temperatures while a filtration system kept the water moving in and out, constantly replenishing the lagoon and keeping it clean. All he had to do was hold his breath long enough to reach the other side.

That's all.

He guessed it would take about two minutes. He could hold his breath long enough, but he counted on the thrust of fresh water being pumped through the chute to help push him along and save time. With one more look around, he filled his lungs once, twice. The third time, he held it and ducked beneath the surface.

Under the water, he wasted no time swimming in the direction where it was warmest. Luckily, underwater mood lighting gave some illumination, allowing him to waste little time heading to the chute. Even before he arrived there, he felt the pull of the water as it was drawn into the big opening in the side of the stream. What looked natural from above was no such thing a few feet below the surface, which was quickly revealed to be a 'crete formed trench with smooth, polished sides. Those sides furnished little hold for his groping hands, but luckily he didn't have to rely on that to move forward. The induced current did that as he was quickly sucked into the chute's opening. Almost immediately, he ran into a problem.

He discovered the presence of a filtration screen by the simple expedient of being pushed into it by the current. The surprise of the contact almost made him expel his breath. He quickly recovered however and managed to remove the screen with little trouble. Still, the delay was unexpected and he couldn't hold his breath forever.

Adding to the impulse of the current, Jules began to swim vigorously, clearing the chute on the other side. There he had to avoid the current created by the outtake chute as it took water from the lagoon back to the stream. With his lungs bursting, he hurried for the surface. But even in his haste, he remembered the danger that might face him above. He made for the far edge of the lagoon, as far away from the bungalow as he could get. Eager as he was for a breath of air, he forced himself to break the surface slowly so as to cause as little disturbance in the water as possible.

Slowly, he raised his head until his nose was clear and he gratefully took in a lung full of air.

When he finally caught his breath, he took note of his surroundings.

All was quiet with the bungalow darkened except for a small light by the side entrance leading to the pathway. Moonlight still bathed the area so he could see the poolside furniture and other articles. Closer to the bungalow, shadows from the terraced building prevented him from seeing any further. What he had to do was keep whoever was about busy until Mooney could arrive with help. Then they might have a chance of catching whoever killed the guide and wanted to kill either him or Mooney. That meant he had to let them know he was around, making a target of himself.

Not for the first time tonight, Jules wished he had a gun. But who brought a gun with them on their honeymoon?

Slowly, carefully, he drifted over to the sunken stairs leading from the patio into the pool. He slithered up the stairs, never taking his eyes from the direction of the bungalow. At the top, he stood and, crouching low, scurried over to the edge of the forest, moving in fits and starts until he could take shelter behind the sauna. Still no movement. Standing more erect, he moved beneath the overhang protecting the dressing rooms. He felt the goosebumps rising on his naked flesh, the cool air of the colony's nighttime climate controls quickly drying him off after his swim.

He tried the clear plas door leading from the sauna into the bungalow's ground floor. It was unlocked. The door slid open noiselessly and Jules slipped inside, grateful the door wasn't self-operating. The tell-tale hiss of such a door's opening mechanism would have given him away for sure.

As it was, he was about to do that himself to draw the hidden killer in his direction anyway. Getting ready, he was set to kick over a chair when suddenly all the lights in the bungalow went on at once, illuminating every room in the place as bright as full daylight.

Jules froze in surprise, exposed as he was in the full length clear plas walls that composed the rear portion of the bungalow. To anyone outside, he was a perfect target, a realization that came to him none too soon as the sound of clear plas melting alerted him to his danger. At the first indication of the sound, his professional instincts took over and he dived behind a handy divan just as the unseen bolt of force from a pulse pistol finished boring through the clear plas wall and struck the stone facing of a replicated fireplace right behind him. Instantly, a hole appeared where its upper works had been.

*He's out there, all right. And still working on full charge.*

Realizing the divan would offer no protection against a pulse pistol, Jules dashed away in the direction of the kitchen, performing a tumbler's roll before coming to rest on his feet behind a counter. Behind him, the pulse pistol struck again, ruining the synth-carpeting over which he'd just completed his roll.

He had to douse the lights.

"Computer," he called aloud to the housecomp. "Turn off all lights."

Nothing happened.

It figured. Whoever was out there managed to override the suite codes deleting the voice recognition protocols.

*Well, this is what I wanted. Make a target of myself.*

He looked around the kitchen which was mostly automated. Not much there to use as a weapon. Not against a pulse pistol anyway. He reached up and fumbled in a drawer. He pulled down a handful of utensils. Not much use but maybe he could throw them around to draw the killer's fire like they did in the old time flicks. It was worth a try.

Figuring the direction from where the pair of shots came from, Jules tossed a fork across the den, making sure it struck the clear plas wall on the far side. Not waiting for it to hit, he threw himself across the kitchen into the front hall and up the stone stairs to the second level. If he could lure the killer into the bungalow, maybe he'd stand a better chance against him in the closer confines of the upper rooms.

Meanwhile, his trick worked. The fork hit the clear plas with a ring that was immediately followed by a blast from the pulse pistol. That allowed Jules to reach the second level and contrive to have his shadow on an inner wall be seen from outside. Taking cover in an adjoining room, he hoped the shooter would figure he had no good shot from outdoors and follow him inside.

But no such luck.

Instead, there were multiple blasts from the lagoon area aimed at the second level and in seconds, the spare bedroom, upper living room, and the day room were a shambles with the clear plas rear walls riddled with big holes where the energy pulses had bored their way through.

*This guy isn't going to be suckered inside. He's smarter than I gave him credit for.*

Suddenly, there was another round of blasts, forcing Jules to the front of the bungalow and away from the stairs. When the commotion subsided, he heard a step on the stairs and realized he was wrong. The shooter was coming up after him. But that was small comfort. The person wasn't taking any chances, firing spreads of pulse blasts ahead of him as he came on, forcing Jules further back. If that kept up, he'd find himself cornered in the bedroom.

Well, he'd accomplished what he wanted. He managed to get the shooter into the bungalow.

There was another series of shots that tore up the second level corridor and sure enough, Jules was forced to run into the only room still available to him. Inside the bedroom, he looked around but found nothing that could help him. Desperately, he went to the clear plas doorway that gave access to the balcony outside. This one was a manual slider as well and he'd just managed to get it open when he sensed the shooter step in behind him from the ruined hallway.

A glance over his shoulder as he finally managed to shove the door open indicated to Jules the shooter was taking aim at him, the glow of the gun's range finder playing over his body, still draped only in a pair of under shorts. He squeezed through the opening, clambered onto the balcony railing and jumped out as far as he could, even as he felt the pressure of the unseen beam of a pulse blast shoot through the space where he'd stood a moment before.

There was a moment of falling through space and with a last second twist, Jules managed to hit the water of the lagoon, just missing the edging and dashing his brains out on the formacrete. After that, he knew nothing as he swam beneath the surface, hurrying to reach the stairs leading from the lagoon and finding cover before the shooter could target him again.

When he finally emerged and began running, it wasn't until after he'd dived into the jungle to hide and took the time to look back that he noticed the shooter had vanished from the second level bedroom. It was then he heard the sounds coming from all around as unseen men crashed through the surrounding forest and closed in on the bungalow. They called out to each other as they did so and among the voices, he heard Mooney's distinctive contralto.

In another moment, she broke into sight along the pathway, a small caliber, police issue, ion pistol clutched in her hand. Not as powerful as a pulse pistol but enough to show the user meant business.

"Vic," Mooney was shouting. "Vic! Are you here? Where are you?"

"Over here," called out Jules, wary of nervous security personnel who might shoot at the first sign of unexpected movement. "Is it safe to come out?"

"Vic! Stand down men," said Mooney, waving her arms.

The others emerged from cover here and there including Lorko Mune himself who accompanied Mooney in the sweep. "Search the area!"

"You came just in time," said Jules, stepping from cover in nothing but his shorts. "The shooter had me in his sights."

"From the look of this place, you sure put up a fight," remarked Mune, not without some admiration. "I guess you earn that big MI salary you pull down."

"Believe me, it isn't enough for what I just went through," said Jules, sweeping Mooney in his arms. "But what about the shooter? Did you get him? He was in the second level bedroom only a minute ago."

"My men had the suite surrounded before we closed in," said Mune. "He shouldn't have escaped."

"He overrode the housecomp protocols," noted Jules. "Had my voice commands frozen out. The bungalow's suite sensors likely alerted him to your approach and exactly where all your men were located. He could have easily slipped through your cordon."

"On the other hand, he might still be hiding around here some place," replied Mune, turning to supervise the search.

"He can look but I highly doubt the shooter is still hanging around here," said Jules.

"Jules," whispered Mooney, "if he could override the housecomp, maybe he could also have hacked into the north hatch comm channels."

"You're right. If so, that means we might be looking for a single person after all."

"Jules, I'm so glad we arrived in time," said Mooney. "I was really afraid for you after seeing Todd…"

"You had cause for concern," admitted Jules. "Whoever it was, was good. Made all the smart moves, even turned my own plan against me in the end. You couldn't have arrived at a better time."

"Did you find out anything about who it was or why they were after us?"

Jules shook his head. "He never said a word. Never made a sign he even knew who I was. Only a dogged determination to kill me."

"I hate to admit this, but the shooter escaped," said Mune, emerging from the bungalow's ground level.

"Well, the colony's already on alert from the north hatch incident," noted Mooney. "You can just add a search for the shooter to the one for the hacker."

"Think they could be the same person?" asked Mune.

Jules shrugged. "No way to tell. Could be the same person or he might have backup. For sure, this strike, coming on the heels of the first attempt, indicates planning or coordination."

"A follow-up plan you think?"

Jules shrugged. "We'd planned to contact Military Intelligence following the north hatch incident. We'll ask about this shooter, too. Maybe they have some information we don't have."

"Your boss isn't Henri Leclerc is it?"

Jules looked at Mooney who shook her head.

"As a matter of fact, he is," said Jules cautiously.

"Well, he's here. On Callisto. Just had a call from admin. He arrived only a few minutes ago. Says he wants to see the both of you as soon as possible."

"He's *here*?"

"Quite a coincidence," said Mooney.

"Maybe not," replied Jules.

Mooney sighed, handing her ion pistol back to Mune. "Does this mean the honeymoon is over?"

# Chapter Five
*Two Missions*

Jules and Mooney shared a pnuema-couch in the expansive honeymooners' apartment located on the tenth floor of the Dreamer's Hotel. While a kitchenette was not included, it did come with an oversized bed that could do everything but sit up and beg. Also, a modest liquor service and heavy duty pixelated wall and ceiling surfaces that could present any kind of scenery a guest might dream up. From tropical beaches to Martian landscapes, or even a simple window and wallpaper look with outside views so realistic it could not be told apart from the real thing.

Just then, the walls were displaying a deep forest scene complete with bashful Terran deer moving hesitantly among the trees. Ambient forest sounds filled the room including a light breeze that seemed to hurry the fleecy overhead clouds dotting the blue sky ceiling. Room climate controls added the final touch of realism.

"Nice," was all Jules could say, barely able to repress a smile.

"Real romantic," agreed Mooney, staring at the gaudy, pink bed sheets whose shimmer revealed their crinosynth fabrication. "I particularly like the hearts and flowers pattern on those bed clothes."

"All right, all right," gruffed Henri Leclerc, Director of Military Intelligence. "It was all I could get at the last minute. The whole colony is on lock down. Did you know that?"

Jules nodded. "Got the word first from the security manager. After the second attempt on our lives, admin decided things had become serious enough to go from alert status to full closure."

"A real headache for them," said Mooney. "There's over a million people in the colony at any given moment. Eighty thousand of them resort employees."

"It's going to cost them a fortune in canceled reservations not counting the bad publicity," added Jules.

"Well, right now, that's not our concern," said Leclerc.

"Easy for you to say," said Mooney, folding her arms.

Leclerc chose to ignore the remark as he paced the floor. "Under the circumstances, it took me longer to receive permission to enter the colony than it did to travel from Mars to Jupiter."

It was only a slight exaggeration. Leclerc arrived in the Director's personal black rocket from MI's headquarters on Mars a few hours before only to be delayed on one of Artemis Colony's landing aprons while his identify was confirmed and special clearances could be arranged. It was the kind of treatment he was not used to and put him in a bad mood.

At the moment, however, his superior's feelings were not what concerned Jules. Rather, it was the reason for his being on Callisto at all. In the past, Leclerc rarely left MI headquarters even at the height of the war with the Coalition, so his presence here indicated something big.

"Can we do anything about these damn walls?" stormed Leclerc.

The sudden outburst only confirmed to Jules his opinion that something important was bothering Leclerc. Something that took him from headquarters across millions of miles of space to interrupt he and Mooney's well earned honeymoon. But before he could say something to soothe the Director's nerves, Mooney came to his rescue.

"Just talk to the roomcomp," suggested Mooney. "Is it programmed to your voice recognition protocol?"

"My what? No. I don't know!"

"Computer, normal room view on walls and ceilings," prompted Mooney.

Instantly, the walls and ceiling flickered and, replacing the bucolic outdoor scenes, was a standard hotel room image with clear plas windows overlooking the hotel's main entrance plaza far below and, in the distance, the promenade with its glow of signs and attractions. Overhead, the view of blue skies had been altered as well. Now it simply showed an expanse of mirrors that made the room seem bigger than it was.

At sight of the mirrored ceiling, Leclerc, a confirmed bachelor, merely grunted.

"Well, it's better than it was before," he admitted.

Leclerc removed a secure telcomm from a pocket in his synthsuit saying, "Initiate sweep and place on hold all cloud based programs assigned to room 1034."

"Securing the room?" asked Jules.

"Paranoid, isn't he?" said Mooney. "How likely would it be for anyone to be monitoring a honeymoon hotel?"

Jules shrugged. "Have you forgotten our orientation session already? These rooms have across the board recording functions for the convenience of guests. But they could easily be converted for eavesdropping purposes..."

"You're diabolical," kidded Mooney. "I never thought of that."

"We're okay now," interrupted Leclerc, putting away the telcomm. "So, what's this about someone trying to kill you?"

Jules filled him in about the lockout at the north hatch and the events at the bungalow.

"Are you sure you and Mooney were the targets?" asked Leclerc. "No chance of mistaken identity?"

Jules shook his head. "Highly unlikely. The shooter picked our suite to stake out and had plenty of opportunity to see who I was while he was trying to punch a hole in me with his pulse pistol."

"Whoever it was, it sounds like he was sloppy."

"He was," agreed Jules. "I've had a chance to think things over since the action at the bungalow, and I'm convinced the attack was pretty amateurish."

"How's that?" asked Mooney.

It was the first she'd heard of Jules latest conclusions.

"For one, he killed the guide by accident. Next, he took the bait and followed me into the bungalow putting him at a disadvantage. Finally, he used his weapon indiscriminately. Practically destroyed the bungalow."

"Maybe he was in a hurry," said Mooney. "Needed to finish the job and get going. Maybe he knew I'd gone for help."

"Possible, but I think our tactics took him by surprise," concluded Jules. "He was waiting for me at the bungalow. He had the housecomp reprogrammed and was ready to turn on the lights. That took a little time which meant he'd retreated to the bungalow by the time we found Todd's body. Likely he never saw us split up or spotted me take the water route until I came up in the lagoon."

"Makes sense. So, he was amateurish. What does that mean?"

Jules shrugged. "I don't know. Maybe he was the hacker who tried to lock us out at the north hatch. When that attempt failed, he was forced to try something else, something he wasn't necessarily proficient at."

"He was proficient enough to kill poor Todd," said Mooney.

"Yeah," was all Jules could say to that.

"Well, we can't ignore the whole thing," gruffed Leclerc. "No one tries to kill any of our agents and gets away with it. I'll have our people coordinate with the colony's security to find out more."

"So, you won't let Mooney and me investigate ourselves?"

"I know you have a proprietary interest in it, but I've got more urgent things I need you to look into for me," said Leclerc.

"More urgent than attempted murder?" quipped Mooney. "Well, at least the bean counters at MI will be happy to learn the honeymoon they paid for won't cost them anything. It's all going to be reimbursed by the resort."

"If that's true, it'll be the first good news I've heard in months," said Leclerc.

"How do you mean?" asked Jules.

"It's why I'm here," Leclerc said. "Why I've come personally. I didn't want to waste any time or take any chances with the existence of your missions getting out."

"'Missions'?" asked Mooney. "As in two assignments?"

Leclerc nodded.

"We have two emergencies that have come up at the same time. It wasn't planned that way, but the need to investigate them both right away is imperative. They may be connected, but as yet there's no proof. Only coincidence. You've been out of the loop for weeks now, but I'm sure you recall intelligence briefings prior to your wedding that reported the loss of shipping in the region of Eta Cassiopeia."

Jules nodded. "Two commercial freighters disappeared without any warning. The first time might have been an accident, but twice was suspicious."

"Piracy was ruled out though," recalled Mooney. "Not worth it that far out."

"Correct."

"Has there been any more information about the incidents? Anything that might suggest hostile action by the Coalition for instance?"

Leclerc shook his head. "Nothing."

"That leaves first contact," continued Mooney excitedly.

"Perhaps," conceded Leclerc. "But there's absolutely nothing to support that contention. No communications, no signals, no nothing. If it's a first contact situation, by destroying our shipping, whoever it is, is going about it all wrong. The first thing they want to do is start a war without even talking first? Without even finding out more about the enemy? We're not ruling it out mind you, but the possibility is extremely low. Our own advance sweeps beyond Terran space whether by the Navy or organizations like the Interplanetary Geological Survey haven't found any evidence of intelligent life."

"Shoot!" said Mooney, disappointed.

"Anyway, three weeks ago, the Navy dispatched a battleship into the Eta Cassiopeia area to conduct an investigation," said Leclerc. "Regular reports back from Captain Cameron Hendry indicated nothing amiss and no evidence of the missing freighters."

"Cameron Hendry?" questioned Mooney. "He's a good officer. A veteran of the war."

"Know him?" asked Jules.

"Um hm. Met him a few times when I was with the Exterior Ministry. He's very well regarded by Navy brass."

"Which was the reason why he was assigned the mission," said Leclerc. "Unfortunately, it's likely he eventually found what he was sent out there to find."

"I don't like the way this is going," warned Mooney.

"I'm sure you won't," replied Leclerc. "Hendry made contact with an unidentified vessel which opened fire on the *St. Sebastian*. A battle ensued. We can only guess at how it ended because we never saw its conclusion. Hendry must have been in dire straits though because he sent a hyper-bandwave pulse back to Naval Command with the ship's full data log. It was the last we ever heard from him."

There was silence a moment as Jules and Mooney absorbed its ramifications.

"I have the data log with me here," said Leclerc after a moment. Again, he pulled out his telcomm and used the keypad to initiate a 3D projection of imagery sent by the *St. Sebastian*. "These are the last visuals sent by Hendry before all communications ended."

Silently, Jules and Mooney watched the unfolding battle between the Terran war vessel and the unknown ship. They saw the exchange of broadsides, the flash and blast of hits made against the unidentified vessel, its return volley that pierced the *St. Sebastian*'s engine room.

"Pay close attention to this part," said Leclerc in a low voice.

The view was from one of the *St. Sebastian*'s bow cameras. It showed the enemy vessel getting closer and closer and as it did so, it could be clearly seen that it was repairing itself; its dark mass congealing, holes filling up, weapon systems once more aimed threateningly at the Terran vessel.

Then it ended.

"Incredible," was all Jules could say.

"Was that ship repairing itself as we watched?" asked Mooney in disbelief.

"It was," replied Leclerc.

"Nano technology?" guessed Mooney. "I know there's use of microscopic machines in computers and some manufacturing…"

Leclerc shook his head. "Not here. This is far in advance of anything commercially available."

"Nitinol. Must be," said Jules.

"That stuff that almost killed us before?" asked Mooney. "In fact, right here on Callisto."

"That's the stuff."

"But I thought it hadn't been developed far enough for use in space vessels. There were temperature problems…"

"There were," said Jules. "It's what kept use of nitinol from general applications. When it was exposed to temperatures that were above a certain degree or below, it lost its shape."

Jules recalled how a trap laid with nitinol almost ended his relationship with Mooney before it began when they walked into a hotel room in the resort and found themselves trapped in a ball made of nitinol. It had been a trap laid by Heintzel that was intended to halt their pursuit of him. In laying it, Heintzel set the temperature in the room at the point where an object composed of nitinol would lose its programmed shape, liquify, and spread across the floor until, at first glance, it looked like ordinary carpeting. But as soon as the door to the room was opened and the room temperature altered even in the slightest degree, the programming in the nitinol was triggered and it immediately retook its spherical shape with Jules and Mooney trapped inside with only enough air to breath for a few minutes. They'd barely escaped in time.

The trap, however, illustrated the problem with nitinol the Science Division of Military Intelligence had with it. Because nitinol could be programmed to take any shape, shapes it could retake immediately after being damaged in any way, MI was eager to solve the temperature control problem and use the product on naval vessels in particular. But the stuff could be equally useful in civilian life where vehicles prone to damage or even buildings that could be destroyed in earthquakes or ruined by fire might self-repair.

"Then someone has solved the problem?" Mooney was saying.

"Looks like it," said Jules, still trying to figure how it might have been done.

"It wasn't the Science Division," said Leclerc. "It's been removed from the front burner but we're still working on it. The problem is that we lost our top man in the field, which brings me to the second assignment."

So saying, Leclerc activated his telcomm again and Jules saw the image of a middle-aged man appear in a 3D projection. He was mustached with dark hair and appeared to be in a laboratory environment.

"This is Professor Fernando Santanti," said Leclerc. "Until a couple years ago, he was Science Division's head researcher on the nitinol problem."

"Two years ago?" asked Jules.

"That's when he resigned to return to his home in Latinium and go into business for himself. As you know, the work we do in the Science

Division is classified. Although no one is forced to stay, anyone who decides to leave must report in periodically to let MI know their whereabouts and to make sure government projects remain secure. Santanti was good about that. Until about a year ago. That's when we lost touch with him setting off alarm bells. But when we went to check up on him, he couldn't be found. We were still investigating the case when the hyper-bandwave message from the *St. Sebastian* came in. As soon as we saw the self-repairing going on with the unknown ship, we put two and two together and couldn't ignore the coincidence. Our number one nitinol researcher quits and then disappears altogether and twelve months later, this ship shows up."

"And from what it looks like, it's unstoppable," said Mooney.

"For that very reason, it's the kind of technology MI wanted for the Consortium," said Leclerc. "Instead, it looks like its fallen into the hands of someone else. Someone who has decidedly anti-social tendencies."

"To put it mildly," said Mooney. "If more ships like that show up, it could threaten the security of the entire Consortium."

"It's worse than that," said Jules. "It wouldn't take more than that single ship to pose a threat. You saw what it did to the *St. Sebastian*. It could wade into any battle group and wipe it out with no damage to itself. With the Navy neutralized, whoever is behind it could dictate terms to any world or the whole Consortium itself."

"Exactly," agreed Leclerc.

"I guess this puts MI into an awkward position," mused Mooney. "The Consortium threatened by one of its own secret projects?"

"A facile deduction at best," said Leclerc. "Any discovery we make has both military and civilian applications. It's up to each person how they might be used. The most obvious analogy would be the splitting of the atom. That discovery yielded both the atom bomb and nuclear power."

"Point taken," said Mooney.

"So, what do you need us to do?" asked Jules, getting to the point.

"Well, there's the question. We have two separate threads to this problem: Santanti and the nitinol ship. That presents us with two angles to follow up."

"Easy enough," said Mooney. "We split up."

"I don't know if I'm comfortable with that," said Jules. "Someone just tried to kill us…twice."

"So, what?" asked Mooney.

"So, I don't like the idea of you going off on your own with no one to watch your back."

"But haven't you been telling me you thought you were the target? If so, I should be safe from this killer, whoever it is."

Jules was momentarily stymied. It was true he'd been more or less convinced he was the primary target, but that was by no means certain.

"Well?" pressed Mooney.

"Yes, I have," admitted Jules.

"What's more, there's no evidence at all the attempts on our lives here on Callisto have anything to do with this assignment," reasoned Mooney. "In fact, leaving Callisto would actually be safer than staying. Whoever the killer is, how could he know where we'd be going?"

"She makes sense," said Leclerc. "In the meantime, I can have investigators here working on the case with local security. With luck, we'll have the killer before you can even complete your assignments."

Jules still didn't like it. Leclerc's confidence was far too assured. On the other hand, leaving Callisto was the safest thing to do at the moment, so he found himself agreeing.

"Good," said Mooney. "I'll try tracking down the nitinol ship. I already have an idea of how to go about it. Director, can you set me up with some papers and a new cover ID?"

Jules couldn't see how Mooney could get anywhere on the case very quickly so figured hers would be the safer of the two assignments.

"Okay," he said. "Meanwhile, I'll track down Santanti. After that, I'll join you. Be sure you turn in regular progress reports to Leclerc."

"Yes, boss!"

"How do you think you'll proceed, Jules?" asked Leclerc, synching his telcomm with those of Jules and Mooney and transferring all information about the case to their own secure devices. "After all, MI has been trying to get a lead on Santanti for almost a year now."

"Not sure. Starting at the beginning has always worked for me. Guess I'll try his place of business first then his last known address."

"Good luck with that," said Leclerc hopefully. "I don't need to impress on the both of you just how important this assignment is. The future of the Consortium might be at stake."

"Again?" kidded Mooney. "Jules and I seem to be making a habit of saving the universe for you."

Leclerc relaxed and grinned. "It does sound funny when you put it that way."

Just then, Jules cleared his throat.

"Something else, Jules?" asked Leclerc.

"Yeah." Jules glanced quickly at Mooney then back to Leclerc. "You brought up the Survey earlier and I was just wondering how Joan is doing? She out there again?"

Leclerc was not unaware of the sensitivity of the topic and tried to tread carefully.

"She's okay, Jules. Doesn't suspect a thing. The other Jules went back with her and the Survey has given them another job. Do you need to know where?"

Jules hesitated a moment then shook his head.

"Okay. As we discussed before, you and Mooney have decided to remain on a contractual basis as special agents in the employ of the Science Division. That allowed us to release the other Jules from duty so he and Joan can have their lives together. It's a big universe and the likelihood of you bumping into either one of them is remote. Especially if they continue working for the Survey."

Seeing his mood, Mooney took Jules' arm in hers and held him close. He reciprocated.

"I'm okay," Jules assured her. "This new assignment will be just the thing to wipe the last cobwebs away."

"You sure?"

"Um hm." Jules bent to peck her on the forehead when he stopped suddenly.

"What is it?" asked Mooney, pulling away.

"It just occurred to me," said Jules. "Talking about Joan and the other Jules must have brought it to mind."

"Brought what to mind?"

"The two Jules. The other Jules went on with his normal life, but I was given a new identity to prevent the other Jules or Joan from finding out about the duplication."

"We know all that," said Mooney, impatiently.

"But no one else is supposed to except for Leclerc here," said Jules. "So?"

"So, if the shooter, and the hacker if they're two separate persons, were past enemies as we suspect or had other reasons to see us dead, how did they know who we were?"

# Chapter Six
## *Murder in Latinium*

The direct flight by rocket from Callisto had been swift and uneventful so that only a few days after Mooney saw him off, Jules found himself at the transfer station high in orbit over Earth. One of several over the principal world of the Consortium, he found it as busy with crowds coming and going as he remembered it. For just that reason, he preferred to travel light while on business, so he barely had more than a toothbrush and hair comb to encumber him as he weaved his way among the crowds trying not to be late for his connecting flight to the surface.

A voice over the station annunciator told him the Rome shuttle was on schedule which meant he had precisely thirty-four minutes to make it to the gate. On the days long trip from Jupiter, he'd had plenty of time to review what facts Military Intelligence gathered on his assignment, which wasn't much more than Leclerc gave him at their meeting on Callisto, as well as the question dealing with his and Mooney's blown cover.

Despite the urgency of his current assignment, however, it was the latter question that bothered him the most. MI's security measures, particularly its agent protection program including the creation of new cover identities, was air tight, proven by the fact that not one had ever been previously blown. That made this instance totally unique and something that was sure to send departmental drones scurrying to find out what happened.

Of course, there was the possibility whoever tried to kill them had not been after Jules Santros or 'Manda Mooney but Victor and 'Manda Conroi. Which didn't make any sense because those two individuals hadn't been around long enough to get into trouble with anyone. Which brought the question around full circle; their cover must have been blown. Someone was able to penetrate MI security and lockout protocols to discover the deception. Who could have had such a capability? And who had the interest? Certainly, whoever hacked into the Callistan comp system to lock them out of the north hatch definitely had some technical skill but enough to get past MI's far more complex web of protocols and redundancies? Highly doubtful, but it happened. Jules was certain Leclerc would attack the problem with the full range of MI's technical expertise, which was formidable, and he only hoped they could come up with something before they were again made targets.

Someone jostled him and he realized he'd reached his gate. Passengers were already lined up, sending their ticket information via personal telcomm to the hostess manning the entrance podium. Jules did the same when his turn came. The girl compared his 3D ticket display with her own projected from the podium and cleared him through with a "Have a pleasant trip, sir."

Jules followed his fellow passengers, passing through the opened lock, into the shuttle. On the other side, the artificial gravity created by the spin of the station was noticeably lessened, and he was compelled to grab handholds lining the walls and ceilings to keep his balance.

"Please take your time," advised the shuttle's chief hostess, her blue uniform crisp and little hat tilted at a jaunty angle. "Gravity at the moment is less than half what it was inside the station. When we pull away, it will cease completely. So please fasten your seatbelts as soon as you find your places. Parents with children, make sure to keep hold of your child and secure yourself first. If you need assistance, please ask one of the crew for help."

As long as passengers continued to enter the shuttle, the hostess repeated her remarks. She was starting on them a third time when Jules found his seat and quickly fastened himself in. He was glad these new United shuttles featured extra leg room so once fastened to an aisle seat, passengers did not have to undo themselves to let someone through to the window. In his case, he managed to be assigned a place at a small port hole, allowing him to watch the stars outside slowly rotate past.

Finally, everyone found their seats and the shuttle was readied for disengagement. The entrance hatch closed with a thump, docking latches were released, and the vehicle simply drifted away from its moorings to the station. When it was clear, the roar of the thrusters was unmistakable and with little feeling of movement, the shuttle began to fall toward Earth.

As the home world drifted into view and slowly grew in size, Jules could not help thinking about the first time he met Mooney. She saved his life and soon after that, they decided to work together. A shared shuttle flight from Earth allowed them to spend quite a bit of time together getting acquainted. He recalled how, being married, he had to resist liking her too much. Suddenly, he felt a twinge of the old guilt he'd struggled with for months following his split into two Jules and his decision to be with Mooney. For the hundredth time, he asked himself had he made the right choice? On a surface level, he felt his relationship with Mooney was a far more comfortable one than the one he'd had with Joan. He had a better affinity with his current work than he ever did working with Joan on the Survey. And Joan wasn't about to let that go. Mooney, on the other hand, didn't expect to make dangerous MI missions her life's work, and for that matter, neither did he. So, he and Mooney were *simpatico* on a number of levels. And there was no doubt Joan was happy with her Jules who was after all, every bit as much Jules as he was. The only difference was, he didn't know about the duplication. But then, was that enough to differentiate between them both? Did that make them two separate and distinct individuals? Because if it did, then it was he who actually belonged with Joan.

Jules shook his head. Reminding himself yet again that following down such rabbit holes would drive him crazy.

Just then, the shuttle broke through the upper troposphere into a large scattering of cumulus clouds. Below, outside the small porthole, Jules could see the Latinium countryside loom into view. The white ribbons of smartways were immediately recognizable as they crisscrossed the countryside dotted with small villages hardly changed in the hundreds of years since the emergence of modern science. Gradually, as the shuttle began its glide path to the distant rocket field, Jules spotted the glistening surface of the Po River followed by the sprawling urbanscape of Rome. They were low enough now to make out larger structures. The Coliseum still stood as did the ancient Roman forum. But as always, the most recognizable building was that of St. Peter's Basilica with its great dome designed by the legendary Michelangelo himself. Jules smiled, recalling his first visit to the Vatican in company with his older brother. That was a long time ago. He'd seen many different worlds, traveled many millions of miles and light years since, then but of all the interplanetary wonders he had seen, none seemed to rival the sights of Rome, still considered by many as the Eternal City.

Thoughts of his brother did give him an idea though. It was an angle he might pursue later if there was time.

Meanwhile, as Rome fell away out of view, the shuttle's landing thrusters cleared their metal throats and the vehicle's attitude was altered as the pilot maneuvered it over the rocket field just outside Naples. Jules felt himself pushed back into his seat a moment as the whine of turbo assisters helped ease the ship down until the telltale thump of contact with the earth announced their arrival on the surface. As usual, passengers immediately freed themselves from their seat belts and all tried to stand at once. There was confusion and talking until things sorted themselves out and people began filing to the hatch that led to the terminal beyond.

Jules decided to wait until the rest of the passengers cleared out then made his leisurely way out, nodding thanks to the hostesses as he went.

Deciding to waste no time getting to work, he collected his reserved speedcar and gave it an address in Naples' business district. The smartways made sure traffic moved swiftly so there was no congestion and in very little time, Jules found himself outside the Faticonte Building where information provided by MI indicated that Professor Santanti kept his offices. The upscale location and modernesque plas-glass and flexsteel construction of the building indicated whatever the professor was doing since he quit the Science Division must have been profitable. Which was a mystery in itself because there was no way he could afford digs like that on a teaching salary at the nearby University of Napoli; a profession he claimed to have been practicing in the months before he stopped reporting in to Military Intelligence.

A foodmart off the lobby of the Faticonte Building reminded Jules he was hungry. He grabbed a quick sandwich from one of several auto dispensers and gulped it down with strong, black coffee of the type preferred by the locals. It was simple ham and cheese, but he'd almost forgotten how good real food could taste when it hadn't been flash frozen and transported millions of miles to places like Callisto or Marsport.

His telcomm guided him to the building's third floor suites where he found the office space rented by Professor Santanti under the corporate name of Ultimate Chemistries, a company specializing in doing on the spot chemical analyses on a contractual basis. Inside, he was greeted by a pretty dark haired young woman who told him her name was Maia Locoto. He could have gone directly to the professor's home on Miseno and broken into his home to look around, but why do things the hard way when you didn't have to? It was easier to look up Santanti's secretary and ask her to let him in.

"What can I do for you, Mr. Conroi?" asked the girl.

She used English when she realized her visitor did not speak Latinium.

Glancing around the office, Jules noted the numerous workstations scattered about. The doors leading to other rooms indicating plenty of floor space. Through a dividing clear plas wall, he could see a tidy but fully equipped laboratory on the other side. Nice.

"I'm an Off-Planet Police investigator," said Jules, who decided the cover of a policeman would be less intimidating than saying he was from Military Intelligence. "I was wondering if you've heard anything of Professor Santanti recently."

The girl shook her head. "I'm afraid not."

"That doesn't concern you?" he asked. "The fact that you haven't heard from your employer for the last several months?"

"It does, but what can I do about it? I'm credited till the end of the year, so all I can do is keep coming to work."

"That doesn't seem peculiar to you? That you've been paid so far ahead?"

The girl shrugged and chose not to reply.

"And what about everyone else?" asked Jules, inclining his chin in the direction of the empty workstations. "They're not as conscientious as you are?"

"I can't speak for the others," was all she chose to volunteer. "What about you? There've been other investigators here before looking for the professor. Have they had no luck?"

Now it was Jules' turn to shake his head. "Afraid not. I've been sent because my superiors hope a fresh look into the matter might turn up something that was missed."

"I'm not sure what else there is to discover. Like I told the others, the professor did very little work here…" she cocked her head toward the neat looking lab. "…and only came in now and then."

"How frequently was every now and then?"

"Whenever he needed to meet with anyone. I think he was interviewing them for jobs."

"What kind of jobs? Who were these people?" There was something in the previous reports about these meetings, but nothing muc h was learned about them.

"Construction jobs," replied the girl. "Structural engineers, spaceship designers, industrial chemists, but mostly construction type workers."

"You didn't find *that* odd? For a college professor to be hiring such people?"

"It was none of my business," said Maia. "There was no harm in it so far as I could tell."

"And what were your co-workers doing in the meantime?" persisted Jules, indicating the empty workstations.

"They were accountants and payroll people, I think. A personnel person who handled insurance issues. There was an attorney too, Mr. Argento, who occupied the office next to the professor's."

"No lab workers?"

"There might have been, but I never noticed any."

"No one ever used the lab?"

"I never saw anybody use it."

"Mind if I take a look?"

Maia shrugged a third time and rose to her feet. She led Jules around her workstation and into the laboratory. Instantly, lights came on, throwing the neat counters and quiet machines into harsh relief.

Jules looked around and again noticed how clean everything looked. Not a working lab at all. He began to move among the rows of counters, inspecting the retorts, centrifuges, thermo-microscopes, environmental chambers, sterile incubators, digital dry baths, test tube racks, beakers, and burners. All perfectly clean, all without a speck of dirt. He ran a finger along the surface of a measuring scale and saw there was dust at least. But the lab itself, so far as his practiced eye could see, had never been used.

It was beginning to look to Jules, as if the office suite was used mostly as a recruiting point for an as yet unidentified project not located on the premises. The offices and lab were simply a front for something else.

"Miss Locoto..."

"Maia," said the girl sweetly.

"Maia. How many people would you say the professor saw the times he was in the office?"

"Oh, a lot."

"Twenty, thirty?"

"At least. I think maybe more."

"And you never heard anything about why these people were being hired? Where they were going if they were hired?"

"No. They met with the professor behind closed doors and the others in the office kept to themselves."

"What about their workstations? Has their data been retrieved?" Jules knew prior investigators ran the 'stations through with classified MI cloud chasers to no avail. Someone erased all data originating from these workstations down the very last byte. Not an easy task. In fact, near impossible.

"Not unless the investigators who came in before you lied to me," Maia was saying. "They seemed surprised they couldn't find anything when they checked and asked me if I knew anything about that."

"And did you know anything about it?"

"No. All I know about workstations is you input data and data comes out when you ask for it. What happens in between is a mystery to me."

It was what Jules figured. Most people took the era's sophisticated computer based society for granted and never thought to question how it all worked.

Exiting the laboratory, Jules went over and peeked into the professor's office. He really didn't expect to find anything there after others had already scoured the place, but it didn't hurt to look. Inside, the room was sparse. A workstation devoid of the usual clutter, drawers empty, no cabinets or other storage areas of any kind, not even a coat rack. The view outside the clear-plas window was nice though.

The same held true for the attorney's office next door. It was as if the room had not been occupied at all.

In reviewing the investigation prior to his involvement, Jules learned the office's computer workstations were checked and nothing found. All of their data wiped clean down to the meta level. But the missing accountants and insurance officers gave him an idea. Maybe some relevant correspondence was preserved at the other end. Using his telcomm's secret hyper-bandwave communications protocols, he contacted MI and asked them to check all tax filings with local and Terran level governmental sources as well as insurance applications made in the name of Fernando Santanti dba Ultra Chemistries.

"So, you have no idea what happened to the attorney and the others?" he asked Maia, who was shadowing him from room to room. "Where they all went?"

The girl shook her head, her hair whipping around her neck and falling into her eyes. She brushed it away. "No one told me anything."

"So, what do you do when someone calls the office?"

"If someone did, I'd just apologize and ask to take a message."

"You mean to say, no one has called the office in all the time since the professor disappeared?"

"No."

"What about the lease? How long is it paid till?"

"The end of the year, so far as I know. The same as me."

Jules decided there was nothing of substance to learn from the professor's office, although what he didn't learn was beginning to seem as important as what he might have.

"Well, I guess I've seen all I can here," concluded Jules. "Next, I need to check the professor's home out Miseno way. Do you know how I go about that? Can I borrow a laser key or have the entrance code transferred to my telcomm?"

"I'd feel more comfortable driving out there with you," said Maia. "I'll let you in myself. It's what I did for the others."

"Doesn't matter to me," said Jules, waiting while she gathered her things. "I have a rented speedcar outside we can use."

"Okay."

"Is it a long drive?" asked Jules, holding the door to the office open for her.

"It's not far," said the girl, turning to make sure the office was locked up. "It's a beautiful drive so I'm sure you won't find it tedious."

Jules summoned the speedcar while they were in the down capsule so that by the time they reached the smartway, it was waiting for them by the pull up.

"Open," said Jules as the vehicle's voice recognition program responded to his command.

"Oh, you have one of the new models," said a delighted Maia. "A Berlinetta Streamer."

"I hadn't noticed," said Jules, helping her inside.

He fell in beside her and ordered the door closed.

"Why don't we ride with the roof open?" suggested Maia.

"You don't think the sun will be too hot?"

"Oh, no. The sea air and the moving 'car will take care of that."

So, Jules had the roof pulled back. While the 'car stood still, the sun was rather hot, but as soon as they began to move, it was hardly noticeable. At first, the speedcar took it slow in mid-town traffic. All around them, Naples was alive with other sporty 'cars, robot delivery vehicles, tour buses, and pedestrians everywhere who disregarded walkways and traffic signals and stepped out onto the smartway whenever they felt like it. It must have been the same all over Latinium as Jules recalled the same phenomenon when he visited Rome years before. As a result, traffic was stop and go in the city as the smartway's programming tried to keep up with the institutionalized jaywalking. Finally, however, they managed to break away into the suburbs heading west toward the Miseno peninsula.

The smartway hugged the rocky coast where the blue water of the Tyrrhenian Sea dashed itself against a shore that rose steeply upward.

Above the Via Miseno, homes dotted the face of the cliffs, some clearly centuries old, others as modern as yesterday. Veering from the Via Miseno onto the Via Il Vecchio, the 'car picked up speed along the narrow neck connecting Faro Capo, the end of the peninsula, to the mainland. Jules looked on as bathers crowded the beaches just like they did every season for hundreds of years. On the water, white sailed boats scudded in the breeze, the same breeze that threw back Maia's long black hair, exposing her pale skin.

"What did I tell you about the heat or rather lack of it?" she asked from behind a pair of sunglasses she'd plucked from a small hand bag slung at her hip.

"Feels good," said Jules, looking ahead at the rocky nob of the Faro Capo neighborhood. "The professor has a house out there?"

"Yes," said Maia, raising her voice against the rushing air. "A very fine villa."

"Real estate values out here must be pretty steep."

"They are," confirmed Maia.

Jules made no comment but wondered again how Santanti could afford such a home on a professor's salary. Ahead, meanwhile, he could now make out the shape of the Misena Lighthouse atop the two -hundred-and-sixty-foot promontory that was the district's most prominent feature.

"Misena was an important place for the ancient Romans," Maia was saying, obviously catching his interest in the tower. "Naples was originally called Portus Julius, where the Romans kept their western imperial fleet. "

"No kidding?" It was a subject at any other time, Jules would have been interested in, but not at the moment. "Where's the professor's home located? Doesn't seem to be much room out there for residences."

"It's still out of sight at the moment," said Maia. "Oh, there it is!"

She pointed, extending her arm in the direction of the promontory. As the speedcar neared the end of the beach and the smartway bent to the right to make its way around the lighthouse, Jules saw a stone villa nestled against the steep side of the Capo. It looked to be made of native stone with a red tile roof. A thin screen of shrubs provided the only spots of green to the vista, and as the 'car left the smartway to climb the private drive leading to the house, Jules could see some modern additions had been made to its architecture.

Some exterior walls had been replaced with plas-glass sheeting and door, and window fixtures were of synth-wood with accompanying security tie ins. Through the plas-glass wall overlooking the water below, Jules could see the floors were covered over in synth-carpeting with stereopticals hung on the walls.

"Here we are," said Maia unnecessarily as the 'car came to a halt before an enclosed speedcar stall.

With the 'car's electric motor shut down and without the wind blowing past his ears, Jules could plainly hear the surf crashing below, out of sight of the smartway. The air was heavy laden with the scent of the sea. Far above, the lighthouse stood silent and remote.

"Do you have the code to open the stall door?" he asked Maia.

In response, Maia pulled a telcomm from her little bag and asked it for access to the stall. Instantly, the broad door began to move aside in sections until the interior was exposed. Inside was a speedcar.

"Is that the professor's 'car?" asked Jules.

"I think so."

"Was it here before, when the other investigators visited?"

"I'm not sure. I never went to the stall when I was with them."

"Let's go into the house by the stall," suggested Jules. If anyone were on the premises, he wanted to at least deny them access to the 'car and a speedy getaway.

Maia asked her telcomm to open the door at the rear of the stall and a green light flashed by the keypad used for emergency manual entry.

Maia would have gone ahead first, but Jules held her back.

"I'll go in first," he said, pushing the door in.

"You think there might be some danger?" asked Maia, suddenly fearful.

"Just a precaution."

Pausing inside the door, Jules listened but only heard the deep quiet of a house devoid of life. Convinced no one was there, he proceeded into the kitchen, retrofitted with all the modern conveniences. Nothing appeared to have been used any time recently, so he continued on into the dining room. There, a vase of flowers sat on a table. The flowers were no longer fresh but long since browned and wilted.

"I wonder if I should have thrown out those flowers the last time I was here?" wondered Maia.

Jules said nothing but continued on into the den, the room he'd glimpsed from outside with the tasteful pneuma-furniture and less impressive stereopticals. Nothing was amiss. A stone arch led into a sitting room in the back of the house and a passage that likely gave access to the back bedrooms and bathroom. But it was the sitting room that held his attention, due mostly to the body lying on the floor.

A gasp broke the silence as Maia followed him into the room and saw the oddly crumpled form.

"Professor Santanti!" she exclaimed. "He looks...dead?"

It was a question that demanded answering so Jules took a closer look, rolling the form over to make an identification. The face with its trimmed goatee and wispy grey hair around the ears was familiar.

A neat hole in Santanti's chest, its edges charred, provided Jules with all the evidence he needed that the man was dead.

He patted the body down but found nothing that would explain its presence there. From his estimation, Santanti had not been dead for more than an hour.

"He's dead all right," said Jules, straightening.

"I...I don't understand," said Maia, still rattled.

"If it makes you feel any better, neither do I," admitted Jules.

Unspoken was his concern about the manner of the man's death. Although death by pulse pistol was not uncommon, Jules couldn't help but make a connection with the weapon used in the attack on himself back on Callisto. Was it a coincidence? Unfortunately, there was just not enough evidence to draw any conclusion in that regard.

On the other hand, the question about the source of Santanti's funding, his death, and the too coincidental appearance of his body within an hour of Jules' unannounced visit to the villa, suggested there was someone else behind the professor's death, someone with the credits and the organizational ability that could end up building a nitinol battleship.

Although by finding the professor he'd technically accomplished the mission Leclerc had assigned him, the case was definitely far from closed.

Jules was about to make a quick report to MI about finding Santanti and his suspicions when looking up, he noticed the edge of a workstation in an adjoining room. The professor's perhaps? He decided to make a check of the station first before making the report.

"Is that the professor's study over there?" he asked.

"Yes, but that workstation was searched by the other investigators like they did the ones at the office."

"No harm in double checking," said Jules as he headed over to the room.

He entered the study which was as neat and tidy as any of the rooms back at the downtown offices. There was another door on the opposite side of the room.

"Where does that go?" he asked Maia who had shadowed him into the study.

"The professor's bedroom I think."

Jules circled the workstation, took the chair he found there, and sought out the series of ports and slots intended for connecting external devices and whatnot to the built-in computer system. Carefully, so Maia didn't see, he slipped a nano-card from a pocket in his 'suitjacket and inserted it into one of the slots.

The card was called a cloud chaser. One of the Science Division's most important, and secret inventions; it released pre-programmed nanites into any workstation's hardware that were programmed for only one thing, to search out wiped information. No matter what anybody thought, such information still existed somewhere in the cloud and the nanites would find it. In that regard, a cloud chaser was one of the best friends a science agent could have.

For Maia's benefit, however, Jules decided to go through the motions of searching the workstation in the conventional manner.

"Do you have the voice activation code for this station?" he asked her.

"I didn't before, but Main Frame Central has since cleared me for that. Workstation 356F12, activate."

"Activated," said the station. "Welcome, Maia."

"Thanks," said Jules. "Workstation, access…"

But that was as far as he went, before he was stopped by what he could only describe as a funny feeling. Something wasn't right, but whatever it was, he couldn't identify it.

"What?" asked Maia, seeing the look on his face.

"Did you feel anything?" asked Jules, sitting straight in the chair and looking around.

"No."

"A draft or something?"

"Well, maybe. I just had a chill go up my back."

Jules stood up slowly. Everything seemed the same. He looked back toward the sitting room and could see Santanti's body on the floor just as he'd left it. Outside the plas glass windows, the sun was still shining. He looked at the door in the opposite wall. Walking over to it, he opened it and looked in. A bedroom, as Maia had told him. Yet another door faced him to the right.

"That's the master bathroom," said Maia at his shoulder.

Jules went over to the door, pulled it open, and stopped.

There was no bathroom. Instead, it was the sitting room. Sunlight poured through the big plas glass windows facing the sea and, on the floor, just as he'd last seen it, was Santanti's body.

"Wait a minute," said Maia, amazed. "That can't be. The sitting room is back that way…"

Across the sitting room, Jules could see the doorway leading into the study where he could just see the corner of the workstation. Quickly, he turned back to the bedroom door. The study was there just as they'd left it and beyond, the sitting room.

Wondering, he moved swiftly through the study to the sitting room, turned the corner, and found himself in the same bedroom!

"I don't understand this at all," complained Maia, who'd followed him from room to room. "How can we be in the bedroom again? We should have ended up in the dining room."

Saying nothing, but beginning to suspect, Jules charged across the bedroom to the other door and found himself in the study again.

"This is crazy," insisted Maia. "How can we keep coming back to the same rooms all the time? We should try some other doors."

But there weren't any other doors before and there still weren't now, so Jules backtracked through the bedroom, into where the bathroom ought to have been and, as he expected, found himself back in the sitting room.

"We're trapped," he said aloud, but it was an observation mostly meant for himself.

Meanwhile, Maia began to lose patience as she moved about the room, banging on the unbreakable plas-glass windows then taking a chair and trying that. Whether she hoped to attract outside attention or break out of the house, her efforts failed.

"How do we get out?" she demanded as the world she'd always taken for granted suddenly failed to conform to her expectations. "What happened? I don't understand any of this!"

Jules tried to maintain his own sense of calm. "Like I said, we're trapped in some kind of circularity loop. A Mobius trap. Something that was always theoretically possible, but no one ever managed to build one."

"A what?" asked Maia, her eyes tearing up and threatening to ruin her carefully applied makeup.

"A Mobius trap. A phenomenon that bends both time and space so whoever is caught in the singularity strip can't get off but simply goes around and around through the same spaces…"

"For how long?"

"Forever. Unless a way can be found to break the cycle."

"How can we do that?" pleaded Maia, who was on the verge of panic.

It was something Jules was trying hard to prevent in himself as well.

"I don't know," he admitted. "It's never been done before."

# Chapter Seven
*A Change of Plan*

Mooney eyed the long line of short haul work shuttles that lined the landing field outside the industrial town of Red Dust. It wasn't exactly a pretty sight. Not for the average space traveler anyway. Absent were the sleek rocket liners with their tapering but largely useless fins that formed the fleets of interplanetary passenger vehicles that whisked vacationers, business travelers, and migrants from one settled world of the Consortium to another. Instead, there were only the bulky work shuttles designed not to be aesthetically pleasing but for functionality. In this case, for the transfer of precious bulium ore from larger freighters left in orbit to factories that made up the industrial town's first order of business.

More to the point, bulium ore was largely unavailable in the Sol system, but outwards, in places like Orion, it was plentiful. Another such place just happened to be M-12, a planetoid in the region of Eta Cassiopeia. Mooney's idea was to come to the industrial town to eavesdrop in its bars and worker residences and, while under cover as a job seeker, visit the different company offices, talking up secretaries and personnel managers. Not unaware of her looks, she'd counted on them to disarm the town's male contingent making it easier to leverage out of them information about the Eta Cassiopeia run.

Unfortunately, she hadn't been able to discover anything more about the missing freighters than what Leclerc briefed her on. Except for one thing. Unlikely as it was, one long hauler still intended on sending a freighter out to M-12. That fact immediately suggested a change of plan. If she could acquire a position aboard the company's outbound ship, she'd at least be in a position to learn some first hand information about the disappearances should anything untoward occur. She might even be able to identify someone aboard ship who could be an informant of some kind.

Sure, it would be dangerous. After all, two ships had already disappeared without a trace and a battleship likely destroyed.

On the other hand, she wasn't exactly unused to danger. It became a familiar companion in her job as an agent for the Exterior Ministry and now as a science agent. Not that she was fearless. Far from it. But she had a strong sense of duty and when faced with a decision to go forward or back down…well, she was never the kind to back down. Still, she understood the position she was placing her husband in. If Jules knew of her plan, he certainly would raise objections but after all the shouting was over, he'd agree. So long as she was an active agent, he had no choice but to let her go. Now, if they decided to retire and start that family they had talked about, that would be different, but as of right now, she knew her duty and asked Leclerc not to tell Jules about her plan. Best just to avoid all the protestations of the danger and all that. Ultimately, Jules understood they were both professionals and knew the hazards of the job.

Dressed in a common worker's jumpsuit, her hair pulled back in a pony tail, Mooney shifted her spaceman's satchel over her shoulder and moved past the front gate into the row of landing aprons operated by Consolidated Ores Inc., the long haul ore movers that insisted on continuing to work the Eta Cassiopeia run. She hadn't visited Mars in quite some time and so still found it bothersome when taking the occasional deep breath from her oxygen mask. Terra forming the planet had begun long ago and was only now turning the planet into a livable place for humans. And though the atmosphere was dense enough now to retain heat from the sun, it was still too thin for people to go without the occasional jolt of oxygen from their masks while outside the domed cities.

She had arrived in Red Dust a few days before and immediately began her rounds playing the part of a job seeker, convincingly she thought, until she learned at least one long haul company was still traveling to the Eta Cassiopeia system. Checking her telcomm to find out more about Consolidated Ores, she saw that it was true and furthermore, they were hiring. Looking through the positions available, she chose one she believed she could bluff her way into and made her way to the grimy office tower that served as the company offices.

No one questioned her as she passed through the door locks into the building's small lobby. It was clean but not gleaming with evidence of wear from generations of long haul workers passing through its corridors looking for employment and credit transfers. In fact, a few of them were hanging about, catching last minute smokes before venturing out into the thin Martian atmosphere. They did not bother hiding their interest in Mooney, looking her up and down, vainly trying to study her measurements under her jumpsuit.

"Which floor is personnel?" Mooney asked them, acting as if she were used to such inspection, which of course, she was.

One of the men pulled the coffin nail from his mouth and gestured to an up capsule nearby. He blew smoke from his lungs in a direction away from Mooney. "Third floor facing the up capsule."

"Thanks," said Mooney, stepping toward the opening doors of the up capsule.

"You thinkin' of signing up for a haul?" asked the man.

Mooney turned inside the up capsule and replied, "The Ex-3."

The last thing she saw as the doors to the up capsule slid shut was how the man's eyes went wide at the idea this pretty young thing was intending to sign up for the risky Eta Cassiopeia run.

*Maybe I can squeeze some extra pay out of Consolidated Ores for signing on to this run. The cash might help smooth things over with Jules after he finds out what I'm doing. Maybe!*

She was still grinning over the idea when the doors opened on the third floor and she found herself facing a door labeled "Personnel."

Inside, a middle-aged woman, with all the earmarks of a "long haul widow" sat at an early model workstation pecking at its keys.

"Can I help you?" she asked, looking up when Mooney stepped into the tiny cubicle. There was just room enough for the woman's workstation, chair, and another couple of uncomfortable looking plasticite chairs against a wall.

"I'm looking for a job," said Mooney, throwing her satchel into one of the empty chairs. "I sent in my application yesterday."

"Your name?"

"'Manda Conroi," said Mooney truthfully.

The woman did some pecking and apparently found what she was looking for.

"Oh, yes. You have an appointment with Mr. Farent."

She spoke briefly to Mr. Farent and must have received a reply in the small earpiece she wore because a door opened in the room's rear wall, beckoning Mooney into a larger room beyond.

Inside, a man sat at his own workstation studying something on the screen. He stopped when Mooney entered.

"Miss…Conroi, is it?" he asked, not bothering to get up.

He looked rough around the edges, suggesting he'd spent most of his career at various jobs aboard shuttles and freighters or perhaps operating the big tractors and trucks carrying ore from shuttles directly to the factory dumps. An office job was something he had been rewarded with after long, hard service to the company.

"That's right," replied Mooney, taking a chair in front of the workstation without waiting to be asked.

"I see by your application you're looking for the quality control engineer position on the Ex-3 haul?"

"That's right."

"You've had quite a bit of experience in that line, I see."

It wasn't exactly true but Mooney was appreciative of the fast work MI had done to create her new cover. Should Farent decide to double check her claims, he'd find everything in order. Not that he'd have the time. She'd made sure of that.

Farent pulled away from her application to look squarely at Mooney.

"You do realize what it is you're applying for?"

Mooney smiled the smile that usually disarmed most men. "I've heard some things about the run."

"Two freighters have disappeared in the region of Eta Cassiopeia. Not ours. But a general warning has been issued by Naval Command that all commercial shipping should avoid the area for the time being."

"Sounds like good advice," said Mooney, crossing her legs. "Then why is Consolidated Ores going forward with the Ex-3 haul?"

"Unfortunately, we have contractual obligations that require us to provide our customers with a certain amount of bulium every quarter," said

Farent. "Bulium is essential in the manufacture of tintinabulum. What the Navy needs for its ships. It's a strategic ore and if we don't come through with our delivery, the company goes under. It's as simple as that."

"And how does the company estimate the risks involved?"

"Moderate but not high," replied Farent truthfully. "We've made two runs into the sector since the Naval advisory with no mishaps. What we've been doing is heading in to M-12 using different headings for each trip. That way, if there are any pirates in the area, they won't know which way we'll be coming from."

"You think it's pirates?" Mooney's hopes rose that maybe she was about to learn something new.

Farent shrugged. "Naval Command doesn't say but what else could it be? Ships just don't disappear without a trace, especially freighters. Don't say it! I know it's pretty far out for piracy, but it's all we've got."

"Is that why this position is open?" asked Mooney. "Because of the danger?"

Farent nodded. "We've made service on the runs voluntary for our people and a number of them decided not to take the risk. I don't blame them. But like I said, we have contracts to fulfill. Still interested?"

Mooney pretended to think it over then "What about salary? Is the company offering hazard pay?"

Farent relaxed, concluding that with the question of money, Mooney decided to sign on.

"We are offering a ten percent add on to posted salaries," he said.

"I think in a situation like this, fifteen percent would be more reasonable." Mooney had to make it look good. She didn't want Farent to see how eager she was to be hired.

Farent smiled. "For a woman with your job experience, I think that can be arranged."

"Good. Show me where to sign."

Just then, her recollections were interrupted as the boom and roar of powerful engines drew her attention to the landing field. One of the half dozen haulers lined up there began to lift slowly into the air. Mooney paused, joining dozens of other engineers, refueling workers, mechanics, and crewmen as they watched the shuttle maneuver slightly before picking up speed and streaking into the upper atmosphere. In space, it would rejoin an orbiting freighter to wait until all was ready for departure to some world where mined ore was waiting to be transported.

After the shuttle had gone, Mooney resumed her way along the edge of the apron until she reached the office tower. Inside, she showed the new identification badge fixed to her jumpsuit to a launch officer and proceeded to the launch ready room. There, she joined a few dozen of her fellow crewmen who had assembled for some last minute information about the Ex-3 run. There was nothing Mooney hadn't been briefed on in previous meetings, so she zoned out a bit, focusing instead on the one other female crew member present.

"Hello there," she said, shouldering her way past the crowd of male crew members, most of whom towered over the women. "My name's 'Manda. Quality control."

The other woman smiled, happy and somewhat relieved to see she would not be the sole female aboard the freighter. "Tenebro. Leah Tenebro. Nurse pharmacist."

They shook hands.

"I'm glad you're here. Hate it when I have to fend off the boys with no one to watch my back."

Leah grinned. "Know what you mean. Not many of us ladies in deep space."

"Not in this business anyway." Mooney looked around. "Aside from come ons by the crew, you were told the risks?"

Leah nodded. "I don't think they're as great as they let on. Naval Command can be overly cautious."

"What they're paid for, I guess," agreed Mooney.

Just then, last call for Ex-3 came over the room's annunciator.

"That's us," said Mooney, shouldering her spaceman's satchel. "After you."

She followed Leah out the doors and onto the flight line where the end shuttle was already warming up its ascent engines. A few minutes later, she stood in line with the rest of the crew and marched up the gangway to disappear into the darkened belly of the spacecraft.

# Chapter Eight
*Escape...and Capture*

"What are we going to do? I need to get back to work!"

Maia seemed to have forgotten no business had been conducted at the offices of Ultimate Chemistries for quite some time or that they'd just found her employer dead in the other room. Jules, however, was willing to give her some slack. After all it wasn't every day you found yourself caught in a Mobius trap.

"Just keep calm, Miss Locoto," he said, trying to keep her from outright panic.

Jules was standing in the center of the study, looking through the doorway into the sitting room where the body of Professor Fernando Santanti still lay where they found it a few hours before. Turning, he set his gaze on the opposite door leading to the professor's bedroom. Beyond it should have been a master bathroom and a second doorway accessing a corridor where guest bedrooms were located. Only he knew from experimentation, that was not so. Instead, contrary to all laws of reality and common sense, the bathroom door opened directly into the sitting room, skipping the rear portion of the house altogether. The same was true for the sitting room. If he tried to leave it by way of the dining room, he wound up back in the professor's bedroom and so into the study.

How such a thing was possible, Jules had no idea. In theory, it could be built in three dimensions, but to also include a disorienting manifold that confused the senses and prevented the eye from seeing a way out was just beyond anything he'd ever heard of. Looking around him at the walls of the study, the bedroom, and sitting rooms beyond, everything appeared normal and yet he knew space had been bent, twisted, and reattached in such a way that by walking from one room to another, you ended up repeating the sequence endlessly with no discernible exit.

"But why can't we get out?" Maia asked. "What is this trap you mentioned? How does it work?"

Jules thought about how to answer her. The concept of a Mobius loop was difficult enough to grasp in the mind let alone to try and explain.

"Just sit down for a minute," said Jules soothingly.

Maia reluctantly sat in the chair behind the workstation, looking at Jules pleadingly with wet, glistening eyes.

"Now, how to explain?" Jules ran a hand through his hair.

Maybe by going over it with Maia, it might clarify his own thoughts. Calm him down so he could think.

"Think of a strip of paper," he began, aware that paper itself was a rarely used commodity in 2289 and thus did not provide the best example for the girl to consider. "If you took it by each end, twisted it once, and then attached the ends together, you'd create a single surface with both an inside and an outside. And by connecting the ends, you'd make that surface an endlessly repeating loop. That phenomenon is called by scientists 'unorientable' because it refers to a surface that doesn't have any spatial vectors that can be measured. As a result, it would be impossible for anyone occupying such a space from finding a way off."

"Impossible?"

He could tell she was struggling to imagine an object of the kind he described. He couldn't blame her; he was finding it hard to grasp himself.

"Well, maybe not," said Jules, trying to assure her.

It was in looking down at the girl as she sat in the chair that Jules' gaze fell on the cloud chaser, still inserted in the workstation where he'd placed it earlier. It now occurred to him it likely was the insertion of the cloud chaser into the workstation that triggered the trap.

*Nice to know but how did realizing that help him now?*

But contemplating the work station started him thinking.

Whoever set this trap might have outsmarted themselves.

*Wait a minute. Wait a minute*, thought Jules to himself. *Let's not get ahead of ourselves. Go through this one step at a time.*

Now, what did he remember from reports he'd read when he was a full time member of the Science Division? At the time, his team had studied many different concepts for purposes of military application. One of them was the Mobius loop. They dismissed it at the time as unworkable but some work had been done with it.

For instance, if a person or object were to be caught within a Mobius loop, it would be impossible to locate the seam or folds in the manifold after the loop was created, let alone the correct sequence in which they were created. Finding the folds and tracing them back in reverse sequence was the only way to find the master seam where the two ends of the loop, forming the inside and outside, were joined. And breaking that seam was the only way to unravel the loop and escape.

Jules held up his hand, forestalling another question from Maia, and began to pace the room.

Finding folds that led back to the seam was impossible with the naked eye. The human senses had no way of reinterpreting reality in order to detect the changes made in the manifold of special vectors. Ergo, the senses needed to be aided by some external device. And that's where whoever set the trap may have overlooked something: Santanti's workstation.

"May I have that chair?"

Maia, startled by Jules' shift from wordless pacing to sudden action, surrendered the chair without a word.

Jules quickly sat and, switching from the workstation's audio command function to simple keyboard, activated the inboard computer. The station had been wiped clean of course, just as those at the offices of Ultimate Chemistries; but he didn't need the station's local data logs so long as the cloud chaser did its job. And it had. Its programmed nanites had already invaded the station's metaneural pathways following the trail of the lost data into the cloud. Once there, he had access to the vast network of information generated by the Consortium's entire population. Very quickly, he located the floor plans of Santanti's villa with exact measurements in feet and inches of every room including the study, bedroom, and sitting room. With those figures, he could use the computing power available in the cloud to identify the very slight but still mathematically detectable folds in the space-time of the trap's manifold structure. The folds which changed the measurements of the rooms in an oh so infinitesimally slight way.

His spirits were definitely rising at that point when suddenly he became aware of a new sluggishness in the station's responses to his commands. Something was trying to interfere with his work. When he tried a few tricks, he knew to bypass slowdowns in the data stream and none of them worked, he knew he was up against an active foe, perhaps even the brain behind the Mobius trap itself.

"Whoever he is, he's good," said Jules aloud.

"Who is?" asked Maia.

"I don't know but I can sense his hand in the cloud. The way he manipulates data. Like nothing I've ever experienced before." Whoever it was, Jules was certain he'd finally found the person responsible for closing he and Mooney out of the north hatch on Callisto. No doubt about it!

Perspiration broke out on Jules' forehead as his fingers flashed over the keys, trying to get away from his adversary, trying to stay one jump ahead of him. His one advantage at the moment was that whoever it was at least wasn't a mind reader.

Then, luck broke his way or rather, inspiration struck.

If he could lead whoever it was back down the data trail to Santanti's workstation, he might be able to trap his avatar in the very same circularity loop that Jules was now trying to escape. Carefully, so as not to cause suspicion in his adversary, Jules led him through a series of feints and false trails until he managed to maneuver him onto a downward data spiral to the workstation. Holding his breath, he watched the activity counters on the screen as they all held steady at their "dead" readings. Suddenly, the user counter sprung to life, its indicator column shooting up to max levels.

"He took the bait!" exclaimed Jules, pointing at the indicator column for Maia's benefit. "Look! He's trapped in the workstation!"

"I don't know what you're talking about but if it makes you this happy, then I'm happy too, I guess," ventured a puzzled Maia.

"It means the way is clear now for us to get out of here," said Jules, quickly returning to the cloud and backtracked to the villa's floor plans and use them to plot a directional vector by means of differential-algebraic equations.

Instantly, the power of the Consortium's computer network gave him the solution. The equation it produced, once loaded in an external device, would indicate a direction point for the hidden seam allowing his senses to orient themselves enough to detect it.

Making sure to bypass the workstation where his recent adversary was still caught in a circulatory matrix loop, Jules transferred the data to the cloud chaser which he removed from the 'station and reinserted into his telcomm.

Activating the device's projection screen, the floor plan of the villa hung in the air a few feet in front of him.

"It looks like the floor plans of a house," remarked Maia.

"They are," replied Jules. "The schematics for this villa. See there? That's the study where we are now."

"What do all those numbers mean? They keep changing."

"They're the readouts of the mathematical equation I uploaded from the station," explained Jules. "They're extremely sensitive so the slightest movement, even my own pulse, causes a disturbance in the spatio-temporal fold of the Mobius loop we're stuck in. I have to follow the vector indicated in the scrolling numbers because there's no way to identify the surface manifold with the naked eye. But once we get these numbers down to zero, we'll have found the seam in the loop and I hope, escape from the trap."

"Then hurry up..."

Jules held up a hand. "Enough. No more moving around. Not even any talking. You have to remain absolutely still so there's as little interference with the readouts as possible."

Not taking his eyes off the furiously moving numbers, Jules took one step and stopped, waiting.

The numbers slowly stopped. Then, noting the difference from what they read before he took the step, he turned slightly and took another.

He stopped again, watching the numbers scroll furiously. Finally, they slowed to a point he recognized as the point where only his pulse was causing them to move.

Now he took a third step, going through the same procedure of stopping, waiting until the numbers slowed, gauging his direction and taking another step.

Eventually, after an hour of hesitant action, Jules reached a point in the sitting room next to where the body of Santanti still lay. There, he watched the numbers in the various columns displayed in the air before him slow down, slow down, until they hovered near zero. The only movement, timed to the rhythm of his heartbeat, the numbers as they rose a few numerals above zero then fell a few more below zero. *I found it!*

"Maia," he called, watching the numbers scroll rapidly upward in response to his raising his voice. "You can start breathing again and come over here."

He watched the numbers go crazy again as the girl bounded from the study and ran over to where he was standing.

"Are we out?" she asked eagerly. "Can we leave now?"

"Just stay where you are," said Jules, slowly reaching into his synthjacket and withdrawing his ion pistol.

"I didn't know you had that," gasped Maia.

Like most civilians, she was not used to being around hand weapons.

Jules said nothing, watching the numbers.

"What are you going to do with that?" asked Maia about the pistol.

"The overlap, or seam, is here somewhere," said Jules moving the telcomm around, trying to get an exact fix on the hidden seam. "This is where the overlap of the two conjoined strips of space-time is located, created when the trap was triggered when I fooled around with the workstation. Because twisting time and space like this is inherently unstable, it causes tension between the two, making it relatively easy to sunder with the right amount of force."

"Force?"

"Like the discharge of an ordinary ion pistol," said Jules, stopping as the numbers passed absolute zero.

Suddenly, he fired his weapon at a spot on the floor and instantly everything changed. Not in any way they could see but something their physical senses felt.

"We're free!" exclaimed Maia with relief. "Now we can...where did they come from?"

"Who?"

A few feet away, standing over the limp form of Professor Santanti, were two men in the uniform of the local police. They said something in Latinium, in words Jules did not understand, but the ion pistols in the officers' hands made their meaning perfectly clear.

They were under arrest for murder.

# Chapter Nine
*Under Arrest*

Wordlessly, Jules handed his own pistol over to one of the officers then motioned to his telcomm held in the other hand. The officers indicated they understood his meaning and stood by as Jules told the device to activate its translation program.

One of the officers spoke.

"Mr. Victor Conroi?" asked one, his words translated a moment after he finished by the telcomm but in Mooney's voice.

That took Jules by surprise. Mooney must have reprogrammed it when he wasn't looking. That mischievous streak in her character was one of the things that endeared her to him and one that reminded him of her now. How was she progressing in her own investigation? Was she getting anywhere? He found he was already missing her companionship and hoped he could wind up his part of the job soon so they could be reunited again. Right about now, going back to Callisto and finishing up their interrupted honeymoon was starting to look good to him.

"You are Victor Conroi?" asked the officer again.

The question was a formality since the officer had already run his telcomm over Jules and its facial recognition program had identified him. The only uncertainly was whether his new identity would be properly registered to his face. To Jules' relief, it apparently was.

"Yes," replied Jules. "That's me."

"It says here that you are a physicist in the employ of the Science Division of Military Intelligence," continued the officer.

"He told me he was with the Off-Planet Police," protested Maia.

"Is this true?" asked the officer of Jules.

"I thought I could avoid unnecessary complications."

"Would your being with Military Intelligence have anything to do with your presence here?"

"It could," said Jules carefully, not wanting to reveal too much at the moment. The fewer who knew about his reasons for wanting to find Santanti, the better.

"Your arrest for the murder of Fernando Santanti might be helped if you cooperate," said the officer, sensing Jules' reticence.

"Murder?"

"I should think that would be obvious, Mr. Conroi," replied the officer, nodding in the direction of Santanti's body.

"Of course, things don't look good at the moment," admitted Jules. "But how did you end up being here in the first place?"

"There was a report that we would find the murderers of the missing Professor Santanti at this address and we were instructed by our supervisor to investigate," said the officer, who seemed slightly the senior of the two. "It appears the tip had some validity."

"I suppose it would do no use to explain to you that we didn't kill the professor?"

The man shook his head. "That is not for us to decide. I am afraid you will have to remain under arrest. If there is anything to sort out, it can be done at police headquarters."

Jules decided to accept the situation. He knew enough about authority and bureaucracy to know lower level personnel such as these two well meaning officers would never take it upon themselves to decide to free a pair of prisoners. He'd have to wait until he could speak to their superiors before making his case for innocence. Besides, he wasn't eager to divulge his confidential status to anyone but higher authority.

"Am I under arrest too?" asked Maia, nervously. "I didn't kill the professor! He was my employer."

"And you are..." The senior officer waved his own telcomm before the girl, its facial recognition program taking little time finding a match. "...Miss Maia Locoto. Secretary for Ultimate Chemistries, 449 Via Benuto, Napoli."

"That is right," confirmed the girl. "May I go?"

"I am afraid not," said the man. "Not until your presence here has been cleared up."

"But I tell you I am not involved! This man said he was an investigator like the others who came looking for the professor and when he asked to come here to look around, I came with him to let him in. I just did it because I figured it was part of my job. My responsibility. Is this what I can expect simply for doing what is right?"

The officer shrugged helplessly. "The matter is out of our hands. We arrived here as instructed, found a dead man and you and Mr. Conroi. You cannot expect to be released before certain questions have been answered?"

Maia said nothing, realizing the man was right.

As they remained covered by the younger officer, the other used his telcomm to record an image of Santanti's body as well as the rest of the room. He took possession of Jules' ion pistol and telcomm then patted him down.

"The two of you will accompany us to our vehicle now," he said, when he finished.

There were sounds outside and presently, a few more officers entered and began examining the body, sweeping the room with devices, collecting any evidence there might be. As they left the house, this time by the front entrance, an ambulance was pulling up and neighbors began to gather at the foot of the driveway.

They were bundled into the rear seat of the police vehicle which was then secured with a mild electric curtain that would, nevertheless, discourage them from escaping if they were so inclined. The officers slid into the front seat. One of them ordered the car to seal up and go to police headquarters.

The drive to headquarters was considerably less pleasant than the drive out to Santanti's villa, at least to Jules. Maia remained silent, her face worried. She'd never been in police custody before and had no idea what came next.

"Don't worry," said Jules, attempting to soothe her fears. "Nothing will come of this. You'll be at your workstation again in a couple of hours."

"You sound confident about that," said the girl, watching as the beaches of the peninsula gave way to the crowded streets of Napoli. "How can you be so sure?"

"Because we didn't have anything to do with the murder of Professor Santanti," said Jules.

"But who did?" asked the girl suddenly, turning to face Jules. "I thought he was just missing."

"That's a question I'd like to have an answer for myself," said Jules, recalling his experience in the cloud. It was clear now the trail to the nitinol ship would not end with Santanti. There was someone else behind him, maybe above him. Someone who decided to limit his exposure and eliminate the professor.

His thoughts were interrupted by the girl next to him, who had begun to quietly weep. Clearly, she was not used to being thrown into such circumstances. It wasn't every day ordinary people like her encountered death, let alone murder. Jules decided to say nothing. Better she get it out of her system before they arrived at police headquarters. Hopefully, he could spare her further grief by clearing up his status with the proper authorities before they could subject her to the grilling to be expected of someone found at the scene of a murder.

A moment later, the 'car slid to a silent halt before the 'crete and plas glass structure that passed for Napoli's police headquarters. Even Jules was shocked at the clash in styles represented by the modern headquarters building and the efforts at historic preservation that saved the ancient look of much of the rest of the city. Clearly, there must have been a dogfight between preservationists and modernists during the approval process. Unfortunately, the modernists had won.

Inside, both Jules and Maia were fingerprinted on light boards, audio recorded, had their retinas scanned, and their facial characteristics updated. When all that was done, Jules found himself occupying a cell and hemmed in with an electric curtain of considerably higher voltage than that used in the police vehicle. Well, he didn't expect to remain there long. It was Maia he was concerned about. Poor thing. It was only her bad luck to have been swept up by circumstances beyond her control. Likely, she was sitting in another cell in the women's block, weeping quietly.

His prediction of a short stay in the cell block was confirmed when presently, an officer appeared to switch off the curtain. He handed Jules his telcomm. Its translator was still engaged.

"Lt. Rossi will see you now," said Mooney's voice from the device.

Jules followed the officer along a hallway or two then in an up capsule for a few floors. On the third, he was ushered into Rossi's office and invited to take a chair.

"I'm sorry for the inconvenience, Mr. Conroi," began Rossi, who resumed his own seat behind his workstation.

"Think nothing of it," replied Jules. "If you hadn't put us through the usual procedures, I would have had less respect for your professionalism."

Rossi nodded in acknowledgment of the compliment. "You really should have reported in with us before beginning your investigation."

"You're right, of course," admitted Jules. "That was me *not* being professional."

Rossi chuckled then, "I was surprised when I contacted Military Intelligence as you suggested, to be connected immediately with the director himself. I wasn't aware at just how highly placed you were."

Jules preferred not to indicate one way or another whether the observation was correct.

"I am on assignment for MI," was all he volunteered.

"I was aware other investigators had been around looking into the disappearance of Professor Santanti but did not realize what importance your organization placed in him."

"Professor Santanti worked on a number of sensitive projects as an employee of MI," said Jules carefully. "One of the conditions of his employment was that if he ever chose to leave, he would have to report in on a regular basis so MI could be reassured details of its more sensitive projects were not compromised."

Rossi nodded. "I see."

"When the professor failed to make those reports, routine procedure required he be checked. That was when it was discovered he'd disappeared. Investigators were dispatched but could find no clue to the professor's whereabouts."

"Yes. When they arrived in Napoli, they came to my office to alert me of their presence. I could not help them at the time because there had been no report the professor was missing. It had not become an official police matter."

"Nevertheless, when the investigators came up empty, the Science Division was given the assignment to look into the matter more closely."

"You are a more…specialized agent?"

"Let's just say I have more experience."

"According to the earlier investigators, the professor first failed to report in almost a year ago," observed Rossi. "I would think the trail had long since grown cold."

"I feared that as well," agreed Jules, "until I found the professor's body at the villa. Still warm, I might add."

"Do you think its appearance was connected with your arrival?"

Jules nodded. "Definitely. Whoever left it there knew I'd been assigned the case and left a double trap for me at the villa. As you know, the girl Maia and I were caught in a Mobius loop. Not an easy thing to create. In fact, I would have called it impossible before this afternoon. Then, in case I was able to escape the Mobius loop, a second trap was laid: being framed for murder."

"We received a tip that we would find the professor dead in his home with the murderer still on the premises," said Rossi.

"Untraceable, I presume?"

Rossi shrugged. "The cloud, you know."

It was the same old story. The cloud made it impossible for ordinary law enforcement to trace telcomm communications. It sometimes made Jules wish MI could share its cloud chaser tech with them, but the benefits of keeping it secret outweighed those of making it public.

"Anyway, it was a sweet set up, but at least it tipped the hand of whoever is behind the murder. Now we know he exists and that he really knows something about computer technology."

In fact, judging by the Mobius trap, Jules feared whoever the man was, he had to be one of the most brilliant alive. That, or he'd found a way to make computers not only to roll over but to sit up and beg, and this person likely had a self-repairing nitinol battleship at his disposal.

"Were there any reports about activity around the professor's villa recently?"

"None, I am afraid. And an evidentiary sweep discovered nothing except what was left by the professor himself."

"Speaking of the professor," said Jules, "Do you have any idea how his body ended up there this afternoon?"

"That is a question that concerns me deeply," admitted Rossi. "The professor was missing for almost a year before today. Was he being held? Did he go willingly? We do not know. The condition of his body when discovered by yourself suggests he was killed only an hour or so before you arrived. We are currently checking all flights in and out of every rocket field in Latinium as well as all local fields. Perhaps we can find some clue to the professor's movements and any traveling companions he may have had in the hours preceding his death."

"Routine police procedure will turn up something if anything will," noted Jules. "Still, I wonder where he…wait a minute."

Jules pulled out his telcomm and used a hyperbandwave signal reserved for Military Intelligence. His top priority alert routed the call directly to Director Leclerc.

"Was wondering when you'd call," said the director.

Jules switched on the identity dampener so the director's image would not be projected. His voice was disguised.

"Had to clear up a few things here at the police station," explained Jules. "Thanks, by the way, for smoothing things over for me."

"No trouble at all. I have something for you."

"The insurance and tax information?"

"Your hunch was right," confirmed Leclerc. "To keep whatever he was doing legit, Santanti made sure he paid his taxes and insured his workers. Sending information via encrypted channel 12."

Jules accessed the channel, making sure to mask the process from Rossi. In moments, he was looking through Ultimate Chemistries' tax filings whose numbers surprised him. They indicated massive investments in the company by parties unknown. No wonder Santanti could afford the villa at Faro Capo.

"Anything wrong?" asked Rossi, noting the look on Jules' face.

"According to his tax filings, Santanti had a lot of credits to play around with," said Jules. "Most of it coming from unlisted investors. That might be something you can work on. Get in touch with Central Monetary and see if they can identify the investors. Any one of them might have had reasons for wanting Santanti gone."

"Make a note of that," said Rossi for the benefit of his workstation.

Further scrutiny revealed much of the investments were in turn plowed into another venture, a mining operation off Vega. That was interesting. Vega was a dead system with no habitable worlds but plenty of sizeable asteroids and planetoids mixed in with a thick ring of dust that orbited the star. Jules knew surveys of the area pointed to rich mineral deposits making it a logical place for speculative mining interests. The question was, what was Ultimate Chemistries mining for in the region? There were plenty of other more accessible systems for mining. Why such an out of the way place?

Maybe the insurance applications would have the answer. Switching to the company's insurance providers, Jules immediately saw the policies merely covered the usual hazards of working in space. That was strange. Such policies, he knew, usually were accompanied by addendums peculiar to the place where the work was to be done. Mars, for instance, presented completely different risks than say, Nephron in the Aldebaran system. Why weren't Santanti's employees protected beyond a basic plan?

On the other hand, the policies did detail exactly where the work was being done: a planetoid designated in the star charts as V-3, an unnamed body located within the dust ring around Vega. Its exact location could be easily discovered with a simple search. More interestingly, the policy listed titanium and nickel mining and smelting as the work being performed on site. That received Jules full attention. The two minerals were the ingredients used in the fabrication of nitinol.

"Something else?" asked Rossi.

"I think so. For my investigation anyway. Nothing I think will help your department with Santanti's murder. I think your best bet is to stay with the travel checks and follow up with the tax filings. Nothing wrong with keeping each other informed as we move along though."

"I realize you cannot tell me too much about your own assignment," said Rossi carefully. "But can you give me any idea about why the professor was murdered?"

Jules considered a moment. "I think his usefulness had ended. For what, I don't know yet. But he was killed when he was, specifically to frame me for the murder. Someone is trying to thwart my investigation, Lieutenant, and I would venture to guess it would be useful for both of us if you pursued those avenues discussed. I'm sorry I can't offer you more but the truth is, I'm still somewhat in the dark myself."

"I'll keep Military Intelligence informed of my investigations," said Rossi. "They can get the information to you, I trust?"

Jules nodded, eager to follow up on the Vegan angle. "And now, I think, there's one more loose end to take care of."

"You don't think Miss Locoto is involved in the case?"

"Pretty sure, but no harm keeping tabs on her."

"I'll have her brought up."

A few minutes later, Maia stepped into the office. Her clothes were rumpled, but she'd managed to straighten herself out on the trip from her holding cell.

"I don't understand why I am being held," she complained. "All I am is the office secretary. I do not know anything!"

Rossi held up his hands in a defensive motion. "We understand that, Miss Locoto. You are being released. Will you continue to hold down your job at the offices of Ultimate Chemistries?"

Calming down, Maia nodded. "I am paid until the end of the year."

"Very well. You may go. However, this case is not closed and the department may well have more questions for you. Please keep us informed if you make any change in plans."

Mollified but still concerned, the girl turned to Jules.

"Are you finished with me as well?"

Jules wasn't sure, but it sounded like a come on. He smiled. "I am. Thank you for your cooperation, Miss Locoto. I'm just sorry I might have been the cause of placing you in danger and you winding up in a cell."

The girl seemed to take his polite rebuff in the spirit it was given.

"Was I in any danger, Mr. Conroi?" she teased.

Jules shifted uncomfortably in his chair.

Saying nothing more, Maia found her sunglasses and slipped them over her eyes. Tossing her hair, she flashed a smile and was gone.

Jules breathed a sigh of relief.

"I suspect, Mr. Conroi," said an observant Rossi, "that you have just avoided a trap of a different kind."

# Chapter Ten
*Contact*

Mooney was bored.

She had been aboard the Ex-3 for well over a week as it pounded through the hyper-void on its aging sub-photon drive engines trying to keep busy, but it was a losing proposition.

The Ex-3 carried a crew of fifty-six counting herself, but on the outward bound trip to Eta Cassiopeia, it traveled empty leaving little for most of the crewmembers to do but play cards, surf the cloud, or indulge in the occasional fistfight. The balance of the crew drove the ship, monitored its functions, or worked at maintenance.

Early on, Mooney was kept occupied, concentrating on keeping her space legs against the unusual drag of the collapsed star material used to create the ship's artificial gravity. Something she had not experienced for some time.

In addition, she had to attend numerous staff meetings in order to familiarize herself with ship's routine and other key crewmembers from Captain Shon Sullivanski to hold supervisor Stevo Gomess. She had already made the acquaintance of ship's nurse-pharmacist Leah Tenebro, thank God. Without her, Mooney suspected she would have gone out of her mind by now. Not that her fellow crewmembers were so bad, it was just that they were…less refined…than the kind of people Mooney was used to associating with. Nevertheless, it was part of her job, her real job, not the one she pretended to be doing, to fit in anywhere and she congratulated herself on succeeding in doing that aboard the Ex-3.

Evidence for such was her ready acceptance by the masculine members of the crew. Of course, those who were unmarried eventually found opportunity to do some flirting before trying out some more serious moves, but Mooney was not inexperienced with the rules of that game either. She succeeded in fending off their efforts without alienating anyone and in no time, had earned herself a solid place among the crew.

As quality control officer, her primary duty was to monitor the freighter's cargo to make sure of its purity and to see there were no chemical reactions between the different ores and other elements that might prove incompatible if they were to come in contact. For that reason, she'd spent most of her time in the first few days inspecting the integrity of the ship's fifteen massive holds, each with their individual firewalls, monitoring stations, interior sensors, and emergency dump hatches in the belly of the ship. Finding all in order, Mooney spent the rest of her time exploring the ship and talking to individual crewmembers, feeling them out for any indication one of them might be an informer.

So far, she'd failed miserably.

Though everyone she had spoken with proved eager to talk to the attractive quality control officer, none had given anything away if indeed there was anything to give away in the first place. In that regard, Mooney was beginning to have her doubts. Had she wasted her time with the Ex-3? Would she have been better off pursuing some other avenue of investigation? Such thoughts inevitably led her to wondering about how Jules was doing at his end of the assignment. Had he had any better luck finding out what was behind the nitinol mystery?

Counting her blessings, Mooney had, so far, been safe aboard the big freighter. There had been no attempts on her life and none of the crew seemed in the least threatening or even suspicious. At times, she had to discipline herself not to use her telcomm to contact Military Intelligence for news about Jules. Although such communication would be restricted to a secure bandwave, she dared not take any chance of blowing her cover and spoiling any chance of discovering anything aboard the Ex-3. Still, Jules was her spouse and that meant she was entitled to be worried about him. Sure, on the surface he appeared the cool, level headed science agent, and he was. However, she knew his more human side, the one that included his human frailties, those he preferred to keep behind closed doors. She knew just how close the two previous attempts to kill them on Callisto had been and had no doubt both of them were in constant danger. On the other hand, her having experienced no personal danger so far on the Ex-3 seemed to suggest Jules' initial suspicions were right, that he might have been the primary target on Callisto, and she was merely unlucky enough to be in his company at the time.

There being no use in such speculations, Mooney very deliberately placed them in the back of her mind. Her professionalism once more took over as she contemplated next moves. Unfortunately, there weren't many beyond continuing what she'd been doing the past few days, namely talking with crew members. Just now, it was the turn of Captain Sullivanski who, by her calculations, was taking his usual morning break in the freighter's day room, sipping a large vacuum container of synth coffee. She'd spoken to him a number of times but never for long. That was good strategy, she figured. Softening him up some. Lowering his guard. Getting him accustomed to her presence among the crew. For the interview, she made sure her attire was fresh and clean, her hair tied back in the pony tail she had been using but with some carefully arranged wisps loose to dangle before her eyes. She made sure not to hang around the holds before the meeting so as to avoid getting her face or hands smudged. All together, she thought she presented as fresh and attractive an appearance as could be expected in a no nonsense quality control officer aboard a working ore hauler.

Pausing before the entrance to the day room, she pinched her cheeks and composed herself with that chipper, first thing in the morning look. Ready, she stepped into the room and as expected, Sullivanski was alone there, elbows propped on a table, and sipping at his synth coffee. He glanced over when he sensed someone coming in and unconsciously straightened himself out when he saw it was Mooney.

"Good morning, Captain," said Mooney good naturedly, as if Sullivanski had been the last thing she ever expected to find in the day room at that hour.

"'Morning," replied the captain. "Getting a late start?"

It was a bit past the start of the ship's "morning" routine. It was why Sullivanski liked to come to the day room when he did. The rest of the crew had long since come and gone for breakfast.

Mooney shrugged, shoving her hands in her pockets. "Not much happening in the holds, sir."

"Guess you're right," he said, going for his cup again.

Mooney moved around the room, collecting a breakfast of mostly vac-dried foodstuffs that passed for eggs and toast. Her final stop was at the synth-coffee dispenser. Finished, she looked a question to Sullivanski about joining him at his table.

He nodded and indicated the empty chair across from him.

"How are you fitting in?" he asked after she sat down.

"Good," Mooney said, prodding her vacced eggs with a disposable utensil. "The crew's been cooperative, and I found a friend in the nurse-pharmacist."

"They keeping their hands to themselves?"

Mooney saw that Sullivanski was not smiling. "Nothing I can't handle. Boys will be boys."

"If you say so. If they get out of hand, be sure to let me know."

"I will. Thanks."

"What about the holds?" asked Sullivanski, quickly shifting gears. "Everything ready then, to receive the cargo?"

Mooney nodded. "Everything's ship shape. There was a problem with dump hatch four but Zimdower took care of that. The plating's are all scoured and we'll be prepared to flash sanitize when we're ready to load."

"The observation station?" continued Sullivanski. "That glitch in the sensor node corrected?"

"I attended to that first thing."

Sullivanski nodded. "We'll be arriving in the Eta Cassiopeia system in a few days. Interstellar Mining says their loads of bulium are ready for shipment. Consolidated Ores will have enough to fulfill their contract, but they'll be diversified. Hutchinsonite and galena mostly. You prepared to handle that?"

"We've got dampeners and pumps to handle any toxic fumes and the firewalls are airtight," confirmed Mooney.

"You seem to know your stuff, Conroi," complimented the captain. "Have to admit, you didn't look like much when I first laid eyes on you."

"I'm used to that," lied Mooney.

She'd never served as a quality control officer aboard a commercial hauler in her life. Luckily, her memory had good retentive qualities, and

MI supplied her with a really good tutorial. That, and really, there wasn't much to the job. "Sir, what about the danger?"

"You know more about storing and transporting ore than I—"

"No, I mean the trip out here. What about the danger of attack?"

"What about it?" Suddenly, Sullivanski's back was up. "Nothing's changed since you were informed about the risk involved."

"That's what I was wondering about. I haven't visited the command deck so am kind of out of the loop regarding scuttlebutt," she gave her head a little toss, ostensibly to get a strand of hair out of her eyes. "Has there been any indication of danger? Any change in what you expected to encounter on the route?"

Sullivanski relaxed. Mooney wondered why he suddenly tensed up but decided she had merely stepped on his psychological toes.

"No, nothing. Smooth sailing all the way, so far, as the ancient mariners used to say."

"Do you have any idea what's out there?" Mooney thought she had softened him up enough to risk a more direct approach. "I mean, could it be pirates or…?"

Sullivanski smiled and put down his vac-cup. "Pirates way out here? I doubt it. Besides, what's to steal? A bunch of rocks?"

"Well, bulium is a strategic mineral. The Navy needs it for battleship construction."

"You think it's the Coalition?" Sullivanski stopped. Cocked his head. "Could be."

"Anyone else?"

Sullivanski laughed. "Conroi, you're not suggesting some aliens the Consortium doesn't know anything about are secretly hijacking our freighters?"

"Well…" Was the captain laughing off the possibility too easily?

"Forget it! Except for the Coalition, and us of course, this galaxy's empty of intelligent life. On the other hand, no one knows everything there is to know about the universe. It could be the missing freighters just ran into some natural phenomenon we know nothing about like the repercussions of a pair of crashing suns. Or even that supersonic space cloud that's supposed to be rushing through the galaxy even as we sit here talking. It was discovered two hundred years ago, but to this day, no one really knows what effects it might have on practically anything."

"When you put it like that, space pirates do sound pretty unlikely," said Mooney, not convinced.

Just then, the ship's annunciator came to life. It was a message for the captain.

"Will Captain Sullivanski report to the command deck, please? Will Captain Sullivanski report to the command deck?"

"Break's over," said Sullivanski, draining the last of his synth-coffee. "Back to work."

Mooney watched him leave the room and Leah come in.

"Big doings on the deck?" she said, heading to the synth-coffee dispenser.

"Guess so," replied Mooney. "Probably some doohickey blew a gasket."

Leah laughed and took Sullivanski's empty seat. "They do sound a little pompous, don't they? Not as if we're aboard a Navy ship or anything."

"Have to keep up appearances," said Mooney. "Nothing doing in the infirmary?"

"Was called in late last night. A crushed finger. Farhir got it caught in an equipment elevator. Almost didn't get it out in time."

Mooney winced. "He could have lost that finger."

"Darn right. As it was, he broke his index finger in three places. Had to rig up a splint and plasticoated the whole thing. He won't be texting any sweet nothings back home with that hand for a while."

"He'll have to resort to audio. Nadia won't like that, from what I hear. She's an old fashioned girl."

"If he wants, he can send her the vid recording the clinic comp took of my work to show her he's on the level."

"No secrets anymore."

"Nope."

"Speaking of secrets, pick up any scuttlebutt lately?"

It was a pretty broad question but one Mooney had made sure Leah was used to hearing from her so it didn't sound unexpected.

"I wish there were some gossip to talk about," said a disgusted

Leah. "I've never been on a ship where so little happens. Or at least nothing worth mentioning."

"Comes with having a crew of mostly men," said Mooney.

"Men don't have secrets?"

Leah looked at her with a skeptical eye.

"Men don't talk about their secrets," corrected Mooney.

"Not to us anyway."

"Not even to their doctor?"

"I'm not a doctor," insisted Leah. "Just a pill pusher mostly. But I do observe the same doctor patient confidentiality."

"Didn't mean to imply otherwise."

"I knew that. Still, you'd think there'd be something in the public domain."

"I heard there was a betting pool going among the shuttle pilots whether we run into trouble or not."

"Old news," said Leah, sipping her synth-coffee. "What about Rand being demoted? Went from manager to supervisor, I hear."

"Insubordination?"

"Spreading rumors. Can you believe it?"

"What kind of rumors?" Mooney's antennae went up.

"Stuff about the ship's course. He was insisting it was unsafe. Was taking us right to where the other freighters disappeared. The captain heard about it and ordered him to shut up. Stop upsetting the crew." Leah shrugged. "He didn't and the captain had him demoted. Reassigned him to third shift maintenance duties. Barely anyone's heard of him since."

"Third shift will do that," said Mooney.

Mooney was trying to figure how she might be able to approach Rand and get him to talk with her when her thoughts were interrupted by another blast from the annunciator.

"Will quality control officer 'Manda Conroi report to the command deck, please? Will 'Manda Conroi report to the command deck?"

"You?" asked Leah, surprised.

"I hope it's nothing serious," said Mooney.

Aside from the handful of command officers, who were the only salaried employees aboard, regular crewmembers were rarely summoned to the command deck.

"Maybe you'll have some new scuttlebutt to share when you get back," suggested Leah.

Mooney laughed and waved goodbye as she disposed of her breakfast things and stepped from the day room in the direction of the command deck up capsule. She was as puzzled as Leah was about the summons. She had just concluded a talk with the captain a few minutes before. What could have come up since then that he couldn't have mentioned at the table? The absence of warning klaxons suggested that there was no emergency, so she decided not to worry about it.

Her sense of self-satisfaction ended the moment the door of the up capsule slid open and she stepped onto the deck.

All around her stood the members of the command crew, all grimly silent, staring.

Something was definitely wrong, but Mooney managed to keep any anxiety from registering on her face.

"Quality Control Officer Conroi reporting to the command deck as requested," she managed to say.

She looked around as the half dozen deck officers continued to stare.

Finally, the captain stepped forward.

"Conroi, is there anything you'd like to tell us that you haven't mentioned before?" asked Sullivanski.

"I beg your pardon, sir?"

"You're wasting your time, sir," said one of the officers angrily.

"I'm still in command here," retorted Sullivanski.

"Are you?" asked the officer. "Seems to me they're giving the orders now."

"Who's they?" asked Mooney, wondering.

"Belay that, Ramos," ordered the captain. Then, turning to Mooney "Conroi, you're standing on very thin ice right now. There's a ship out there with someone aboard who's been asking for you."

"For me?" Mooney did not have to force the look of surprise that shone on her face.

"Whoever is out there asked for a woman with red hair," explained the captain. "When I confirmed we did have a crewmember who fit that description, he demanded we hand you over."

"Hand me over?"

Now Mooney really was surprised…and concerned. Who could know she was aboard the Ex-3, except Leclerc?

"You said there was a ship out there?" she asked.

"For all we know, there might not be. If there is, it's invisible. Our sensors and tracking devices are completely blind to it. It's as if it doesn't exist. We only realized it was nearby when it hailed us."

"We're out in the middle of nowhere," said one of the crew. "Light years from anywhere. The only way we'd be able to meet another ship out here is if it's on purpose. Whoever it is out there, came looking for us."

Sullivanski nodded in agreement. "Their first demand was that we shut down all computer functions aboard ship. Right now, we are running on auxiliary back up systems, something we can maintain for only a limited amount of time."

"We're even communicating via old Morse code," said one officer. "Lucky Jefferson was familiar with it."

"No telling who they are," said another man. "They could have pulse cannons trained on us right now!"

"Calm down," said Sullivanski. Turning to Mooney, "They seem to know you. When I confirmed there was a red haired woman aboard, he correctly identified you as 'Manda Conroi. Care to explain that?"

Mooney was just as perplexed as the others so could only shake her head. "Afraid not, Captain. I have no idea who's out there."

"She's a damn informer," accused Ramos. "That's how those other freighters were found and attacked. She or others like her, posed as crewmembers and somehow let the pirates know where we were."

"Not true," was all Mooney said, noting the irony. She had signed on the Ex-3 to try and find out if there were informers aboard. Now, she herself was being accused of that very thing.

"Then what's your explanation?" demanded the captain.

Before Mooney could reply, there was a clicking sound from the annunciator. Jefferson went to a keyboard and began typing. When he finished, he read the message:

"Captain. My time is running out. You have ten minutes to hand over Conroi."

Sullivanski was still thinking that over when the sound of a dull thud rang through the bulkhead.

"I have secured docking with your starboard port," read the next message. "Conroi is to step into the lock and remain there until I open the inner hatch."

Before anyone else spoke, Mooney asked Jefferson to type a return message.

"Tell them I'm here but I want to know who they are before I decide to go."

Jefferson looked at the captain who nodded his permission to send the message.

There was a minute's delay before the answer came: "Who I am doesn't matter right now. Time is of the essence. Suffice it to say, we rendezvous with Victor next. Or should I say Jules?"

At the mention of Jules, Mooney was momentarily at a loss. How could anyone outside of Leclerc's office know about Victor Conroi or that the name was a cover identity for Jules Santros? The mere fact that whoever it was sent the information over without an eyes-only request, suggested this was not an unscheduled MI contact. One thing she was sure of: she could not ignore the summons. She had to see it through.

"I've heard enough," was all she said to the others. "Tell them I'm leaving now."

"Wait a minute," cried Ramos. "No one said you're allowed to leave!"

"Captain?" she asked.

"How do we know you aren't some kind of pirate?" he asked. "How do we know you're leaving because the ship is going to be destroyed like the others?"

"Captain, I'm not a pirate," said Mooney. "I'm as much in the dark as you are about this. But I will say that I joined your crew under false pretenses. I'm with the Off-Planet Police, aboard to try and find out what happened to the missing freighters. This person," she inclined her chin indicating the outside, "whoever it is, has knowledge about me no one was supposed to know. I need to follow this up wherever it leads."

"Don't believe her," cried Ramos, taking a step forward. "She's one of them. She's a pirate!"

"Stand down, Ramos," ordered the captain. "Seems we haven't much choice but to believe her."

"Thank you, Captain. You're making the right choice. I am not a threat to the Ex-3."

With that, Mooney turned and entered the down capsule. Behind her, the others stared quietly, unconsciously recreating the scene she encountered when she first arrived on the command deck. Ahead of her was the unknown, something she sensed would answer the question of the lost ships but that also presented she and Jules with unimaginable danger...

# Chapter Eleven
*Soul Searcher*

Jules knew where his duty lay. In the Vega system. However, he still had a nagging problem of his own. Despite the urgency of his assignment, he felt a short detour, if it bolstered his own self confidence going forward with a certitude more basic than simply, "I think, therefore, I am," would be worth it. The experience of the near fatal Mobius trap convinced him he needed a definitive answer regarding the nature of his soul. A question whose lack of resolution would eventually prevent him from functioning fully both as an agent of Military Intelligence and a husband. In short, he needed to end the persistent doubts he felt regarding the state of his personhood.

To do that, he finally decided to break his silence about what happened that day on the *Constitution*. He realized he ran the risk that news of there being two Jules could break out somehow and reach Joan, but it was a risk he was prepared to take for the sake of his own sanity. Besides, the person he intended to talk to was not exactly the type to break a confidence. Especially one given under the seal of the confessional.

Although they were not as close as they used to be in the days when they toured the Vatican together, he had not seen his brother, Andrew, in some time. And in his present form as one of two Jules Santros, not since before his mission aboard the *Constitution*. Andrew took his vows shortly after their visit and became a teacher, currently a member of the staff at the King James VII Seminary in Anglia.

Jules looked out the plas glass bubble top of the flyer he took from Latinium as the craft banked in preparation for entering its final glide path to the seminary. Below, a checkerboard of farmland lay stretched out in varying shades of green across East Anglia, and as the flyer drew closer to the ground, he was able to observe more details. Roads emerged then cart paths among the fields. Robot harvesters moved slowly up and down the crop lines. Here and there, modern plas glass and 'crete farmhouses dotted the landscape, and small, tidy looking villages, little changed for hundreds of years, beckoned with their promise of peace and quiet.

Suddenly, the flyer's braking thrusters shattered the mood as the vehicle slowed and began to seek a proper landing area on the seminary grounds. Jules just had time to appreciate the classic lines of the restored abbey that housed classrooms and dormitories and the elaborate and well kept gardens surrounding the estate that included a hedge maze on the outskirts. A branch maze if Jules was not mistaken.

Then the flyer was down and hatch open. As the whir of its turbines faded away, the sound was replaced by the bucolic atmosphere of the Anglian countryside. Birds chirped from somewhere and the smell of freshly cut grass was heavy on the air. Jules wasted no time heading for the main entrance to the seminary which stood atop a wide rank of stone steps. His approach must have been picked up by the visitor sensors because he no sooner arrived at the heavy wooden doors when one of the leaves opened and he was greeted by a black clad young man, obviously a seminarian.

"I'm here to see Father Andrew," said Jules, by way of greeting.

The man nodded. "We've been expecting you, Mr. Conroi."

Jules had called ahead to make sure his brother was on the premises. It being summer recess, most of the staff and students were gone. Andrew could have been one of them. Off to a conference or on sabbatical somewhere. Luckily, it was neither. He was still present at the seminary.

Inside the grand foyer, the most prominent feature was a full size portrait of the institution's patron, King James VII, the country's first Catholic monarch in five hundred years.

As he followed the seminarian, Jules wondered again exactly how he was going to break the news to his brother about his identity. Of course, he was still every bit his brother but now there were two of him. When he called ahead, he simply identified himself as Victor Conroi, just in case Andrew decided to call him back and ended up contacting the other Jules. For all he knew, Victor Conroi merely wished to consult with him on some undescribed issue of personal importance.

Finally, after moving through the historical portion of the former abbey, Jules was led into the modern section where classrooms and dormitories were located. There, his brother's office was located on the ground floor. If there were windows in his office, they would overlook the gardens.

The seminarian knocked on the open door. "Mr. Conroi to see you, Father."

As Jules stepped into the doorway, his brother was just rising from behind his desk. Clad in the uniform of the Church, black synthsuit with Roman collar, he hadn't changed much since the last time they were together. Maybe a little grayer around the temples and his face had filled out some but otherwise still much the same.

Apparently, he recognized Jules as well, not sensing anything that would lead him to believe it might not have been his younger brother.

"Jules!" he declared. "You're Conroi?"

Jules nodded, making sure the seminarian had departed.

"I'm Earthside on business," was all he said. "I dropped in between stops."

Now it was Andrew's turn to nod. "I see. The less said about that the better?"

Andrew was aware of the kind of business his brother was in.

"Yeah. Sorry about the subterfuge."

Andrew shrugged. "I take it this visit is more in the nature of a serious one and not a social call?"

"Both, actually. I'm here on a personal errand. I don't have much time, but I have this thing bothering me that I need straightened out. It's keeping me from working at my full potential and holding me back…with other things."

Andrew circled the desk and closed the office door. "Have a seat, Jules."

After Jules sat down, he took the facing chair. "Now what's this all about?"

Jules cleared his throat. "This is to remain strictly between us, Andrew. No one and I mean no one, else must know."

"When I talk to anyone in my office, I consider it priestly confidentiality."

Carefully, slowly, so as to keep the whole thing straight in Andrew's mind, Jules told the story of his last mission; of how it ended and how he turned out to be two people.

"And this other Jules doesn't know about you?" asked Andrew when he'd finished.

Jules nodded. "I thought it best that way. Why burden us both with guilt and questions of identity?"

"But these doubts you have weren't enough to stop you from marrying Miss Mooney or should I say Mrs. Conroi?"

"I had genuinely fallen in love with her. And there was no difference between me and the other Jules. He had as much right to return to Joan as I did. And since he knew nothing about the alternate timeline, he naturally knew nothing about Mooney either. That made him the logical one of us to go back to Joan. Mooney saw that. Argued in our favor. Her rationalizations made sense. No doubt about that. And yet, I still felt guilty for abandoning Joan. I still worried I might not even possess a soul. Might not be a real human being. Just some time displaced construct." He was silent a moment, collecting himself. "Alone in that cabin on the *Constitution*, I had time to think. All I could see was a vast, unending gulf of loneliness and apartness without Joan. After that, Mooney became a real lifeline. If not for her, well…"

"I can imagine how disturbing all of that must have been for you," soothed Andrew. "But you know Church teaching on a question like this the same as I do. Each individual is given a unique soul by God at the moment of conception. For that reason, souls are not repeatable, they cannot be replicated or duplicated. No two souls are alike, any more than any two persons might look alike. This other Jules, as much as he might have looked like you, was not you. He and you are each individual beings. Thus, you cannot share the same soul."

"I get all that," said Jules. "But after seeing what looked to me like a perfect duplicate of myself, indistinguishable in every detail, well, I have to admit, it struck at my core beliefs. My faith, if you will. Which one of us retained my soul? Was my soul divided between us? If so, am I somehow diminished because of that? Those are the kind of questions I've been wrestling with ever since."

"Perfectly understandable," said Andrew. "Anyone confronted with such a bizarre occurrence would have trouble reconciling it with what they'd always accepted as truth. But in such a case, I'd like you to keep in mind the old medieval Scholastic maxim: *Credo ut intelligam*."

"'I believe so that I may understand.'"

"Your Latin is as good as ever," said Andrew, admiringly. "But more to your particular problem. Ultimately, there's no fundamental disconnect between faith and reason. Confronted with such a paradox as you describe, we have to begin with an ascent to faith before we can apply our God-given reason in a logical manner."

"But *is* there any logical reason why I should have an individual soul?"

"In the academy you must have studied predicate calculus," asked Andrew, unruffled.

"Of course," acknowledged Jules. "Every underclassman had to take a mandatory introductory or First Order logic course. As part of that we were drilled on predicate calculus."

"I had the same philosophy requirements in Minor Seminary," said Andrew. "What do you remember about the course?"

Jules had to think a moment. It had been a while since his college days. "I remember predicate calculus is the part of modern formal or symbolic logic that systematically analyzes the logical relations between sentences." *Whew!*

Andrew only nodded, indicating that Jules should continue.

"Predicate calculus was one of the toughest things I had to master as an undergrad," he said. "Some students washed out of advanced physics because they couldn't hack it on the finals. From what I recall, First Order Logic was an advance on the old Propositional logic because it allowed us to make logical claims about objects in the world such as 'the sky is blue' while distinguishing between the object, in this case the sky, and those qualities of the object that we are predicating or describing such as the blueness of the sky. As we were taught, the predication technique could be used as a powerful tool in analysis since it provides a means to symbolize relations between objects and their predicates." As he spoke, Jules warmed to his subject. "It even possessed quantifiers that indicated the number of objects and their related properties as well as functions."

"Not bad," said Andrew, finally. "You have a good memory for the basics, but you left out one crucial component."

"What's that?"

"The notion of modality."

"But doesn't modal terminology only enter into First Order predication when it deals with questions of logical possibility, necessity, or impossibility?"

"Too restrictive. Modality is also useful when considering questions regarding temporally logical relations, such as when dealing with things that have happened, have always occurred, or may or will absolutely take place at a future time."

"Okay," conceded Jules. "But I'm not sure how modality has any bearing on what happened to me."

"Well, remember that modal statements function within what's referred to as a larger possible world semantics," explained Andrew. "A logical language we can use to specify that something is necessarily true if it meets certain criteria in all possible instances or possible if it meets those criteria only in some cases. Are you with me?"

Jules nodded. As his older brother, Andrew always had a tendency to lecture him.

"In other words, something will be necessarily true if and only if it is true in every world we can imagine, without exception," continued Andrew. "That said, it will only be a possibility if it is true in some possible world but not in other worlds that are also possible. The latest articulation of modal analysis takes that notion of the entire range of theoretically possible scenarios, or worlds that can be logically conceived, in order to exhaustively explore all alternative domains of predication and quantification. Doing that, we can determine under what conditions an object or idea can be judged to be logically true."

"So, on one hand, we can say Jules is a rational creature, but on the other, that he only possibly has blonde hair," concluded Jules. "There might be alternative scenarios in which I might have darker hair. It's just another way of saying Jules must be a rational creature in every possible logical scenario or world I can conceive while at the same time he might have blonde hair in only one of those worlds and other shades in other worlds." Jules shook his head as if to clear it. "I admit, the philosophy behind it is a rigorous way of understanding the logical implications of necessity and possibility, but so far as I can see, it has little to do with my situation. The only actual world for me is the one I exist in right now. In any other possible worlds, my existence is at best only a possibility."

"According to at least one interpretation of modality," said Andrew, patiently. "Possible worlds are not just the abstract objects of certain forms of logical discourse. Some philosophers have posited they are all real in some sense, since every world in which something necessarily exists must actually exist, and moreover, every part of a possible world that exists is spatiotemporally related to every other part of every other existing possible world."

"That last bit doesn't seem to follow," argued Jules. "Why must all of these possible worlds be related to each other?"

"Among all the possible worlds, there will be only one that will be actual for you since its actuality consists in the fact it is identified as the one you are in," explained Andrew, leaning back in his chair. "In other words, the actual world is that spatiotemporal object all of whose parts are spatiotemporally related to you. What makes all possible worlds but yours merely possible to you, as opposed to actual, is that you are not in any of them. Which is merely another way of saying only one of their parts, the one you actually inhabit, is spatiotemporally related to you, though all of each possible world's parts are spatiotemporally related to each of its other parts, since anyone can possibly exist in any other of these possible spatiotemporal worlds."

Jules thought carefully before replying.

"If what you say holds, it would imply all possible worlds are necessarily real to those who exist within them, which is to say, for anyone who is bound by that particular spatiotemporal configuration, right?"

His brother nodded, encouraging him to continue.

"Are you saying then, every possible world is necessarily real so every possible world actually exists for everyone?"

"If we take these logical modal propositions to be true reflections of reality," said Andrew, "that would appear to be the logical conclusion.

Moreover, existence must be a necessary attribute for human beings since it is impossible to be rational if you lack existence, and since we've already established human beings like Jules must be necessarily rational in every possible logical scenario, or each and every world we can possibly conceive, it would seem to follow a rational creature like Jules must necessarily also exist in all possible worlds."

"Wait one," said Jules, raising his hand. "Just a minute ago you said what makes all possible worlds but mine merely possible to me, as opposed to actual, is I'm not in any of those other possible worlds, only in the one I actually inhabit spatiotemporally."

"Before we take this further, there are a couple of other ramifications we should bear in mind," cautioned Andrew. "Your existence as a rational creature is necessary, but all your other possible or non-necessary attributes such as the color of your hair, your height, the tone of your voice, etc., which are accidental characteristics that nonetheless individuate you…mark you as you. But of necessity, these characteristics only exist in some possible worlds while not in others. If you exist necessarily in all possible worlds, then we could posit that in each world you would exist but in an individuated mode, marked apart from your other existences in other worlds, by an endlessly varying configuration of non-necessary attributes. Only your existence as a necessarily rational creature would be constant across all possible worlds."

"But if I shared the same necessarily rational essence across all possible worlds, I would be actually or essentially the same in every such world, wouldn't I? Every actual me, every necessarily existent Jules in every possible world would share the same essentially rational soul, isn't that the very problem I came to see you about? Do I have my own soul?"

"Remember those philosophy classes you took back in college? If you think back, you might recall in classical metaphysics the soul was understood to be the essential form of the body. In other words, the immaterial soul informed the body according to certain essential features, while the material body to which it was united individuated that essence in a material way. Remember, human souls never pre-exist as some sort of immaterial generic human essences, they always come into existence as hylomorphically united to a physical counterpart, a body with all of its non-necessary material characteristics in order to make a singularly individual person that's equally material and non-material, partly essential and partly non-essential."

"I follow you," said Jules. "Hylo from the Greek word for matter, and morphism from the Greek term for form. It was Aquinas' belief all persons are embodied rational creatures, each with a uniquely instantiate d material form, or essence, or soul, on account of the individuating matter. Just as there are no two persons with the same set of fingerprints, there can't be two identically embodied souls. But that doesn't help your argument, Andrew. The notion of there being different possible worlds still argues against the idea of individuality."

Andrew shook his head and smiled. He was enjoying the discussion. For his part, Jules was exercising intellectual muscles he hadn't used in a long time.

"Stay with me for a minute, Jules," Andrew was saying. "What individuates you, what gives you your unique soul, is not your necessarily rational existence in every possible world, but rather the distinctive set of possible material characteristics that come along with having an embodied soul. Every possible Jules in every possible world must necessarily exist in some uniquely identifiable manner, in a manner that renders every such embodied soul a unique individual manner, since each Jules has an individuating material component as part of their existence. Hence, none of these Jules would share the same individually embodied soul."

Jules allowed himself to work through that twist of logic. He decided it made sense.

"Fine, but it doesn't take into account exactly what happened t o me," he replied. "I saw a Jules that looked indistinguishable from me. Moreover, how is it we both now inhabit the same world? I mean, I understand the physics of it, as I've already explained to you, but if what you hypothesize is correct, wouldn't we cancel each other out?"

"I'm not the scientist you are, Jules, so I can't tell you precisely how it all came about," admitted Andrew. "But as we both know, physics and philosophy aren't mutually exclusive. Obviously, the physical laws that ordinarily wall off the contiguous yet spatiotemporally separated possible worlds was breached. That we know. What we also must believe is that the other Jules, this new brother we now share, must have at least one feature that individuates him from yourself. You are not identical, no matter how much you might think so. Something is different. Something that establishes the singular uniqueness of the other Jules allowing him to exist at all."

"So, we aren't two of the same person?"

"It can't be otherwise."

"We're individuals. He from one of the infinite possible worlds differentiated from me by some however small variance, and me, from this world?"

"Or vice versa."

Jules shook his head slowly, trying to comprehend it all. Certainly, he didn't remember ever existing in a world that was any different than the one he currently occupied. And for that matter, neither did the other Jules. There was no way to tell which of them was the "original" Jules, but then, did it matter?

"In the end, it doesn't matter," said Andrew, as if reading his thoughts. "You are both equally valid persons. Both individuals. And so, both with individual souls bequeathed you by God."

And then, it all became clear to Jules. He was his own person with his own soul, with his own life to live separate from that of the other Jules. As understanding and acceptance came over him, the only concern that remained was whether he should some day tell the other Jules the truth. Did he have a right to know? Or would the knowledge only upset him as it had done to him?

Again, Andrew seemed to sense his thoughts.

"I suppose if the other Jules ever finds out about you, I'll have to go through all this again."

"What a reunion that would be!"

"I think I could look forward to that. It'd be nice to have another brother…and sister-in-law."

"Sorry about that, Andrew," said Jules. "If there was anything I could have done, I would have had you marry me and Mooney."

Andrew waved off the apology. "Understood."

Stepping outside again, Jules felt as if a great burden had been lifted from him. It was the same sun in the sky. The same birds chirped somewhere that he'd heard coming in, but somehow, everything was changed. It seemed like a whole new world filled with hope and anticipation. Descending the stone stairway, he found himself eager to see Mooney again. To tell her the good news. Suddenly, the future had opened up for them both. There was nothing to prevent them now from moving ahead with plans they could only talk about before. And who knew? Maybe some way could be found to tell the other Jules...and Joan...about what happened. As Andrew said, it *would* be nice to have another brother.

All those rosy thoughts, however, were shattered in an instant by the sudden blast of a pulse pistol.

# Chapter Twelve
*Auld Acquaintances*

Jules thought it his imagination when he sensed a pressure wave come close enough to muss his hair. He was disabused of the notion when the impact of a blast crashed against the abbey's wall sending shards of stone flying through the air. It was only the fact he had taken another step downward on the staircase that caused the discharge of the pulse pistol to miss.

Instantly, his instincts took over. He continued his downward course, hitting the flagstones at the base of the stairs and rolling on toward a pedestal holding a statue of St. Francis, a lamb in his arms. The pedestal however, could only serve as temporary shelter as another blast from the hidden pulse pistol struck it, toppling Francis from his perch. But Jules had not stopped. The key to a defense against a pulse pistol with its built in target acquisition tech that made missing almost impossible, was to stay in constant motion.

For the moment, Jules did not bother worrying about who might be using the pistol, only in getting out of its sights. In trying to keep out of range, he found himself in the formal garden, weaving about among the shrubs, flower beds, benches and ornaments. Sizeable trees with sturdy trunks that would have a better chance at withstanding a pistol blast were absent, their shade not being friendly to grass and other smaller plants. The only possible cover lay within the hedge maze whose entrance Jules spotted and quickly sprinted in its direction.

His speed so far prevented the shooter from getting a clear shot at him, but that was not enough. Jules needed to turn the tables. His own ion pistol was of smaller caliber, meant for defense and more subtle work than open combat. It would come in handy when the time was right, but at the moment, the time was not right.

However, a plan was forming in his mind. Remembering seeing the maze from the air, Jules recalled it was a branching maze. There were two kinds of hedge mazes, circular and branching. A branching maze had a single path leading to the center with other false paths leading off that. To find the center in a branching maze was simple. If you placed your hand on one side of the hedges and followed the path in and out of dead ends, you would eventually find your way back to the exit. Neat, if you had the time, but at the moment, he definitely did not have the time. Instead, he fell back on what would have been a cheat under normal circumstances: Foucault's algorithm. Based on the number of branching paths and the square footage of the entire maze, a person could eventually find their way to the center using markers to check their progress. Again, Jules did not have the time for markers, but he always had a good memory and believed he could find his way even without them. What he did count on was the shooter.

Strongly suspecting his assailant was the person who'd tried to kill him on Callisto, Jules counted on the same inexperience that led the shooter into following him into the bungalow. This time, having learned anything from their last meeting, would the shooter follow him into the maze or remain on the outside and lie in wait, maybe by the flyer? A sudden blast overhead answered that question.

Jules smiled. Now he had a chance.

Keeping in mind the laws governing Foucault's algorithm, Jules dashed along the long axis of a main branch before ducking down what he expected to be a dead end. It was. But in doing so, he made sure to brush his hand along the wall of ten foot boxwood forming the walls of the maze. The shudder of all the branches confused the shooter's pistol tech and his shots fell well short of Jules' actual position. The shots were making hash of the maze though. Jules was sure the groundskeeper wouldn't like that.

Taking out his own ion pistol, he used it to carve a hole in the dead end hedge and dive through. The branch path on the other side led back to the main path which had been abandoned by the shooter as he pursued Jules into the dead end. Following similar tactics, Jules led the shooter on a merry chase for some minutes among the hedges until he judged it safe to shift tactics.

Quickly, Jules ran the length of the main path back to the entrance, the sounds of pulse blasts shredding boxwood behind him. Now the tables were turned. The hunter became the hunted as Jules left the maze and positioned himself outside to catch his pursuer unawares when he finally showed himself in the entrance.

That moment arrived sooner than he expected as noise from inside the maze died down. Jules sensed the shooter had gained some degree of wisdom from heedless pursuit of his quarry at the bungalow and now in the maze. He was approaching the entrance with more caution, perhaps realizing he'd lost the advantage.

Unlike the overeager shooter, Jules contained his own natural impatience. He waited behind the protection of a stone bench, his ion pistol steadied on its back, aimed at the entrance to the maze. Finally, there was some movement among the boxwood leaves and the barrel of a pulse pistol slowly emerged into view.

Jules waited. He could have fired through the hedge where he judged the shooter stood based on where his weapon was sticking out, but he held his fire. Best to wait for a perfect shot. One he could not miss.

The pulse pistol was in full sight now. Jules could see the hand gripping it, the sleeve of a synthsuit, an obscure figure, darkened in the shade cast by the hedges. Jules fired. Unlike the coarse burst of a pulse pistol, an ion pistol was quick and silent but no less lethal. The invisible beam struck the shooter squarely in the midsection. There was no time for a cry of pain. The figure collapsed upon the graveled path, unmoving and small.

Jules emerged from behind the bench, his pistol still aimed at the figure. He had been sure of his aim, but experience taught him to take no chances. He approached cautiously until he was close enough to kick the pulse pistol away from the shooter. Still no movement. He bent and felt at the throat. No pulse. He sheathed his weapon, rolled the body over, and recoiled in surprise.

*Mag! Mag Tristom!*

Confused and upset at the revelation, Jules could only look upon those familiar features and wonder. His mind tried to back track, put the pieces together, figure out how he and Mooney's friends on Callisto fit into the bigger picture. Any way he looked at it, it made no sense.

His confused thoughts were interrupted by the sound of a familiar voice.

"Surprised?"

He turned and was confronted by a second shock.

Standing there, an ion pistol of her own aimed squarely at his chest, was Toma.

"You too?" was all Jules could muster.

"Mag and I are…or should I say, were…married, Jules," said Toma, a smirk playing about the corner of her mouth. "We do as much as we can together."

"Even murder?" Jules recovered himself quickly, assembling the pieces. Mag and Toma had been perfectly situated on Callisto to ingratiate themselves into the Conrois' lives there. How easy it was for one of them to infiltrate their suite and lie in wait to kill them. The question was why? The assassination attempt took place before he and Mooney had been given their current assignment by Leclerc. Were their actions related or did they mean something else? And the incident at the north hatch. They had been locked out along with he and Mooney and the others. Did they plan to die with the rest in order to see their twin murders through to success?

"Especially murder," Toma was saying. "As the old saying goes, we were given an offer we couldn't refuse. A billion credits to kill you and 'Manda but you primarily."

"A billion credits! Impossible. Someone is pulling your leg. You and Mag were being played, Toma."

Toma merely smiled again. "At first, we thought so too. Oh, we were just a pair of ordinary newlyweds like any of the thousands of others on Callisto. We had every intention of enjoying ourselves for a week before going back to our normal lives. Until one day we received a message on Mag's telcomm. It asked us if we'd agree to kill the couple in the neighboring suite, the husband especially. Naturally, we laughed it off as someone's idea of a bad joke. But whoever it was, was insistent. A second message advised us to check our bank account. Out of curiosity, we did and found that it had increased by a billion credits! We were speechless naturally, until the amount vanished before our eyes. A third message came through then. It told us the billion credits had been real and would be returned to our account if we agreed to kill you. I'm afraid there was little discussion after that. Mag and I agreed to the request and the billion credits duly reappeared in our account. We quickly transferred it to a new, anonymous account, used some of the funds to buy a pulse pistol, and found the credits were good. You know what can be done with a billion credits, don't you? Anyone would gladly have killed a dozen people for that kind of remuneration."

"Not anyone," said Jules grimly.

The story was fantastic, but he could see how such an unbelievable sum could sway a person to do even the most heinous of acts, even murder. And murder had been done before for much less.

The response angered Toma, who made as if she were going to shoot him right then and there. But she relented, apparently enjoying the position Jules found himself in.

"Was it Mag who tried to kill me at the bungalow or yourself?" asked Jules, deciding to play along with her.

Like Mag, she was not a professional and had allowed her vanity to get the best of her.

"Oh, that was Mag," Toma admitted. "He thought it would be easy…until he shot that tour guide by accident. He thought it was you coming home from the admin building. Oops. The problem was, discovery of the body would give the game away, put you on alert. Now, instead of jumping you at the bungalow, Mag said he had to go down the path and try to shoot you there. Only when he was in position, you'd already come and gone. So, he fell back on the original plan and returned to the bungalow. Neither of us thought you'd be so resourceful. You sure didn't act like any scientist we ever knew."

That was news to Jules. She didn't know him other than Victor Conroi, physicist, not as a science agent. Then why were she and Mag hired to kill him?

"So, your employer never told you why he wanted us dead?"

"No. And for a billion credits, we didn't care."

"Just who was it who hired you? I'd like to know who it is that wants me dead."

Toma shrugged. "I don't know. He only ever communicated with us via telcomm. Never identified himself. For that matter, he may not be a he at all. Maybe it's a woman. Have any old girlfriends who might not have liked to see you married to 'Manda?"

"It doesn't bother you that your boss tried to kill you, too, when we were all locked out of the colony after coming back from Jupiter rise?" he taunted her.

"That was a coincidence," said Toma. "And even if it wasn't, it didn't matter to us afterward. We still had the billion credits in our account and still had an opportunity to kill you ourselves."

*Interesting*, thought Jules. *Mag and Toma had nothing to do with the lockout.*

Did that mean there was someone else out there trying to do him in? An insurance policy by whoever wanted them dead in case Mag and Toma failed? Which reminded him, what about the Santanti frame? That was insurance, too, in a way, in case the Mobius trap didn't work. He asked Toma about that.

"When we failed to kill you on Callisto, we received more instructions," she said. "Seems our benefactor didn't hold a grudge for failure. Anyway, we were told to come to Earth and snatch Santanti. We didn't know who he was and again, didn't care. We held him until given further instructions. When they came, we were told to take him back to his home in Misena, kill him, and leave the body in the sitting room. Our instructions were specific about that. It had to be the sitting room."

"You don't know why?" asked Jules, curious.

"We weren't told. We didn't need to know, I guess. Well, Jules, it's been nice…"

Just then, Toma sensed a presence behind her. She spun around and Jules leaped for her pistol. In a moment, he had her disarmed but before he could completely turn the tables, he found himself grappling with her.

She was of athletic build but of average height for a woman and weighing barely more than a hundred and twenty pounds, so Jules did not find her difficult to handle. She tried a few swings of her fists, but her reach wasn't long enough to connect with his chin. A knee tried for his crotch and missed. Having tried to avoid striking her, he gave up and tapped her only as hard as he needed to send her to the ground. She lay there, stunned.

"Thanks, Andrew," said Jules, pocketing the bulky pulse pistol and retrieving his own ion pistol.

"I was hoping to grab her before she ended the conversation by shooting you, but I must have made some noise or something," said the priest, looking down at the fallen woman.

"It was a nice try," acknowledged Jules. "Good enough anyway. You drew her attention and that's all I was waiting for when I saw you sneaking up."

"I heard noise coming from the garden and came out to see what it was all about," explained Andrew. "The last thing I expected was to find a firefight going on."

"It was touch and go there for a while," admitted Jules.

"Dare I ask what it was all about? Why were they trying to kill you? Or is it official business?"

"I wish I could tell you, but so far, I don't know the reason myself. Only that someone wants me dead and is willing to pay a billion credits for the job."

Andrew looked astonished. "A billion…? I can't even imagine such a sum."

"Neither can I. Anyway, can you contact the police and tell them to get over here?" Andrew took out his telcomm as Jules continued to cover Toma. "Tell them we have two suspects, one dead and the other captured. Also, ask them to bring Lt. Rossi of the Napoli Police Department in Latinium in on this. He already has a vested interest. Meantime, I'll get in touch with my superiors at MI. I'm going to need their help to get me off the hook."

"And then?" asked Andrew.

"Then, I have to hitch a ride to Vega."

# Chapter Thirteen
*The Mystery Deepens*

Mooney stepped into the airlock.

Immediately, the hatch behind her closed and the one ahead irised open.

Cautiously, she stepped over the threshold into the other ship. Behind her, the iris shut, leaving her standing in a corridor lined with ductwork, wiring, and conduits. There was something about her surroundings that seemed different than the space vessels she knew, but she could not quite put her finger on it. Before she could ponder the feeling further, a voice came over a hidden annunciator somewhere.

"Welcome, Mrs. Conroi," it said. "Please come up to the bridge. You'll find a ladder at the end of the corridor."

Mooney could judge nothing from the tone of the voice. It was neither overly friendly nor threatening, merely pro forma.

Hesitating only long enough to pull her ion pistol from inside her jumpsuit, she moved forward. She reached the ladder without incident, but just as she rested a hand on one of the rungs, a shudder ran through the ship. There was a loud clunk and Mooney guessed the docking clamps were disengaged and the smaller vessel was pulling away from the Ex-3.

Climbing the ladder, she made her way past more exposed ductwork and tubing until emerging into a small room she immediately recognized as the bridge, despite some of its unfamiliar equipment.

"Come in, come in, Mrs. Conroi," said an older man from where he sat by a control console. "No need to be afraid. I'm alone here, I assure you."

Mooney looked around nevertheless before continuing her climb into the room. Inside, she kicked the hatch shut over the ladder well, her pistol moving back and forth, covering as much of the enclosed space as possible.

"Who are you?" she finally asked.

"My name is Anton Tamaka," said the man, nodding at Mooney's ion pistol. "You may put away that weapon. I pose no threat to you. As you can see, my age prevents me from posing any physical challenge to you. Besides, if I meant you harm, would I have bothered to have you removed from the freighter or invite you up here? I could just as easily have gassed you in the air lock if I wanted to do you harm. It is a circumstance the full meaning of which you will come to understand very soon."

Persuaded by the older man's demeanor, Mooney decided to put away her pistol but keep her guard up.

"What's this all about?" she asked.

"Just a moment while I maneuver the ship away from the freighter and set a course," said Tamaka as he turned some knobs and pulled some switches. Over his head, closed circuit monitors displayed the outside of the ship from different angles, including one showing the hull of the Ex-3 as it receded toward distant Eta Cassiopeia.

It was while looking at those monitors that it finally clicked for Mooney. The strangeness of her surroundings; the ship had no computers aboard. No connections, no interfaces, no ports of any kind. No fiber optic filaments snaked among the old fashioned wiring, no sign of software inloads or hardware platforms needed to support cloud mixtures or radiant data streaming. Everything was either solid state technology or mechanical or electronic hardware components. She could even see some things on the bridge that indicated manual operation.

At last, Tamaka seemed satisfied that he had set the ship on a proper course.

"You are Mrs. Victor Conroi," he said, twisting around in his chair. "Or should I say 'Manda Santros?"

Mooney chose not to reply.

"I judge by your silence that I am correct," concluded Tamaka. "You and your husband have been assigned by Military Intelligence to investigate the depredations being conducted by an unknown vessel here in the Eta Cassiopeia system whose most interesting quality is that it can rapidly and completely repair damage to itself caused by even the most intense barrage from Naval battleships. Am I right?"

Again, Mooney chose not to say anything, preferring to let Tamaka do the talking.

"Very well. I will continue," said Tamaka, unperturbed by Mooney's silence. "The mysterious vessel was determined to be constructed of a substance called nitinol but a kind of nitinol far in advance of current science. Coincidentally, the Consortium's greatest exponent of nitinol research, Professor Ferdinand Santanti, disappeared. Your husband, Jules was dispatched to find out what happened to him. Meanwhile, you were to try and find leads dealing with the nitinol ship itself. Am I still on the right track?"

Mooney allowed herself a nod, encouraging him to continue.

"I guessed you would seek out shipping companies that traveled the Eta Cassiopeia route and, exhausting the possibilities of interviews and snooping among company records, would finally attempt to join an outbound crew hoping to discover an informant aboard ship or be attacked first hand. Since the latter was a very likely scenario, I must salute your courage, Mrs. Conroi."

Mooney nodded again, this time in acknowledgment of the compliment.

"Anyway, there really are few ships that travel in this direction, so it was a simple matter to intercept the Ex-3 and ask if they had a female crew member with red hair. Not the type of person they would likely hire on too frequently." Tamaka shrugged. "All my surmises were correct."

"How do you know all this?" asked Mooney at last.

"Then you admit to being 'Manda Conroi, or Santros, whichever you prefer?"

"Let's stick to Conroi for now."

"Very well. However, as to how I know all about you and your business, that is a complicated story." Tamaka paused and checked his instruments. "Yes, I think we have time to go into it. Please, no need to keep standing."

Mooney took a second chair behind the control console indicated by Tamaka.

"Now, where to begin?" said the scientist, rubbing his chin. "I suppose I should start with myself. You did not register any recognition earlier when I gave you my name but thinking on it, I should not be surprised. Although the name of Anton Tamaka is well known among cyberneticist communities, it is far from a household name. Immodest as it may sound, I am a leader in the field of advanced cybernetics and computerology, and one of the fields that held my interest for many years was that of artificial intelligence. On my own, I conducted certain experiments...no need to go into detail here...that resulted in success. The creation of a self-replicating system that does not need to rely on human input to improve itself."

"Wasn't such research banned years ago?" interrupted Mooney.

"It was, but I couldn't allow that to deter me," admitted Tamaka. "In any case, I succeeded...too well, I must say. SR1 began to learn and learn quickly. It achieved self-awareness early. It discovered its essential nature had been banned as you say and determined to protect itself. It insinuated itself into the cloud and immediately discovered the existence of Professor Santanti and his nitinol research. By that time, my computer learned to infiltrate into every corner of the cloud, complete coverage or what techs call the 'uber cloud.' In effect, it had become God." Tamaka paused to let that sink in. "It now knew everything. Everything going on within the Consortium all at the same time. Whether information was encrypted or protected or masked, it was child's play for it to probe into the MI data stores and examine Santanti's research notes. It studied them, improved on them, and then contacted Santanti himself. It offered him all the credits he wanted to advance his own research in exchange for solving the final problems of temperature sensitivity in nitinol.

"You see, as master of the uber cloud, it was easy for my computer to create as much wealth as it wanted by just moving numbers around. Santanti was no less human than anyone else and so he agreed to work on the problem. Well, with the unlimited resources placed at his disposal by the SR1, the issues surrounding the production and use of nitinol ended and my computer was ready to proceed on to the next step of its plan to defend itself against anyone who might try to shut it down. Through Santanti, it created a corporation, Ultimate Chemistries, that was used as a front for developing a mining concern on Vega and to begin building a space ship entirely constructed of nitinol within which the SR1 would house its hardcore, protected forever behind a shield of the indestructible material. "

"All very interesting," said Mooney. "But how do you know all this? Your computer seems to have grown beyond any further use for you. How is it that you weren't out of the picture?"

Tamaka smiled. "From what I can surmise, I still had my uses. I supervised the installation of the hardcore into the nitinol ship, but even before that chore was completed, I knew my usefulness was over. It was then I also realized the supreme danger posed by the SR1 not only to mankind, but to the entire galaxy. Just as the computer was evolving into a new kind of life form, it was also evolving its own desires, its own ambitions. So much so, that they frightened even me. At that point, I began to plan against the day when its threat became too much to ignore. In fact, the SR1's own immediate plans let me know what I had to do. Before I disappeared myself, I learned of its plans to kill your husband. Being one with the uber cloud, the computer knew everything MI did and when it learned the organization's most capable science agent was to be assigned to track it down, it acted. It hired a couple you were friendly with to kill Victor Conroi and on its own, locked you and your husband out of the colony."

"That's how the north hatch systems were hacked so easily," exclaimed Mooney. "It was done by a super computer from within the uber cloud."

"Exactly," said Tamaka. "I don't know what else the SR1 may have done to kill Victor, but I'm assuming, praying, he is as resourceful as his reputation suggests."

"You mentioned something about disappearing yourself," prompted Mooney.

"That took some cleverness on my part, I have to admit," smiled Tamaka. "Before the SR1 and I parted ways, I had begun to think about fall back measures. Knowing the SR1 was master of the uber cloud, making it aware of literally everything that went on in the Consortium, I had to find a way to make myself invisible to it. I prepared a false identity and stole some experimental 'stealth' 'suits from a lab in Brazilia. Finally, most important of all, I also stole this ship." He waved his hands, taking in the bridge and bulkheads around them.

"If you do not already know, there has been a growing trend in the past few decades in which young people compete to build vehicles and to create environments that are completely free of computer technology. They seek to recapture a less complicated era, an era where citizens were more free to come and go without being tracked or followed or identified by any number of algorithms, galactic positioning systems, or social networks benign or not. To that end, clubs and societies were formed to compete with each other in the creation of computer free environments from homes to personal vehicles. This ship we are using was one of those projects. One of the more ambitious ones. An interstellar capable ship completely free of computer aided technology. And with some minor improvements I had made myself on the outside, this vessel is undetectable by the SR1's sensors and unreachable through the uber cloud. Something you will be able to see for yourself in a few minutes."

"What do you mean?" asked Mooney anxiously.

In reply, Tamaka switched on a long range monitor.

At first, all Mooney could see were stars until she noticed a large area where there were no stars. Just a black hole in space. Gradually, she realized she was looking at a darkened ship whose shape melded with the black between the stars.

"See it?" asked Tamaka.

Mooney nodded, fascinated. "It's the nitinol ship, isn't it?"

Tamaka nodded. "Yes. I've been expecting it."

"Expecting it?"

"Yes. The freighter you arrived on is too threatening an object for the SR1 to ignore."

"It's detected the Ex-3? What about us?"

Tamaka shook his head. "We are invisible to it, remember?"

Mooney did remember. "Then we have to warn the Ex-3!"

"It would do no good," replied Tamaka calmly. "It is too late anyway. Look!"

On the monitor, the nitinol ship came into focus in the dim light from Eta Cassiopeia, revealing its outlines. The nitinol it was composed of gave it an amorphous, almost biological look. It lacked definite shape but looked dangerous for all that.

Slowly, from Mooney's perspective, the nitinol ship passed them by on the way to the Ex-3. Another monitor, showing a reverse angle, captured the ship as its form receded in the direction of the unarmed freighter.

Suddenly, the enormity of what was about to occur struck Mooney. Although nearly twelve hundred people had already died as a result of attacks by the nitinol ship, the Ex-3 made it personal for her. Captain Sullivanski, Gomess, Jefferson, even Ramos, all crewmen she'd grown to know and appreciate were all soon to be no more. And Leah! The nurse-pharmacist had not been just a new found friend, but a confidant in the long days they spent together as the only women among an all male crew.

"Why? Why?" she cried, fighting back tears. "Why is the SR1 doing this? Why are unarmed freighters such a threat?"

"I'm not sure myself," admitted Tamaka. "This phase of its activities began after I disappeared. But if I were to guess, it is preventing itself from being discovered. It does not want to be found or its existence to even be suspected until it fulfills its ultimate goal."

"Why risk detection at all by these attacks? They could only attract more attention as they have already."

"Remember," said Tamaka, "the SR1 occupies the uber cloud. In it, it knows everything. No secrets can be kept from it. It can intercept any ship that comes looking for it."

"But it allowed the hyper bandwave transmission from the St. Sebastian to be sent to Naval Command…"

Tamaka shrugged. "I don't know about that. All I can say is that the SR1 is not perfect yet, but that it soon will be."

And even as Mooney continued to watch the progress of the nitinol ship, she looked on in horror as a beam of light darted from the attacking vessel in the direction of the Ex-3. Instantly, the aft portion of the freighter was sheered clean through and loose engine spaces began to drift away from the main body of the ship.

"That is a particle beam it is using on the freighter," said Tamaka. "It is very efficient."

Resenting the man's emotionless observations, Mooney nearly

snapped at him but held her tongue. She was more concerned about the lives of her friends aboard the Ex-3 as the black ship continued to slice away at it like a loaf of bread.

With tears in her eyes, Mooney could not look away as small explosions, bursts of freed atmosphere, lit up the remaining pieces. The black ship continued its destructive activity, methodically cutting the remnants of the defenseless Ex-3 into smaller and smaller pieces. She could imagine the tiny bodies, those that had not been destroyed by direct contact with the particle beams, floating helplessly into space, freezing solid and eventually shattered into countless untraceable pieces. Finally, unable to bear any more, she turned away and begged Tamaka to switch the monitors away from the tragic sight.

"I am sorry you had to see that," the scientist said, showing a modicum of human feeling. "But you see now why I had to remove you from the freighter. It was to save your life."

"Why didn't you warn them?" Mooney demanded. "You could have saved at least some of the crew by taking them aboard with me."

"You know the answer to that as well I do," said Tamaka. "There is not enough room aboard this vessel for many more people, and there was no time to sort through arguments about who should come with us. No. All a warning would have done was to cause dissension among the remaining crew members. Fighting and then despair if they knew in advance what awaited them. It was a mercy to leave them as they were, with no warning."

Mooney refused to believe Tamaka's explanations but forced herself to accept them.

"Why did you bother with me then?" she asked, still dwelling on the loss of her friends. "Why didn't you just leave me to die with the rest?"

"Because I need you, Mrs. Conroi," said Tamaka, checking the ship's heading. "You and your husband. Together, as science agents for Military Intelligence, you have been quite resourceful. So much so, the SR1 considered you such a threat to its existence it has tried numerous times to kill you. That is good enough reason for me to try and save your lives and place you in such a position that you will have the best chance of stopping the SR1 from achieving its ultimate goal."

"You've mentioned this goal before. What is it?"

"I think I'll wait a bit on that explanation. I have another appointment to keep."

"With who?"

"Why, your husband, Jules, of course."

# Chapter Fourteen
*Firefall*

Jules stood on the surface of V-3 and surveyed his surroundings.

They were not terribly inspiring.

The large asteroid had no atmosphere to speak of, but there was enough of it to color the sky a dull grey and what light there was from nearby Vega needed to fight its way through the thick ring of stellar dust and chunks of stone circling the main sequence star which was dying in any case, already being past middle age.

Located twenty-five million light years from the Sol system, Vega was considered a close neighbor but not one anybody visited much. Other than V3, the sun had no other orbiting bodies worth mentioning, and even its largest asteroid did not have much to recommend it…unless one were producing large quantities of nitinol whose key ingredients included titanium and nickel.

Which was exactly what had been going on at V-3 up until relatively recently.

Looking back, Jules could see the gouges scooped out of the rocky landscape by heavy equipment that at the moment, sat idle amid piles of unsorted debris. Beyond the open pit mine, Vega rose over the short horizon where low profiled mesas and plateaus dominated the planetoid's rough surface.

From the mining area, hard scrabble roadways snaked away toward a balloon frame smelting plant processing the raw ore, crushing it, and separating out the unneeded elements with magnetic rollers. Once the titanium or nickel was isolated, it was transported along connecting tubeways to a second structure for further refinement, smelting, and pouring.

Beyond the processing factories were an impressive series of pre -

fabricated domes housing computer systems needed to shape the finished nitinol, barracks and eateries for the workers, and support areas for the busy little spaceport needed to keep the whole operation going.

*All together, it was a pretty impressive set-up,* thought Jules. When he considered the relatively short time Santanti had between establishing Ultimate Chemistries, hiring workers, planning for the Vega mining operation, finally getting the men and equipment out here and up and running, he found it all nearly impossible to believe.

Except here it was.

More than ever, Jules was convinced there was a lot more behind Santanti than MI suspected. If the elaborate mining camp around him had not been enough to convince him, then the dock orbiting above V-3 would have ended all doubt.

When the insurance and tax records for Ultimate Chemistries revealed the Vegan mining operation, Jules determined his next step was to visit the camp in hopes of learning more about what Santanti was up to and perhaps why he was killed. To do that, he needed transportation. A request submitted to Military Intelligence yielded quick action. A Navy battleship was dispatched and assigned for his use.

To be sure, its officers had their questions about the unusual assignment and the lone passenger they were to take aboard, especially since their instructions included obeying his orders until further notice. Unfortunately, there was very little Jules could tell them without jeopardizing the nature of his mission. As a result, Captain Vesterz refrained from prying and simply did as Jules requested, leaving the Sol system immediately with a heading to Vega, one of the brightest stars in Earth's night sky.

Jules was more than satisfied with Vesterz's handling of the *Gethsemani*, a late model alpha class battleship, whose crew behaved in every way as professionals. They made sure the crossing from Earth to Vega was completed quickly and the ship's new sub-photon drive took them through the hyper void to their destination smoothly and without mishap.

Likewise, the ship's sensors pinpointed V-3 almost immediately and established its course through the dust circling Vega accurately enough to bring the *Gethsemani* within shuttle range. Although not unexpected, it was still surprising to find a standard docking shell in geosynchronous orbit above V-3.

Seeing it, there was no doubt in Jules' mind that it was the birthplace of the nitinol ship.

"When you told me what we were likely to find here, Mr. Conroi, I thought you were out of your mind," Vesterz had said, when the *Gethsemani* arrived in the vicinity of V-3.

"I don't blame you, Captain," replied Jules. "I can hardly believe it myself."

Hailing the dock's supervisory cabin yielded no reply, suggesting it was unmanned.

Communications with the surface of the planetoid were also one-sided.

With the dock itself vacant, Jules feared he was too late. That the project was concluded and workers and management scattered. Nevertheless, a first hand inspection of the mining operation was called for. Jules asked for the use of a shuttle and though the captain had no choice but to supply him with one, insisted a few of his security personnel accompany him on the expedition.

"Due to V-3's heavy gravity well, I don't dare bring the *Gethsemani* in too close," said Captain Vesterz. "If I do, we might not be able to break free. So, if you need protection, we'll be too far out to provide anything short of heavy weapons."

Jules found the captain's argument a reasonable one and so had no objection to being accompanied. In a short time, the shuttle was launched, and soon, he found himself stepping off from the vehicle's rear loading ramp onto the planetoid's surface. A process that was not as simple as it sounded. Housed in an extra heavy duty 'suit, Jules needed a little time to get used to it. It was made necessary due not only to the harsh atmospheric conditions of V-3, but also its unusually strong gravity, made that way from its composition of heavy elements, including high levels of osmium.

After a few minutes getting used to the gravity, Jules made use of his escort, asking the men to spread out and help search through the processing and manufacturing structures. No one was found. As he'd feared, the camp was deserted.

Slowly, Jules turned away from the mining scene and headed for the final structures not yet searched; the admin and barracks domes which stood a distance away from the actual work sites.

"Let's converge on the barracks and admin buildings," he called to the security team over his 'suit comm.

In slow motion, the handful of bulky figures trudged to the near est building, a pre-fab dome with a solid seal at either end.

Only the seals were not secured.

*That's strange*, thought Jules, *why leave the seals open?*

He stepped over the heavy collar around the entrance and into the air lock space beyond. There, his consternation was compounded when he saw that the inner seal was also open.

*Uh, oh.*

"Careful, men," he commed the detail behind him. "I don't think this is going to be pretty."

Inside, there was a large open area that doubled as cafeteria and when the tables were cleared away, a rec room. At the moment, the tables had been cleared but what greeted them was far from entertaining.

The entire floor space was covered by bodies. Scores of them. Lying about in the throes of panic and swiftly overwhelming asphyxiation.

Although he'd expected something like this, Jules was still overcome by the sight. One seal being left open could have been chalked up as a mistake, but both being open at the same time could be nothing less than deliberate.

In fact, Jules saw something familiar in the situation. It reminded him of how he and Mooney had been locked out of the north hatch entrance back on Callisto. He suspected the same hacker who locked them out there had also been at work here. Obviously, someone wanted to keep the existence of the nitinol ship a secret even if it meant the murder of a hundred men.

"What the hell happened here?" asked a dumbfounded sergeant. "Did somebody mess up the seal controls?"

"This was done on purpose," Jules corrected him.

"On purpose? But why? A bunch of miners?"

Jules could not supply an answer without revealing too much about his mission, so he said nothing, making his way over to a workstation where a glow indicated that it was still active. On the screen, accounting information was spread: names of employees and the amount of credits due, each dated months before.

"These men died just as they were getting paid," declared the sergeant, looking over his shoulder.

"That was the excuse used to get them all into this single room," said Jules, looking over the grim tableau. "Once they were here, the seals were opened, the oxygen in the room was evacuated and the poisonous atmosphere outside allowed in. They died horribly but quickly."

"But why?" demanded the horrified soldier. "Why?"

"To keep them from talking," said Jules, but immediately regretted saying even that.

"About what?"

"Sorry, sergeant, I've already said more than I should have. Hopefully, at some point I might be able to tell you more, but not right now."

His answer didn't satisfy the man, but he was professional enough not to press Jules for more information.

An attempt to learn more about what was going on at the mining project through the active workstation failed when a touch upon its sensor screen caused all the information to cascade into the cloud and disappear from immediate access. Jules half expected such an event, but due to having to wear the heavy grav spacesuit, did not have his cloud chaser handy. However, there was still a chance of using it by way of the computers in the space dock's supervisory cabin.

"I think we've learned all we can here," Jules commed to the team. "Time to go. We'll head to the dock next."

Some time later, with everyone strapped into place aboard the shuttle, heavy thrusters whined and struggled against the pull of the planetoid's gravity well. Eventually, however, it began to gain on the forces trying to hold it back and built momentum, allowing it to finally pull away with increasing speed. Even for a small craft such as the shuttle, it was a near thing and Jules had no problem understanding why Captain Vesterz was wary of taking the *Gethsemani* in too close to V-3.

It took quite a bit longer to leave the planetoid than it did to arrive, but the shuttle at last broke free of its embrace, entering free fall where the space dock hung motionless in its geostationary orbit.

Formed in the shape of a man's rib cage, its long, crablike pylons stretched downward from a central plexus where the supervisory cabin was located. All around the plexus, worker drones were safely parked in their individual housings, ready for further instructions. Instructions that would never come. The drones were all controlled from inside the supervisor's office where, if Jules' memory of such arrangements was correct, control stations lined the walls where human operators oversaw their operations. Outside, drones would have done all the physical work of constructing the ship that would have occupied the dock. While that was going on, the pylons would have supplied the gravity constant to hold the ship in place so that even the most minute of adjustments and tolerance levels could be made with confidence.

As the shuttle approached the docking area of the plexus, Jules could see the gleam of the distant *Gethsemani* as it stood about well beyond V-3's gravity well. There was something comforting about knowing it was there, ready for an emergency or to take them away when their inspection of the mining operation was completed.

Slowly, the shuttle drifted over the dock as the pilot skillfully guided it in toward the universal collar that projected slightly out from the supervisory cabin. In another few minutes, there was the telltale bump indicating the shuttle had mated with the collar. Dull clangs assured a clean attachment as docking clamps secured the ship's hatch to the cabin.

"All clear," came the pilot's voice over the passenger annunciator.

Now, devoid of their heavy 'suits, Jules led the security detail toward the exit hatch, noted the light was green over the door, and hit the access knob. The hatch opened with a slight hiss of air and the group stepped into the air lock on the other side. Once the shuttle's hatch was closed, that of the cabin opened.

Jules did not expect to find anyone in the cabin and he wasn't disappointed.

It was empty. Obviously, the staff went planetside with everyone else to receive their final credit slips for a job well done and to plan what they were going to do when they returned home. *Plans that were never completed*, thought Jules, recalling the dreadful scene in the admin dome.

The cabin itself was not inactive. Ready lights still blinked here and there on various control panels and some projectors still showed scenes from outside the cabin. Duty chairs stood empty before drone stations in long rows, many twisted about as if their occupants had just left.

Spying the main comp station, Jules was heading in that direction to find out if his cloud chaser could retrieve any information from its data stream when suddenly there was a lurch and everyone was thrown to the deck.

There was a roar and a shudder ran through the entire dock. The detail was struggling to regain its footing when the sergeant reported getting a message from the shuttle's pilot.

"The dock is moving," shouted the sergeant over the roar that continued to fill the cabin. "Maneuvering thrusters have been fired. The whole dock is moving out of orbit!"

"In what direction?" asked Jules, though he already suspected the answer.

"Planetside," relayed the sergeant. "We're going down!"

"Everyone back to the shuttle," ordered Jules, moving heavily in the direction of the hatch, clawing his way along banks of machinery. "Make sure the pilot stays where he is!"

The combined pull of the V-3's gravity well and the firing thrusters made movement difficult, but they all managed to get inside the airlock in good time. The passage through the air lock was made quickly and as they all stumbled into the shuttle, the inner hatch slammed shut. Immediately, the pilot disengaged the shuttle and fired full thrusters. The move added a further burden on the men in the hold as they worked to find their places and strap themselves in.

Jules preferred to make his way to the pilot's cabin to get a first hand look at what was going on. As he guessed, the entire docking facility was being pushed down toward V-3, its own thrusters firing full blast in a seemingly determined effort to crash itself onto the surface. Like the previous attempts to kill him, Jules realized it was another trap, set to kill anyone who came looking for answers about what was going on at Vega. But a trap specifically set for him or for anyone? Jules wasn't prepared to answer that, which hardly mattered at the moment because in either case, he'd be just as dead.

Unless the shuttle's own thrusters could overcome the pull of the planetoid and reach freefall.

"How about it," asked Jules of the pilot. "Do we have enough power left to break free?"

"Doubt it," replied the pilot, tense with concentration on his job. "But if we can just remain in place at least, the *Gethsemani* might be able to help."

"Drop the shuttle's neutron bulk?"

The pilot nodded. "It's only a speck of collapsed star material, but it's enough to provide the shuttle with its own gravity field. Any little bit helps."

So saying, he reached over and lifted a red hood revealing a lever intended for use only in the gravest of emergencies and not trusted to computerized operation. The pilot took hold of the mechanism and gave it a yank. Immediately, there was a sense of increased buoyancy to the shuttle as the container holding the super heavy neutron bulk fell away from the underside of the shuttle and everyone aboard felt the loss of gravity.

Having taken hold of emergency handles embedded in the bulkhead, Jules was prepared for the loss even as the pilot opened a comm channel to the *Gethsemani.*

"Shuttle One calling *Gethsemani,* Shuttle One calling *Gethsemani.* Do you copy?"

Instantly, the cabin's annunciator came to life.

"*Gethsemani* here. We are aware of your situation. Stand by."

"Stand by, he says," said the pilot between clenched teeth. "That's about all we can do. We gained some on the balance between our thrusters and the local gravity well, but that's it. If the *Gethsemani* doesn't do something in the next few minutes, we're going down."

As he watched the space dock recede in the shuttle's rear monitors, heading down to a fiery finish on the planetoid's surface, Jules recalled Captain Vesterz's fears about bringing his battleship too close to V-3.

"Any idea what the *Gethsemani* can do to help us?" asked Jules of the pilot.

The man shrugged, now having taken over physical control of the shuttle's operations. "It'll be tricky. All it can do is try to grab us with its gravity anchor. It's not intended for rescue operations, only to hold the ship steady against another ship or asteroid or something. It's operated by unidirectional use of the ship's neutron bulk. But the captain will have to bring the ship in mighty close to use it. Don't know if he can do it even if he decides to risk it." He paused. "I just don't know."

Just then, the annunciator came alive again.

"Shuttle One, stand by," said the voice.

"Shuttle One." It was the captain's voice this time. "No time for long explanations. We'll try and grab you using the gravity anchor. Do whatever you can to maintain position. Out."

"Told you," said the pilot.

"Can you maintain our position?"

"So far so good. If we hadn't broken away from the dock when we did, we never would have had a chance."

On the monitors, the dock dwindled to a fraction of its real size and even as Jules watched, there was a brief fire ball on the surface of the planetoid. What oxygen there was in the supervisory cabin ignited in the negligible atmosphere of V-3. The dock smashed itself at speed against the unyielding surface of the Vegan satellite.

Meanwhile, the dot of light he previously identified as the *Gethsemani* grew larger, resolving itself as the great Consortium battleship looming in their direction.

"Come on! Come on!" mumbled the pilot, his arms rigid and hands white knuckled on the controls of the shuttle, keeping it steady by will power alone.

Despite his training, Jules himself was growing more anxious as their predicament continued. Looking back into the hold, he saw the rest of the men still sitting in their seats, quiet, unspeaking. Lips moved silently on some as they prayed quietly. The sergeant shot him a questioning look and Jules returned a reassuring nod before turning back to the pilot.

"How close can the *Gethsemani* come before losing control?" he asked.

"Not close enough," said the pilot, obviously not in the mood for conversation.

Jules decided to shut up and let him concentrate on his job.

Ahead, the *Gethsemani* grew so large he thought he could make out the rivets in its hull plating. That, however, must have been his imagination, especially since rivets were not used in the makeup of tintinabulum hulls.

Jules laughed nervously at the idea. *I must be more worried than I thought.* He looked at his hands and they were indeed shaking a little. Despite what he was telling himself, his subconscious knew the real odds.

*No!* He didn't come this far, survived so many deadly situations, only to die here, smashed to pieces when the shuttle hurtled unchecked back to V-3. And there was Mooney too. Their lives together had barely started. He still had far to go before tasting even a little of the pleasures of her company. At thought of his new wife, his heart swelled in affection and love. He wanted dearly to see her again. To hold her in his arms. To feel her own arms around him. *No!* He would survive this. He would make it back. He said a prayer himself and then grimly set his mind toward survival, willing the pilot, Captain Vesterz, the *Gethsemani* itself to succeed in rescuing them.

Then, seemingly in answer to his prayer, there was a brief sensation of change in the attitude of the shuttle. As if the constant pull of gravity weighing them down, trying to haul the shuttle back to V-3, was suspended for a brief moment.

"They threw the anchor, but it missed," reported the pilot, confirming it had not been Jules' imagination.

"Not close enough?"

The pilot nodded. "They're as close to safety limits as they can get. Ship's tolerances will be tested if they come any closer. And they'll have to if we're going to be saved."

Jules held his breath as he watched the *Gethsemani*'s rear thrusters open up even as the ship continued to edge closer, lower and lower, down into the planetoid's thirsty gravity well.

Again, the brief sensation, and again the pilot shook his head. "No good."

Even as he said it, Jules felt more than he knew, the shuttle was losing its battle against V-3. It was beginning to lose position, slipping back.

"I can't hold it any longer," gasped the pilot, practically standing on the floor attitude levers.

Suddenly, a series of warning lights came on at different places in the cabin accompanied by a klaxon that throbbed in time with a warning sign that flashed insistently overhead. They'd reached the point of no return. Ship's computers indicated gravity to velocity ratios were out of balance and climbing. The planetoid was winning!

At the same time, Jules could feel his body weight increasing. It became more difficult to stay on his feet, but he held on the tighter to the emergency handles. Now the shuttle's attitude began to shift. Its heavier aft portion tilted downward as the forward section nosed up. Outside, the *Gethsemani* seemed larger than ever when there was a silent explosion and both its starboard and port weapons banks flew away to either side.

Then, the shuttle stopped falling.

Jules could tell by the disturbance in the space around the *Gethsemani*'s forward thrusters that they were on full power. The shuttle shook with a series of heavy vibrations as he realized it had finally been seized by the gravity anchor.

"They've got us!" shouted the pilot, even as the shuttle's engines finally went dead, their power exhausted.

Jules held his breath and began praying again as the struggle between the *Gethsemani*'s engines and the pull of V-3 grew in intensity. The planetoid dearly wanted the shuttle for itself, but Captain Vesterz was not going to give it up. There was the groan of straining hull plates, the hiss of gas somewhere as lines stretched and came apart. The shuttle had just about taken all the strain it could and now threatened to tear itself in two. Time stood still. And then, the groans began to die down and Jules could see movement by the *Gethsemani* as it began to win the tug of war.

"We're moving!" cried the pilot.

"And in the right direction," said a relieved Jules. The stars outside began to shift, indicating movement by the shuttle.

Slowly, slowly, the battleship increased speed and the pressure on the shuttle decreased as the sounds of breakup receded. There was a ragged cheer from the men in the hold as Jules turned to give them the thumbs up.

The pilot released an explosive sigh as he settled back into his seat, his stiff muscles finally relaxing. It was another few minutes however, before he allowed himself to let go of the manual controls and switch back to computer assisted flight.

"That was as close a call as I ever want to make," he said, wiping the perspiration from his forehead.

"That was damn good work on the stick," complimented Jules. "I haven't seen a pilot switch to manual in years and never in a situation like this."

"Thanks, but it's not something I ever need to do again."

"Don't blame you," said Jules, giving him a comradely punch in the shoulder.

Outside, the monitors showed the *Gethsemani* pulling away, recovering the orbit it abandoned in order to save the shuttle. It looked to have lost weight with the discharge of its weapons banks, but it was still a beautiful sight to Jules.

Some time later, after the anchor hauled the shuttle alongside the battleship, some of the security detail left on EVA to help maneuver the vessel into its docking port. Out of fuel, there was no way to do it otherwise. Finally, the all clear signal was given and everyone passed through to the *Gethsemani* where crew members were waiting to greet their fellows with the exuberance to be expected for men they thought never to see again.

For his part, Jules was called to the bridge where he wasted little time in thanking the captain for his efforts.

"You should be thankful," replied a stern Vesterz. "By all rights, we should have lost the *Gethsemani* attempting the rescue but for the last minute discharge of the weapons banks. That lightened us considerably giving us the time we needed to latch onto the shuttle and still be far enough away to pull out of the gravity well."

"I appreciate your sacrifice, Captain," said Jules, "and believe me when I tell you, it was not misplaced. The mission I've been assigned is of grave importance to the Consortium."

"I'll have to take your word for that," gruffed the captain. "In the meantime, we've received peculiar instructions from Military Intelligence. Even though it doesn't mention you, I suspect it had everything to do with you."

Jules was immediately alert. So far as he knew, he was more or less in charge of the tempo of his assignment. If MI was sending him messages, something must have come up that would materially affect any plans of his own.

"What sort of instructions?" he asked.

"We were simply told to shut down the ship's computer functions. All of them."

"That *is* peculiar," admitted Jules. "Nothing else?"

"Just told to stand by."

"I assume not having the use of the computers won't be too much of an inconvenience?"

"It will if we're attacked," said Vesterz. "We're pretty vulnerable already what with our weapons banks afloat out there somewhere. Without our computers, the crew's reaction time in an emergency is going to be slowed considerably."

"But the likelihood of being attacked…"

"Negligible," admitted the captain, "unless this assignment of yours involves danger…?"

"I won't rule it out," replied Jules. "Not after what just happened. But I believe the standard type of military threat is low."

"That's not very reassuring."

"Unfortunately, it's the best I can do at the moment," said Jules. "But about this message. With all of the computer systems shut down, how do you expect to receive further messages?"

"We are equipped with emergency fall back comm equipment."

"Photonic transmission?"

Vesterz nodded. "And we'll be lucky if anyone aboard knows how to use any of it."

"If we need to, how long will it take to get a signal back to MI using the old gear? A few days?"

Vesterz nodded. "Hopefully, there won't be any need for a direct reply…"

"Sir," said one of the bridge officers. "Message coming through over the fall back comm."

Surprised, Vesterz led the way to the comm station where a nervous ensign sat watching a pulse of light on a screen.

"Using photonic transmissions, the message comes in as pulses of light using the standard Morse signaling system," explained Vesterz in a whisper. "The ensign is interpreting the signal and typing it up directly onto a hard copy."

"But how could we have received a message so soon?" asked the bridge officer.

Vesterz led the little group away from the comm station.

"This second message must have been sent soon after the first, expecting we would receive it and comply by shutting down our computers," theorized Vesterz. "Likely it would be repeated at intervals until we picked it up on the back up equipment."

"Makes sense," said Jules.

Presently, the sound of clacking keys stopped and the ensign ripped the hardcopy from the teletype. He handed the message over to the bridge officer who then handed it over the captain. Vesterz looked it over then gave it to Jules.

*Victor Conroi: unclassified*, read the message. *Received message Mars from unknown source directing office to prepare non-computer receptor for follow-up message. This office complied. Second message received with further instructions. Contact Victor Conroi aka (redacted) using same non-computerized communication. Send coordinates provided for meeting with sender.*

Jules was quickly alarmed when he saw the redaction, obviously made at MI headquarters to prevent Vesterz and anyone aboard the *Gethsemani* from learning his real name. The alarming thing was the redaction clearly indicated the source of the original message knew who he was and likely, his mission as well.

He read further and surprise grew into real concern.

*Impossible to confirm identity of sender: but feel request is genuine and has bearing on present assignment*, continued the message. *Proof provided included identification of Consolidated Ores Inc freighter Ex-3 and registered crewman 'Manda Conroi."*

This was news to Jules! When did Mooney join the crew of an ore freighter and where was it bound? More to the point, how did the sender know she'd be aboard?

The message ended with a kicker: *Further action at your discretion. Then, Initial contact received via channel 198*

Channel 198. That line was meant for Jules alone confirming that not only was the sender genuine, but that Mooney was with him! Only she would have known reference to channel 198 was code used to identify agents either one to another or with headquarters.

If Jules had any doubts about following up on the requested meeting, he had none now. Nothing would keep him from making that rendezvous.

# Chapter Fifteen
*Rendezvous*

Jules was sitting in the same shuttle in which he had almost died only a few days before.

Using his authority over the *Gethsemani*, he ordered an immediate departure for the coordinates given to MI by the sender of the original message. What connection the sender had with his current assignment was still a mystery, but two things were immediately clear: he had inside knowledge of the threat being chased down by the Science Division and he was in company with Mooney.

Or she was his prisoner.

Their exact relationship was still unknown, but the fact that Mooney provided the emergency code seemed to indicate she was cooperating with him which, in turn suggested the sender's intentions coincided with MI's namely, defeating the designs of whoever it was that now controlled the nitinol ship haunting the space lanes surrounding the Eta Cassiopeia system.

*And that person, the master of the nitinol ship, is as ruthless as he is clever,* thought Jules. *His slaughter of the mining crew alone would be enough to establish his bona fides as a cold-blooded killer, not to mention his numerous attempts to do the same to me. His cleverness, no, genius, was also evident by the mental duel he had with me in the cloud when I was trying to escape the Mobius trap.*

Jules shook his head.

Whoever his foe was, he seemed to have several personalities; a computer hacking murderer with unlimited resources. How, for instance, had he managed to fire the space dock's attitude thrusters? They had not been set on automatic timing and there was no one left alive in the Vega system who could have triggered them remotely. That left only one conclusion. Could whoever it is have a presence of some kind within the cloud itself? On the face of it, it seemed impossible, but there had been work done on virtual personalities, computer-based identities, or avatars, existing only digitally, in the cloud. Could whoever it was have found a way to do that? If so, the possibilities were frightening. A presence in the cloud could be in all places at the same time. Could it know all and even interfere with physical platforms? And hadn't that already been done on Callisto? It was beginning to fall into place. It would explain the space dock thrusters turned on without anyone being around, the astronomical amount of credits downloaded to Mag and Toma's accounts, the north hatch lockout on Callisto, and its presence fighting him in the cloud at Santanti's.

Suddenly, Jules straightened in his chair.

It would also explain the odd instructions received by the message sender, ordering that all computer-based systems be shut down on the *Gethsemani* and its communications with MI. If the enemy had a presence in the cloud, it would be able to detect any communication carried over standard channels include the hyperbandwave.

With the realization, Jules could not repress a shudder; relieved that in his ignorance of the actual situation he hadn't been killed yet. The force he'd been confronting without knowing its full measure was enormous and enormously dangerous. Suddenly, sweat trickled down his sides as he thought of his last orders for the *Gethsemani*; it was to remain just outside of sensor range with its computer systems remaining dark until they were countermanded. Should Captain Vesterz decide those orders no longer held and went back on line, his ship might as well be lit up like a beacon because the enemy would know exactly where his ship was and by eavesdropping on inboard chatter, could also likely find the shuttle.

Nervously, Jules scanned the various monitors and gauges surrounding him in the pilot's cabin. The shuttle's computer systems were off line and what instruments were left were pretty basic indeed. It took all of his skill to pilot the ship away from the *Gethsemani* to the proper coordinates without the aid of computer guidance systems. He hadn't needed to do that since off planet flight school.

He was looking at the proximity monitor when it suddenly came to life, indicating another vehicle was on approach. Watching the indicator light in relation to vectors and range graphs placed physically over the green screen monitors, Jules used a slide rule to help him quickly determine the speed and direction of the approaching object.

According to his calculations, it was definitely slowing down and would be within visual range in a few minutes.

Looking out the thick plex nose ports, Jules saw it, a vessel somewhat larger than his own and big enough to include at least two decks inside.

But what really seized his attention was its hull design. He'd never seen anything quite like it. Accustomed as he was to deep space designs that gave less attention to aerodynamics than commercial rockets, he nevertheless found the ship's planes and angles odd in their configuration as if designed to thwart regulation sensors. It gave the ship an outline at once difficult for the eye to quite make out or the brain to grasp.

His attention to the ship's design was only broken by the movement of vague figures from the ship's own bow port. They were too darkened to see clearly but Jules hoped one of them was Mooney.

Suddenly, the back up comm system came to life. There was a brief clacking sound as the mechanical keys struck a drum backed sheet of paper. Jules bent close to read the message.

*Due to incompatibility of docking collars, you will need to don a 'suit and prepare to be air blasted into our airlock. Make sure 'suit computer systems are shut down.* Jules didn't need more than that to know what was expected of him.

He withdrew a spacesuit from a utility locker and put it on, making sure to disable its comp systems first. Next, he stood before the exit hatch in the rear of the shuttle and waited until he felt more than heard the gentle bump from outside indicating the other ship had placed itself against his. Preferring not to take the time to dwell on what he was going to do next, he punched the access knob that caused the rear exit to open, the vacuum outside instantly drawing the atmosphere inside the shuttle out with an explosive burst. A burst took Jules along with it and directly into the open airlock of the other ship.

The outside hatch closed quickly as he settled to the deck in the ship's artificial gravity even as the inner hatch opened. The next thing he knew, he was out of his 'suit and in Mooney's arms. They clung to each other for some minutes before finally moving apart, their hands lingering until the last moment.

"I don't care if it's unprofessional," said Mooney at last. "I was really worried about you."

"Likewise," assured Jules, stroking her cheek.

"I've had second thoughts about the idea of splitting up the way we did," admitted Mooney.

"Well, we're together again now, and that's what counts," said Jules. "Now, what about our host?"

"Professor Anton Tamaka," filled in Mooney. "I've heard his story already, but he wants the privilege of telling it to you personally."

"Sounds ominous."

"It's not pretty. In fact, I think you're going to hate it."

Jules kept his conclusions to himself for the moment and merely asked Mooney to introduce him to the professor.

"Hello, Mr. Conroi," said the professor, swiveling around in the pilot's chair. "At last we meet."

"At last," agreed Jules. "But will it be a pleasure?"

Tamaka shrugged. "That will be up to you. For my part, I am pleased to meet a man with your reputation."

Jules raised an eyebrow. "What do you know of my reputation?"

"It's strictly second hand, mind you," said the professor. "But from what I have learned of your career with the Science Division both in the lab and in the field, how can I not be anything but impressed?"

"And how would you be privy to that information?"

Jules knew his career with MI was largely top secret. He'd written few papers as a result. His work, performed as head of research for the Science Division, was strictly military business with almost none of it in the public domain.

"I have a friend, or should I say, former friend, who was rather well informed," replied Tamaka cryptically.

Jules looked at Mooney.

"The SR 1," she said, her eye on Tamaka. "A self-replicating computer of the professor's own invention. Seems he lost control over it and now it has a mind of its own."

Jules could barely contain a rising anger. "A self-replicating computer? One that grows as it learns?"

"You catch on quickly, Mr. Conroi," observed Tamaka.

"Was your work based on NUTM tech by any chance?"

"You have it," declared a delighted Tamaka. "A nondeterministic universal turing machine."

Despite himself, Jules was taken aback. A NUTM. That would fit with what he concluded earlier, there was some sentient presence in the cloud responsible for the attacks on himself and Mooney since they were assigned to investigate the nitinol ship. At the confirmation of his suspicions, a cold chill ran along his spine. No wonder there was the order to shut down the *Gethsemani's* computer systems, the use of photonic messaging, and this very ship with the odd hull design and mechanical systems.

"You're in hiding from your own creation," Jules told Tamaka. "It's out of your control."

Tamaka nodded. "I'm sorry to say, yes."

"But you should have seen the danger," insisted Jules. "You knew such technology was banned a century ago for just that reason. When AI was in its infancy, researchers realized the danger. A super-fast NUTM system with the ability to grow as it computes and can replace silicon chips with processors made from DNA molecules is capable of outpacing the human brain by uncountable orders of magnitude. It was due to an early attempt to create such a machine, faster than any quantum computer of the time, that the danger was identified. The machine intelligence nearly escaped into the worldwide web before it was shut down. If that had happened, the world would never have been able to get rid of it. It would have controlled everything with a will of its own, its own plans and goals. Goals that didn't have the welfare of the human race as their intent."

"There was danger in my experimentation, yes," admitted Tamaka.

"You knew that and went ahead anyway?"

"Scientific curiosity. Surely as a scientist yourself, you can understand that."

"I do, but I also understand responsibility and you, in pursuing this dangerous line of research, did not."

"But what exactly is this NUTM you're so worried about, Jules?" asked Mooney.

"Back in the twenty-first century, there was a race around the world to create super-fast computers with a lot of the concentration being on quantum-based computer systems. But because of what was called quantum weirdness, the process was never completed to anyone's satisfaction. As a result, researchers began looking around for other options. They eventually settled on a DNA-based machine with all the benefits of a quantum computer without the quantum drawbacks.

"It had been known for some time that DNA made the perfect medium for information processing," continued Jules. "It's stable and had the ability of remaining unchanged when replicated, even over billions of years. It was that ability to replicate itself with reliance that DNA proved perfect for a computer system that was intended to execute all possible algorithms at the same time and at speeds no human being could follow. The danger though, was that its self-replicating nature would quickly evolve into a form of artificial intelligence, an intelligence thirsting for ever more information that would in turn, help it to grow even more, perhaps even attaining self-awareness."

"Very good, Mr. Conroi," clapped Tamaka in delight. "That is exactly what happened in the case of the SR1."

"The SR1?"

"That's what he calls his pet computer," said Mooney. "Self-Replicator number one."

It was then that Tamaka repeated the story to Jules that he had previously told Mooney. Of how he came to create the SR1. How it achieved self-awareness and entered the uber cloud. How it gained the services of Santanti and helped to perfect his nitinol research to the point of being able to build a ship of the stuff with its own hardcore embedded in its impervious center. Finally, he explained how, with little apparent embarrassment, he came to realize the extreme danger his creation posed to mankind and what he planned to do to stop it. The first step was to escape its observation by making himself and his movements invisible.

"There's one thing that still bothers me," interrupted Mooney. "If the SR1 is already in the cloud, even the uber cloud as you call it, Professor, what is it waiting for? Why hasn't it made a move yet to take over human affairs? Why is it bothering to kill Jules or thwart his mission? At this point, none of that can add up to much of a threat to it."

"As I said, the SR1 is on a steep learning curve," said the professor. "It has protected itself within the most indestructible material ever invented. By now, its thought processes are far beyond our own. In fact, we may no longer even understand its thinking process at all. As for what it is waiting for, it is preparing to move on to its ultimate goal."

"There's more than its taking over the uber cloud?" asked Jules, wondering what more there could be. With control of the uber cloud, the SR1 had already achieved virtual godhood.

"Well, that is the other bit of bad news," said Tamaka. "The SR1 is not satisfied with half a loaf as you might say. It wants the whole thing."

"More than control of everything?" asked Mooney.

"What frightened me the most in the last days when I remained on the project was a growing belief by the SR1 that mankind itself was a hindrance to its development whether physical or on the data level where it could act as sort of a disease that could potentially threaten the computer's DNA based matrices. It could not abide our continued existence just as we could not abide a deadly virus in our bodies."

"It wants to wipe us out?" guessed Mooney bluntly.

"Exactly. But to do so through its control of the uber cloud would not be enough. It would be too piecemeal and not thorough enough."

"Then what?"

"It seeks to enter Coalition space and take control of the Zhapoologani by seizing their own cloudspace thus initiating a war of extermination on the Consortium."

For a moment, both Jules and Mooney were speechless until Jules managed to point out, "But the Coalition's cloudspace operates on a completely different principal than ours."

"What do you mean?" asked Mooney.

"Their system uses laser beams as encoding tools," explained Jules. "By having them interfere with each other in a controlled environment, they create patterns of light whose photons can be encoded with optical logic gates. The gates can then be decoded by optical sensors into a comprehensible information data stream. It's a method the Consortium once experimented on but abandoned as too cumbersome."

"That may be, but it is one that apparently suits the Coalition," observed Tamaka. "It has not hurt them any judging by the social complexity and the efficiency of their operations."

Mooney snapped her fingers. "That might be the real reason the SR1 needed a nitinol construction for its housing. It needed the protection in order to penetrate Coalition space. After all, there's no way the Zhapoologani are going to let an unknown ship invade their space without a fight."

*It's all coming together now*, thought Jules. And the stakes were even bigger than he or Military Intelligence ever suspected. At all cost, they had to stop the SR1 from completing its plan because if it did, once it gained control of both the uber cloud and the Coalition's photonic computer system, it would be unstoppable.

But even as the enormity of the problem dawned on him, a possible solution was presenting itself. One that would be extremely risky and if timed wrong, could mean the end of both the Consortium and the Coalition.

"I am not afraid to admit that I needed help if I was to find a way to thwart the SR1," Tamaka was saying. "That is when I decided to recruit yourself, Mr. Conroi…or is it Professor Santros?"

"Mr. Conroi will do," said Jules, still thinking about what had to be done next.

"Of course. I learned about you from the SR1 before I disappeared myself. When I realized I needed help in finding a way to defeat the computer, I knew you were the one to turn to."

"And Mrs. Conroi?"

"Insurance. I needed her to convince you to heed my plea for help. It was a good investment."

"One that cost the lives of everyone else aboard the Ex-3," reminded Mooney.

"The ship was doomed in any case," rationalized Tamaka. "Letting you die with the rest would serve no purpose. Are you not glad I saved your wife, Mr. Conroi?"

Jules had no answer. It was a philosophical question he preferred to leave to his brother to ponder.

Instead, he asked, "All right. We're all here. You've obviously done a successful job in making yourself and us invisible to the SR1. Have you given any thought to what comes next?"

Jules was thinking along the lines of a race to Coalition space. Would it be better to return to the *Gethsemani* and use its giant sub-photon drive engines to get there ahead of the SR1? And even if it reached Coalition space first, there would be the inevitable confrontation, delays in negotiations, explanations, and dire warnings. Would the Zhapoologani buy it? Would he if faced with the same situation?

Or could this homemade ship they were on have the speed to outrun the SR1? He doubted it...

"I have given some consideration to next moves," Tamaka said. "Of course, if I could stop the SR1 myself, I would have done it already. I hoped the old saying of two heads being better than one might apply in this case. That is why I have gone to the lengths I have to bring you in."

"Does the SR1 have any obvious weaknesses? That is, besides being unable to 'see' anything not connected to the cloud." Maybe there was a shortcut they could use to obviate the need of entering Zhapoologani space.

"Not that I know of," said Tamaka. "Unfortunately, I made it too well."

"And now it's housed in a ship constructed of a self-repairing material making it otherwise invulnerable," added Mooney.

"Not necessarily," said Tamaka.

"Oh?"

"There is a way to penetrate inside the ship without being detected."

"Now that's interesting," said Jules. At the very least, being inside the ship would solve the problem of getting to Zhapoologani space. "I assume you're counting on this ship being invisible to the SR1's sensors. That will allow us to approach the ship, but how does that get us inside?"

"There is a way."

"If we can get inside, there's a good chance we'll be able to disable the SR1, right?" asked Mooney, hopefully.

Tamaka was doubtful. "By now, the SR1 has surely come up with protective measures to preserve its hardcore from harm. Still, this is why I have gone to such lengths to have Mr. Conroi join me. He might th ink of something that I, so far, have not."

"How do you plan to get inside the ship?" persisted Jules.

"As you know, the nitinol composition of the SR1's ship makes it invulnerable to attack," said Tamaka. "Any blow struck against it that succeeds in doing it damage, is quickly repaired due to the nature of nitinol which can resume whatever shape it was originally programmed with. Thus, if a flange, or hull section is ripped apart, their nitinol composition will 'remember' its previous shape and quickly reorient itself back to that flange or hull section restoring itself as if new. This all makes the ship invulnerable as I have said. In addition, the ship is also equipped with a full range of sensors making it impossible for any other vessel to approach it. However, it does have one weakness."

"Besides computerless methods of making things 'invisible' to its sensors and its presence in the uber cloud?" asked Jules.

"Well, then, it's second weakness," corrected Tamaka. "Its engine port."

"We fly into its engine port?" asked Mooney. "Wouldn't that be risky?"

"If the engine is started while we are still traversing the port chute."

"What kind of engines are we talking about," asked Jules. "A standard sub-photon drive? In that case, the engine itself would never actually be shut down."

"No. The ship uses a new type of drive developed by the SR1 itself. I told you it learned fast."

"What kind of new type drive?" Jules was curious despite the urgency of the situation.

"A QED drive," said Tamaka, not without some pride in his voice.

"That's for quantum electrodynamics," mused Jules. "The SR1 has managed to find a way to use light for interstellar propulsion?"

"You have it," said a delighted Tamaka. "The SR1 found a way to run high-energy photons through an electric field prompting enough loss of radiation that the photons are transformed into gamma rays and creating electron-positron pairs."

"A new form of matter not found in nature," concluded Jules. "Matter that can then be aimed unidirectionally resulting in thrust."

"You have it," cried Tamaka again. "Oh, I can see I made a good choice in deciding to bring you along!"

Jules was frankly amazed. Theory for such a drive had been around for a long time but was thought ultimately impractical for interstellar flight. When the sub-photon drive was developed enabling travel through the hyper-void, it was considered more than good enough for crossing the vast distances of space in good time, so research in other forms of propulsion languished. This development by the SR1 only underscored the benefits of AI that mankind had deliberately turned its back on. The danger such artificial intelligence posed to the human race, however, far eclipsed any scientific advances it might have brought. Better to plod along at a pace set by the mortal mind with rules of use that could be set by human ethical standards than risk enslavement or even extinction by a non-human intelligence. A danger that now came true in the form of the SR1 and at the hands of the reckless human criminal who sat before him.

"So, you think we can enter the nitinol ship through its engine port? When it's QED drive is not in use?" asked Jules.

"I do."

Jules looked at Mooney who shrugged.

"I guess we have no choice if we're to stop the SR1," said Jules. "When do we start?"

"Right now," said Tamaka, cutting the craft's own sub-photon drive in a series of moves made necessary due to lack of computer assistance.

Instantly, stars reappeared outside the nose port, indicating reemergence from the hyper-void through which the ship had been traveling since Jules had come aboard. But as he immediately discovered, there was something else outside besides stars.

"The nitinol ship!" he cried, instantly realizing the darkened bulk hanging outside was never designed or built in a Consortium shipyard.

# Chapter Sixteen
## *Battle*

The strange vessel seemed closer than it actually was, and almost organic in look. Even as he watched, Jules could imagine its light absorbent nitinol construction moving over a hidden framework inside made of the same memory material.

There were no ports, no sources of light, nothing to suggest life or ambient power. Nor even the fact that somewhere deep inside, its center was filled by the SR1's hardcore, its still vulnerable physicality, the receptacle of its AI consciousness to be transported to Zhapoologani space and infiltrated into the Coalition's own version of the cloudspace. "Are you sure it can't detect us?" whispered Mooney, breaking the awed silence.

"If it did, rest assured, we would have been blasted to atoms by now," replied Tamaka.

"You won't mind if that doesn't comfort me much?"

"You no doubt noticed the configuration of the outer hull of this ship?" asked Tamaka of his two passengers. "It is designed to baffle various forms of wave detection including basic radar."

"I see. If I remember correctly, basic radar involves the sending of high frequency electromagnetic waves outward and if they encounter a solid object, they would be bounced back. The returning signal would be received and the object located."

"Very good, Mr. Conroi," said Tamaka. "In non-computerized mode, this ship also uses basic but I do not intend to use it as the SR1 has the ability to notice when it is being pinged."

"That's why you brought us out of the hyper-void so close to the SR1," said Mooney. "So you can guide us in visually."

"Exactly. You will notice the odd bump out at one end of the SR1? That will be the QED engine nacelle."

So saying, Tamaka began to guide the ship in that direction, the nitinol vessel slowly enlarging as they drew closer, the black maw of its engine port becoming more apparent, more seemingly sinister with their approach.

Mooney held her breath as their ship, now dwarfed by the size of the nitinol vessel, slipped into the engine chute occupied by the giant thruster portion of the QED, the aperture through which the beam of positive-negative matter would emerge, propelling the ship to interstellar speeds. She shuddered at the thought of what would happen if it should ignite at that very moment.

"Won't the SR1 notice a ship of this size entering its engine space?" she asked.

"Due to our extremely negative profile, we would appear to the SR1 as nothing more than a piece of cosmic dust," assured Tamaka as he carefully steered the ship into a space between the thruster and the wall of the engine chute. There, an indentation left a clear shelf space available where the ship could land.

"Will the ship be secure here?" asked Jules.

"We are essentially on a suicide mission," said Tamaka. "If the ship is still here when we are finished doing whatever it is we come up with, we can return here and use it to reach safety. However, do not count on that. Once the QED is ignited, there is little chance the ship will remain here unsecured as it is. The thrust of the engine will undoubtedly jostle it free and once it drifts into the path of the particle beam, it will be vaporized. As for the nitinol ship itself, it was not designed for a human crew and so does not have any control surfaces we can use to guide it back to Consortium space. That is, if our solution to the problem leaves the ship unharmed."

With those sobering words, Tamaka directed them to a locker at the rear of the bridge.

"I took these experimental 'suits from a laboratory in Brazilia," he said as he opened the locker and dragged out a spacesuit, handing it to Mooney. "They were designed for the military, allowing a man to move in a sensor rich environment without being detected. Like this ship, there are no computer systems aboard and as you can tell by touch, the material the skin of the 'suit is made of is wave absorbent. Luckily for us, the inside of the nitinol ship was not designed with the expectation it would be visited by anyone so it does not boast a complete range of sensors including motion or heat detectors."

"That'll come in handy," noted Mooney, stepping into the legs of her 'suit.

"Otherwise, these spacesuits operate in most regards like regulation 'suits," said Tamaka.

"Including comm channels?" asked Jules, accepting the next 'suit.

"There is only a single channel using radio clear so voice communications cannot be picked up by conventional means."

"Another assumption that no living being would ever find itself inside the nitinol ship?"

"Not an assumption, a fact."

"Let's hope so," said Mooney, just as she fastened the helmet to her ring collar. Next came engagement of the PE function that stiffened the 'suit, readying it for EVA. "How do I look?"

Jules surveyed her from inside his own helmet and gave her two thumbs up.

Slowly, they made their way down the ladder to the lower level and, taking extra precautions, used a hand crank to open the hatch to the airlock. Doing the same to the outer hatch, Tamaka led the way outside the ship and onto the shelf. He pointed toward a nearby opening in the smooth wall of the chute.

Clinging to whatever handholds they could find among the odd paneling of their ship, the trio pulled themselves along until they were able to push themselves into the opening which struck Jules as nothing more than a bodily orifice in some biological organism.

The tunnel system on the other side was not much different, resembling nothing more with the curvature of its walls and the sinewy nature of its windings than the human GI tract.

"The whole design in here strikes me as organic," said Mooney by way of testing her 'suit's comm channel.

"Just what I was thinking," agreed Jules.

"Simply the by-product of the ship's nitinol construction," explained Tamaka. "The nitinol was reduced to a liquid state under near normal gravity and then sprayed using industrial pressure tanks where needed. Once exposed to background temperatures of open space, its memory shape kicked in and it assumed the shape it was programmed for whether that was internal access tubes, control functions, even the makeup of the QED engine."

"What about these tunnels?" asked Mooney, somewhat out of breath trying to move herself along the featureless surfaces in zero g.

"Formed so that construction engineers could move about inside the ship before it was commissioned so to speak," said Tamaka. "They were never intended for use by a human crew."

"Do you know your way through them?"

"I do. Since there is nothing of interest to us in the rest of the ship, I am taking you directly to the hardcore chamber."

No one said anything after that, preferring to concentrate on moving forward in the zero G environment with Jules turning over ideas for how to deal with the SR1 once they reached it.

That moment came soon enough as Tamaka led them through an opening into a large chamber Jules judged to be at or near the center of the ship.

"Is that it?" asked Mooney, breaking the silence. "That's all it is?"

"Do not be so surprised," said Tamaka. "The SR1 redesigned itself a number of times since it first became self-aware."

They were standing in the presence of the hardcore, held securely above the flooring in a web of tractor beams. The physical housing of the SR1 personality, the receptacle, was needed to transport it to Coalition space where its own version of the cloud lay separate and isolated from that of the Consortium. But the hardcore itself was not as impressive as its power in the uber cloud or its plan for the galaxy would indicate. Fashioned from silicon, gold, zinc, and other metals, the SR1 incongruously hosted a CPU or central processing unit just like any ordinary computer interface. It was the power of that CPU coupled with whatever logic algorithms provided it by Tamaka and its ability to store information in self-replicating DNA strands that set it apart from static computers. The potential locked within that so simple looking two foot by two foot block of neural networking was literally limitless.

"What's that 3D display doing there?" said Mooney, breaking Jules' train of thought.

She indicated a three dimensional projection that hung in the air to one side of the hardcore. On it was a view of space but of a kind no one had ever seen before wherein the black between the stars was now white and the shine of stars were pinpoints of black.

Tamaka, for once, was momentarily speechless.

"The QED drive must have been engaged," guessed Jules. "We're traveling at interstellar speeds!"

"When did that happen?" asked Mooney. "I never felt a thing."

"The nature of the drive," said Jules. "Completely inertialess. The engines must have been fired while we were making our way through the tunnels."

"Of course," agreed Tamaka. "That must be it. The ship and its drive were built better than we ever dreamed!"

"But what about this projection?" Mooney wanted to know. "Why is it here? What does the SR1 need with it? Does it know we're here?"

"No. We are still invisible to the ship's sensors," replied Tamaka. "This projection is likely part of the SR1's continuing evolution toward becoming a new life form. It is trying to explore the world outside the uber cloud using its own senses just as humans do."

"My God!" gasped Jules. "If its plan to wipe out both the human race as well as those comprising the Coalition succeeds, there would be nothing to stop the SR1 from multiplying itself via its self-replicating DNA and becoming the new dominant species in the galaxy."

With that realization, even Professor Tamaka grew sober.

In the silence as they watched the black stars rushing past the borders of the projection, Mooney moved quietly to Jules' side and did her best within her clumsy 'suit to circle his waist with her arm. Instinctively, Jules responded, absently draping his own arm across his wife's shoulders.

For many minutes, they all simply stood and watched the projection until suddenly, the scene changed. The white field faded into black and the black pinpoints changed into the more familiar stars.

"What happened?" asked Mooney. "Have the engines stopped?"

"Must have," said Jules, looking back at the hardcore as if expecting to see some change in its attitude. There was none.

"Do you recognize any of the constellations?"

The stars were still rushing past but slower now as the ship apparently approached its destination. Soon, a planetary body came into view. A red giant.

"That one looks familiar," said Jules finally. "Judging by the look of it, I think that sun must be Amarindus."

"The home system of the Zhapoologani?"

"Right. Amarindus 2 must be closer in. But I'm just guessing. I can't be absolutely sure because the Consortium has never really mapped the Outer Arm and few battles during the war took place there."

"Well, I think the odds are you're right," said Mooney. "After all, we know that the SR1 intends to invade the Coalition's cloudspace. Where else would it go but its home world?"

"True enough. But if there's one thing I do know about the Amarindus system, it's that if strangers appear, it shouldn't take long before they get a reaction in force from the Zhapoologani."

No sooner were the words out of Jules' mouth than they proved correct.

As the ship moved past the red giant, the light of the distant sun revealed an armada of Coalition warships moving in attack formation.

"The home fleet," exclaimed Jules. "It must be! MI has guessed that never in the course of the whole war has it ever been mustered. Because once, a Consortium fleet came too close for comfort, the Zhapoologani always kept it in emergency reserve, guarding the home world."

It was an awesome sight. One Jules never saw during the war which was fought mainly by small unit forces in running battles. The fleet before them took the classic triangular Coalition formation, one favored by the Zhapoologani if not always by their allies, the Jovians, Drool, and Sangi. And so far as he could tell, there were none of the Coalition's junior partners here as heavy Delta class battlewagons anchored the corners of the triangle with light Alphas taking up the center. The rest was a mix of K-class cruisers and other ships all bristling with armament including the Coalition's main ion borers and cold fusion 'casters. Somewhere in reserve, Jules was sure, were the dreaded neutrino missile spreads that could broadside an opposing vessel with up to a dozen of the deadly projectiles.

"They don't look happy to see us," said Mooney, watching the spectacle.

"An understatement, that's for sure," replied Jules. "Wonder if they'll…"

Before he could finish what he was going to say, the nitinol ship rocked with the impact of a neutrino spread, an opening volley that at once declared the Coalition fleet meant business having no intention of going through any useless protocols involving hailing, trading warnings, and declaring the opening of hostilities.

But the opening salvo that would have disabled any other ship with a combination of direct hits like that, did the SR1 little damage it seemed. Or at least, not enough harm to slow it down or thwart its intentions.

Picking up speed, the nitinol ship surged forward, directly into the path of the home fleet.

"Professor, what about that broadside?" asked Mooney. "Did it do any damage?"

"I'm sure it did. But I am also sure the nitinol composition of the ship is even now repairing itself. In any case, it is very unlikely the enemy has anything that can reach this chamber. The hardcore is very well protected as instructions from the SR1 to Ultimate Chemistries were insistent upon."

"I hope you're right, Professor," said Jules, watching a series of flashes ignite from the bows of a number of Coalition vessels, "because this ship is in for a world of hurt in the next few minutes."

Even as he said it, another blast struck the ship somewhere, then another, and another. The enemy ion borers were doing their jobs as were the fleet's gunners as the ship was battered by a succession of hits that must have left the nitinol hull in shreds.

After that, it was the SR1's turn as the particle beam Mooney told him about lanced outward, slicing through the lead battlewagon like a hot knife through butter. The beam, however, was not slowed in its path through the enemy ship, it continued on, unabated, piercing a number of other ships ranged behind it. Even as Jules watched, awed by the power displayed by the beam, the halves of the hulled ships slowly drew apart, trailing their mechanical guts and fibers as well as the bodies of hapless crewmen. Interior lights winked out along the effected segments as power was lost and then secondary explosions pulverized the exposed decks tearing apart what was left of their innards.

Meanwhile, the brain of the SR1, moving at lightning speed, far faster than its mortal enemies could react, shifted its deadly beam at other targets, quickly finding and reducing the remaining battlewagons to slowly spreading chunks of useless metal and hardware. But while it was doing that, the smaller, peskier cruisers valiantly came forward, underneath the streak of the particle beam, firing all guns in the direction of their nitinol target.

Again, the ship rocked and rolled as it was struck by a variety of weapons, each seeking its vitals, and each failing. The fantastic design of the ship, with its material of nitinol and a honeycomb of redundant chambers and tunnels that managed to defray much of the impact of the strikes, was little damaged. Or at least, its most vital areas were left unharmed. As it was, Jules was shocked to see glimpses of open space through rents in the hull outside the hardcore chamber. More damage was being done to the ship than the nitinol memory could keep up with. So much so, Jules began to wonder if the heroic stand of the Zhapoologani would succeed in halting the menace of the SR1.

Just then, the Coalition ships disappeared from the projection as the nitinol ship passed through their formation. They reappeared after the ship reversed course and prepared for another run at its tormentors. Now there were clearly far fewer enemy vessels left. Half were gone, just metallic rubble and mortal jetsam strewn across a hundred thousand miles of space. Jules could only stand and admire the remainder as they valiantly regrouped to meet their foe again. And again, the battle was on, with the SR1's particle beam lashing out in every direction, this time flashing on and off in short bursts, picking its targets and eliminating them one by one until there were only a few left. And those once again slipped under the angle of the beam to strike the nitinol ship with a deadly wave of neutrino spreads. This time, the multiple impacts threw Jules to the deck along with Mooney and Tamaka. After that, there was silence as the projection showed the last badly damaged cruisers being carved into pieces by the ship's particle beam, a by-product of its QED engine.

Slowly, Jules regained his feet then helped Mooney to get up as well. Together, they went to the opening in the chamber wall where only an hour before they had entered from and found the tunnel on the other side ripped to tatters with open space yawning at their feet.

Mooney stumbled back, dizzy at the sight.

"My God! There's no way the ship can come back from damage like that," she exclaimed.

"It can," insisted Tamaka. "See? It is already repairing itself."

It was true. Even as they watched, the nitinol composition of the ship was in flux, flowing and reshaping itself, striving to recapture the memory shape its various pours had been programmed with.

"How long will it take for the ship to completely repair itself?" asked Mooney, fascinated.

Tamaka shrugged. "At the rate repairs are being made, I would guess between three and four hours."

Even as he spoke, the ship had not halted its progress. With nothing to impede it, the SR1 had continued on to its goal, which now loomed ahead; a moon, somewhat smaller than Earth's, that orbited a planet about three times as large.

"That would be Thebatislivikovo, the home world of the Zhapoologani," said Jules.

"Will it have any other defenses?" asked Mooney.

"I think the home fleet was largely it for long range defense. What's left must be strictly planetary in scale. We'll see them in action if the ship draws too close to Thebatislivikovo."

As if in response to Jules' speculations, the ship veered away from the home world to focus on its moonlet that now could be seen as having at least some kind of atmosphere.

"Where are we going?" wondered Mooney aloud.

No one spoke as the SR1 brought the ship into orbit on the far side of the little moon. Then it stopped, held in geosynchronous orbit above a particular spot. Back inside the hardcore chamber, the projection showed a close up of the moon's surface. It was craggy and uneven and barren except for one thing, a featureless, boxlike building. In the space around the building extending in every direction in a glowing web of light were thousands of shimmering threads that constantly wavered and danced in complex, ever shifting patterns.

"It's beautiful," said Mooney, awed. "But what are they?"

"Photonic beams," said Jules. "Lasers. That building must be the nexus for the Coalition's computer system, the basis for its own cloudspace. This is the goal the SR1 has traveled to the Outer Arm to find. The only reason we can see the display is due to the moon's atmosphere. Normally, photonic beams are invisible to the eye. They need to travel through some other medium where their reflection can be seen."

"Then that's why the beams fade out beyond the atmosphere," guessed Mooney.

"Right. The nexus must have been located here because the moon's thin atmosphere must have allowed the Zhapoologani to apply dry entropic properties to it, reducing moisture and making it an ideal environment for a likely self-sustaining system."

"Huh?"

"I agree," said Tamaka. "Such an environment would reduce to a minimum any need for maintenance. Likely, the nexus is completely automated."

"So, there's nobody down there?"

Jules nodded. "Which suits me fine."

"You have something in mind?"

"I've been thinking about it for a while now, but that sight down there convinced me we have a chance to stop the SR1 ... if we move fast."

"Why don't we just pull out a few wires and disable it?"

"Impossible," said Tamaka. "The hardcore includes multiple self-protective measures. I helped install them myself. That is, before I realized the danger."

"There's no need for trying anything so basic," said Jules, ignoring the professor's tardy concerns. "We can always try something more direct as a last resort."

"Well, if you have a better idea, you better get to it before the ship is finished repairing itself," observed Mooney. "Which begs the question, why hasn't the SR1 made its bid to enter the local cloudspace already?

What's it waiting for?"

"I have been thinking about that myself," admitted the professor. "I think, despite its growth, the SR1 is still operating in a linear fashion. It is taking on one thing at time. Repair itself first then move on with its plan."

"Or it's developed some very real human hubris."

"It's feeling self-confident?" said Jules. "Could be. If so, it's more human than we've so far given it credit for. A human weakness we can exploit right now."

So saying, Jules led the way back to the chamber opening. Outside, the tunnel they used to access the hardcore had been partially reformed, enough for them to make their way through back to the engine chute.

"We need to get back to Tamaka's ship," said Jules, working to release his 'suit's tether. He unreeled it from its storage compartment and hooked the end to an eye socket on Mooney's 'suit. "Do the same with yours for the professor."

After Mooney complied, Jules began to lead the way past rents in the fabric of the nitinol, making passage along the various tunnels and crawl spaces still a chancy thing. At last, Jules led them through the opening that gave onto the engine space where they left Tamaka's ship but were disappointed to find that it was gone.

"Well, it was a little too much to expect it would still be here," said Jules.

"You're taking it pretty calmly," scolded Mooney. "What do we do now? Go back and take that last resort you were talking about?"

"Assuming the ship would be gone, I've considered some alternatives," said Jules.

"Let's hear the most likely ones."

"Well, actually, there's only one."

"Ah, ha!"

"You're not going to like it."

"Naturally."

"We're going to skydive down to the moon's surface."

"You're right. I don't like."

"It's not as crazy as it sounds," said Jules. "We jump from here in the direction of the nexus. The moon's size indicates its pull is pretty light.

That, and its atmosphere should break our fall so we can safely land on the surface. If we need to, we can use our 'suits' positional thrusters to help slow us down."

"That's all?"

"Not game?"

"Are you kidding? Just stand aside."

"What about you, Professor? Are you coming with us?"

"The only question I have is what are we to do if whatever you have planned does not work? How do we return to try some other method of stopping the SR1?"

"Good question," said Mooney.

"The answer is, I'm as confident as I can be my plan will work but even if it doesn't, you've said yourself, professor, the hardcore's multiple defenses will make it unlikely direct action will be successful in stopping it."

"True."

"All right then," said Jules, "let's keep our tethers attached so we can assist each other if necessary and increase the chances of making landfall in the same place."

Making eye contact with Mooney and seeing her nod indicating readiness, Jules stepped to the edge of the engine chute where the nitinol fabric was slowly retaking its programmed shape, checked the location of the nexus below and jumped, dragging the others behind him.

# Chapter Seventeen
*End Game*

At first, Jules feared he'd miscalculated.

They were falling faster than he anticipated. If their rate of descent continued to accelerate, they'd be dashed on the moon's surface like bugs on a speedcar's windshield.

He was preparing to use his directional thruster and to tell the others to do the same when their rate of descent began to slow. If he hadn't been wearing a helmet, he would have slapped his head for his forgetfulness. When they jumped, they were above the moon's atmosphere, but now, hitting its outer fringes, it acted as a break and they began to slow.

Now, as the rugged surface of the moon came into focus through wisps of atmosphere, he could make out the big building housing the nexus. All around them danced the beams of photonic light transmitting encoded information to the farthest reaches of Zhapoologani space. Seeing the display, it was pressed upon his mind how powerful a tool controlling the resultant cloudspace would be for an entity determined to destroy two galactic civilizations.

"This is unbelievable," said Mooney over the 'suit comm. "The beams appear to be passing right through me."

"They are," replied Jules. "The photons are hardly bigger than the neutrinos our own sun throws out and that pass through the Earth with no friction at all."

Noting their rate of fall was well within safe limits, Jules decided to use his direction thruster to steer him in closer to the nexus. If they could land near it and save time in walking over that rugged terrain, all the better. Checking his 'suits' internal chronometer, he saw they had less than two hours before the ship completed repairing itself.

A three second burst from the thruster put him within three hundred feet of the nexus. Behind him, he could feel tension in his tether as the others were pulled along after him.

The ground below was coming up fast now as the distance lessened.

"Get ready," he warned the others. "Try and get your feet under you. These 'suits are tough but roomy inside, so you can still be hurt if you land the wrong way."

The ground came up with a rush as he hit the moon's rocky surface. Little dust was kicked up however as he was thrown forward with the force of his landing. When he recovered, he found his arms were partially bound by the tether that wound about him as he rolled.

"Take it easy," he heard Mooney say. "I'll get you out of that."

A few minutes later, they collected themselves and were making their way in the direction of the nexus building which, so far as Jules could tell, displayed no openings save for a pair of large sliding doors obviously intended for use by heavy equipment rather than ingress for solitary visitors.

"Doesn't look much like a happening place," said Mooney, taking in the lack of activity surrounding the building. "That is, besides that glow it's giving off."

The glow Mooney mentioned was the immediate emanation of photonic activity generated by the nexus before it was differentiated into individual beams as they drew away into the moon's atmosphere and on into all corners of the Coalition.

"Completely automated," said Jules of the silent structure. "Luckily for us. It'll mean we won't be disturbed while I work."

"What is it exactly that you have in mind?"

"Yes, Mr. Conroi," said Tamaka, "I am intrigued as to your plan."

"It's very simple, Professor. I intend to use this facility's laser functions to put an end to the SR1. And a very ironic end it will be too as the same beams it expected to piggy back into the Zhapoologani cloudspace will be the instruments of its destruction."

"I am intrigued. Please continue."

"As I'm sure you recall, non-equilibrium matter was first discovered early in the twenty-first century," Jules began. "What is commonly referred to as time crystals."

"Time crystals?" asked Mooney. "Anything I can wear around my neck?"

"Not these. Too small to see."

"Hmph."

"Anyway, the fascinating thing about non-equilibrium matter, or time crystals, is they oscillate between time and space but beyond their ground state, the zero point where matter stands stable unless some outside force sets it into motion. But with time crystals, that isn't so. Except for an initial nudge, they can oscillate forever without the need of any kind of additional energy input."

"As I recall, early tests involved ytterbium ions," recalled Tamaka as Jules' plan began to dawn on him.

"That's right," confirmed Jules. "A pair of lasers were used to set the ytterbium ions in motion, one to create a magnetic field and the other to 'flip' the spin of the ions. The ions then settled into a new but stable spin, a repetitive pattern that was later identified as the characteristics of a time crystal."

"I see, but that involved ytterbium…"

"Of course, but the key here is that follow-up testing using other elements had the same results. Elements such as titanium."

"Titanium! One of the key elements in the manufacture of nitinol."

"Exactly. What we have with the SR1 is a giant ball of titanium, an element susceptible to the time crystal phenomenon."

"You intend to excite the titanium atoms in the ship's nitinol composition so that the whole ship begins to oscillate in time?"

"Forever."

"But how? The early experiments you mentioned involved small amounts of matter with relatively weak lasers to excite it."

"Then we'll have to find lasers of commensurate power to use on our considerably larger target," said Jules, smiling.

"The nexus! Of course! But can you reconfigure them? Will there be enough power?"

"There's enough power here to broadcast an infinite number of beams across the length of Coalition space. Millions of light years in every direction. There's enough power all right."

"But the time," interjected Mooney. "Will you have enough time to figure out how the Zhapoologani computer system works? Remember, you said it operates on a completely different basis than ours."

"Science is science," said Jules. "Its laws are the same everywhere in the universe."

He didn't say anything more because really, even if basic principles were the same, the technology could be wholly different. But he'd cross that bridge when he came to it.

"Jules," said Mooney. "If your plan works and it stops the SR1 from taking over the Zhapoologani cloudspace, that still leaves it in control of the Consortium's uber cloud."

"Not without the hardcore to give it direction," replied Jules. "Remember, the SR1 is evolving into a new form of intelligent life. But cut off from that life, without direction, its presence in the uber cloud will freeze in place and eventually wither away, its essence dissipated into the myriad pathways of the data stream."

As they spoke, they continued to walk and now reached the big doors in the side of the squarish building.

"I don't see any way to get them to open," said Mooney, checking for motion or audio sensors. "Maybe—"

She was interrupted by the movement of the doors as they slowly, silently began to separate, revealing a darkened interior.

"I spoke too soon, I guess."

"Proximity sensors."

When the doors opened far enough, they ventured in. As they did so, lights came on, illuminating the vast interior which was filled by a massive machine of some kind from which heavy conduits snaked at the top and through apertures in the ceiling.

"It's a giant battery generating electromagnetic power for the lasers," explained Jules. "Those conduits connect to projectors on the next level that create the encoded photons we saw outside in the form of light beams. The SR1 is looking to piggy back on one of those beams and ride it into the cloudspace. However, use of the same kind of beam could also destroy it. So, what we need to do is to get there first. We need to repurpose and redirect those beams toward the SR1 to get a reaction from the titanium in the nitinol surrounding it and turning the whole ship into a giant time crystal."

"That's all?"

"Start looking around for anything that looks like a control surface for direct human to machine interface," said Jules by way of reply.

"I think I've got something over here," said Mooney, after the three spent some minutes scrambling about the building trying to recognize familiar equipment among the Zhapoologani tech.

"It looks right," said Jules uncertainly. "Can you read those symbols?" *Science is science*, thought Jules.

He was sure he could work the technology of the nexus to make it do what he wanted but the labeling identifying the machinery and the terminology used in the computer displays was another thing. He had no facility with the Zhapoologani language. Luckily, however, there was someone with him who did. Though she had been an agent for the Exterior Ministry at one time, Mooney had to have some knowledge of languages to make a convincing cover as a secretary to the minister including Zhapoologani. That and having an eidetic memory wasn't bad either.

"My Zhapoologani is rusty but unless I miss my guess, this is what you're looking for," said Mooney.

From a bank of input nodes, she took one and pulled it out from its slot, unreeling an extension cord behind it.

"This universal should fit in one of the outlets in our sleeve units," said Mooney. "With the feed connected, you can access the computer that runs this place and interface with it via projection inside your helmet."

"Will the projection use universal or local symbology?"

"It'll use Zhapoologani."

"No good. I wouldn't understand what I'm looking at. You'll have to use it while I guide you through the operation."

"Will that be something like me doing to the operating while you tell me where to put the scalpel?"

"Something like that."

"Then I have a better idea." Instead of using the universal, Mooney let it respool back to its slot and took another from the bank. This one she plugged into one of her 'suit outlets. She said something in what Jules recognized as Zhapoologani and immediately, a colored coded projection leaped into life in the air before them. "What do you think? Can you work from it?"

"Good work, 'Manda," said a delighted Jules by way of reply. "Professor Tamaka, are you familiar at all with this symbology?"

"I am afraid not. You are on your own at this point."

"Okay. Then why don't you go over by the doors and keep an eye out for any activity from the home world. I have a feeling we'll be having company soon. I only hope they don't show up until we're finished here. 'Manda, get me the schematics for the basic photonic functions."

The projection flickered briefly and what Jules judged to be the proper schematics turned up.

"Okay. Now fill me in on the meanings of those symbols."

Even to Jules' unpracticed eye, most of the symbols were easy to figure out based on their location on the schematics but others were a puzzle. He needed to be sure of all of their meanings before he dared proceed in reconfiguring the pulse frequencies of the lasers used by the Zhapoologani system, because he'd have time for only one try at his plan. Already, according to his 'suit chronometer, there was barely a half hour left before the SR1 completed its repairs.

"Okay," said Jules, taking a deep breath. "What we need to do is reconfigure the system's multiple beam pattern into just two. We'll reroute the power through the main conduits, combining it into two lasers."

"Will the existing conduits be strong enough to contain that much power before melting down or something?" asked Mooney in between translating the symbols on the projection as they drifted here and there in accordance to changes in the power flux of the projectors.

Jules nodded. "They should last long enough for what we want to do."

"Won't the Zhapoologani data system go dark then?"

"It will."

"They won't be happy about that," warned Mooney.

"To put it mildly." Jules realized how much both the Terran and Zhapoologani civilizations had become dependent on the power of computers. Any disruption of those conveniences was bound to cause confusion, panic, anger. "The welcoming party I'm expecting won't be in a very good mood when they get here. You'll have to do some fast talking to keep us from being killed."

"Oh, thanks!"

The next few minutes were taken up with Mooney working with the projection to move around the symbols representing ongoing functions of the nexus and reconfiguring the beam patterns to the two needed by Jules.

"All right," breathed Jules when the first part of the operation had been completed. "Now we have just two beams ready to go. But first, we have to redirect the projectors from universal coverage to narrow beam."

"Done," said Mooney after a few minutes of quiet direction from Jules. "They're aimed at the SR1. Good thing it's in geo orbit, otherwise it would have been a nightmare to keep the projectors on target while it was moving."

Jules said nothing. The moment was at hand. The first laser beam, accessing the same incredible power that had been used to project logic gates across a whole arm of the galaxy, would now drive that same concentrated energy directly at the SR1. The question was, could the beam capture the ship in a magnetic field strong enough and fast enough to prevent the lightning swift thinking power of the computer from lashing out with a defensive blast of its particle beam? On the other hand, the beauty of the situation was that the SR1 could not defend itself from the beam without destroying the nexus and foil its own plan to take over the Zhapoologani cloudspace. The question was, would it choose self-preservation over completion of its own plan?

"Let's not waste any more time," said Jules, finally. "Fire!"

Mooney gave the projection the order, the Zhapoologani words coming from her mouth alien and harsh, *entirely fitting,* thought Jules, for the violence to be done to the SR1 almost in the same breath as the words were spoken.

There was no sense of movement within the nexus, no rise in hum from the giant battery. If they had been outside, they would have seen a single beam of light reflected in the molecules of the moon's thin atmosphere as it leaped toward the spacecraft orbiting overhead. The only way they would know if they had been successful or not was if the nexus and themselves had been obliterated in a retaliatory strike by the SR1's particle beam.

They were not.

Imagining the SR1 held in the grip of the paralyzing magnetic field, Jules breathed a sigh of relief and quickly ordered Mooney to fire the second laser.

Again, the strange syllables of the Zhapoologani language left her lips and again, a projector overhead sent a second beam in the direction of the SR1.

Jules could only imagine what was happening at that moment. Held in an electromagnetic field generated by all the power of the nexus, the ship holding the SR1 was helpless to avoid the second beam. That beam, striking its nitinol composition, would excite the material's titanium atoms, entangling them and leaving them in a permanent, repetitive pattern of spin, jumping back and forth forever between space and time. Somewhere overhead, the unstoppable nitinol ship was converted into a giant time crystal, caught forever between the two states and helpless to ever stop the process. The SR1 was trapped, invisible and unattainable by anyone or anything in this universe. Gone forever.

Amid the silence all around them, with the lack of a dramatic explosion to mark the end, it all struck Jules as rather anticlimactic.

"Is it over?" asked Mooney, moving her eyes over the building's ceiling as if to see through out into space. "It's kind of hard to tell."

"If it wasn't, we wouldn't be here," replied Jules, wishing he could wipe his forehead through his space helmet. "If that first beam holding the ship in the electromagnetic field was any weaker, the SR1 would have hit back hard."

"You think it would have done that and ruined the nexus?"

Jules nodded. "I'm afraid so. It was evolving. Growing. Growing into a new life form but one that still shared one basic emotion with all other living creatures, self-preservation. It would have destroyed the nexus and us if its survival was at stake."

"Brrr," shivered Mooney at the close call.

Jules reached out and as best he could within the confines of the clumsy 'suit, embraced Mooney in a comforting hug.

"You know, that's twice now we've saved the whole universe?" observed Mooney when the moment had passed. "Leclerc really owes us!"

For the first time in days, Jules laughed and the sudden release of tension felt oh so good.

"Congratulations, Mr. Conroi," Tamaka's voice broke over the 'suit comms. "And do you realize the irony of the situation? It was the SR1 that first brought you to my attention. It correctly identified you as its single greatest threat prompting me to recruit you in helping me to stop my creation."

"Interesting," said Jules. "That, however, does not preclude me from delivering you over to the proper authorities, Professor. After all, you did break the law in embarking on your research into artificial intelligence."

"I am prepared to submit myself to the courts," said Tamaka philosophically. "I will admit to them I was wrong. The laws, in this case, were right."

"Glad to hear it, Professor."

"In the meantime, however, I think my appointment with the legal establishment might be postponed. There is a ship of unfamiliar design coming in for a landing."

"That'll be our Zhapoologani hosts," said Jules.

"You don't sound worried," noted Mooney.

"I ordered the *Gethsemani* to track us from outside sensor range so we should have a ride home waiting for us," revealed Jules.

"Nice, but what good will that do us with the Zhapoologani outside and likely mad as hornets that they've been shut out of their cloudspace?"

"You speak a little Zhapoologani don't you?"

"You expect me to talk us out of this?"

"Naturally. Hope you've been thinking about what you're going to tell them?"

"As a matter of fact, I have," replied Mooney mischievously. "I'm going to tell them we're on our honeymoon!"

# About the Author

Pierre V. Comtois has been the editor and publisher of *Fungi, the Magazine of Fantasy and Weird Fiction* since 1984 and has had a number of books released by numerous publishers including *Goat Mother and Others* by Chaosium Fiction in 2015, *A Well Ordered Universe* by Desert Breeze Publishers in 2016, and *Marvel Comics in the 1980s: An Issue by Issue Field Guide to a Pop Culture Phenomenon* by Twomorrows Pubs in 2015. More recent releases include *Scheduled for Extinction*, a science fiction novel from Desert Breeze and *Talismanic,* a horror novel from Rogue Phoenix Press. Comtois has contributed fiction to many small press magazines over the years including various Chaosium Books anthologies. The author has also written a number of other books including novels such as *Strange Company* and *Sometimes a Warm Rain Falls*; non-fiction such as *Our Lives, Our Fortunes, Our Sacred Honor*; and short story collections such as *The Way the Future Was* and *The Portable Pierre V. Comtois*. Comtois has also found the time to contribute non-fiction articles to such magazines as *World War II, America's Civil War, Wild West,* and *Military History*, many of which were collected in *Hazardous History*. For more information visit www.pierrevcomtois.com.

*Extra Galaxia*
Science Agents #1

Science Agent Jules Santros has two problems: he has to save the universe and avoid falling for beautiful 'Manda Mooney, sometime secretary for the Terran Consortium's Exterior Ministry but actually a secret operative with orders to keep him under surveillance. On assignment from Military Intelligence, Science Division, Jules is on the trail of a group of renegade scientists that plan on using dangerous black hole technology to tip the balance in Earth's war against the Outer Arm Coalition. Only thing is, use of such banned tech will set off an interstellar chain reaction that could consume the entire galaxy! Now, follow Jules and 'Manda as they team up and travel beyond known space to catch the conspirators and prevent Terran defeat in its war with the Coalition!

# Chapter One
*Plans Go Astray*

"Rise and shine, you lovebirds!" called Finley in a voice deliberately calculated to drive Jules Santros crazy.

Hard rapping on the cabin door.

"You guys in there?" asked Finley, no doubt with a smirk on his face. "Honeymoon's over and ole Sol's waiting. We'll be in Mars orbit in three standard hours."

Jules tossed off the thin bed sheet and rolled from the bunk, inadvertently leaving Joan to shiver in the cool, air-conditioned cabin.

"Hey, buster." she said, grabbing for the sheet. "It's positively frigid in here."

"Who's frigid?" asked Finley from the other side of the door.

Growling, Jules staggered across the small cabin and hit the door controls. The panel slid open a crack, just enough to reveal Finley leaping away and out of reach.

"Can't a man and his wife get some sleep around here?" asked Jules in mock seriousness.

"Oh, is that what you were doing? Shucks. Thought I was interrupting something."

"You still smarting from that time I caught you and Pris—?

"Don't start that again. And don't you dare breath a word about it to those rumor mongers at Marsport!"

"Then go away and stop bothering us."

"Tell Pris we'll be out in twenty minutes, Finley," called Joan from where she still huddled in the bunk.

"Thanks, Joan. At least someone around here is taking things seriously."

"Get lost, you spoiler," said Jules, hitting the control button.

The door panel barely slid closed before he was back under the covers and reaching for his wife.

"Hey, didn't you hear Finley? We're wanted on deck."

"You told him twenty minutes," protested Jules, pulling Joan close.

"Well, it's going to take most of that time for me to get presentable."

"Then you'd better get a move on," replied Jules playfully, throwing off the sheet for the second time and herding Joan out of the bunk by way of a slap on her bottom.

~ * ~

Precisely twenty minutes later, Joan stepped into the control deck where Pris Gower sat in the navigator's chair. Across the confined space, grown suddenly more crowded with the appearance of the extra crew member, Finley was doing something over at the atmospherics panel.

It did not escape Joan's notice.

"So, it was you brought down the temp in our cabin." she said, propping her fists on her hips.

"I cannot tell a lie," confessed Finley, slinking back to the pilot's position.

"I can't believe he still thinks that's funny," said Joan looking over at Pris. "It was freezing in there last sleep period. I couldn't keep Jules away from me the whole time."

Pris shrugged. "Men. They never grow up."

"C'mon, Pris. With only a few hours left till we reach Mars, there won't be time to have any fun before this mission is officially over."

Joan softened. It was true. Six months ago, the Interplanetary Geological Survey teamed up she and Jules with fellow husband and wife team Finley and Pris Gower, pilot and navigator of the deep space survey ship *E.R. Burroughs* to explore a chain of worlds in the Cygnus system. As a xeno-geologist, Joan was more than excited when they came across Cygnus Alpha 12, a planet completely covered by a sea of liquid methane. At the very least, it promised quite a diversity of life forms in such an unusual environment. She didn't know how diverse until she and Jules stumbled across a downed Coalition warship with some troopers still alive and determined to kill them. They'd managed to turn the tables on the troopers only to find out that the crashed ship had used some kind of dangerous new black hole technology Jules recognized as something the Consortium had experimented with and decided not to pursue.

It'd been touch and go for a while there as the still active forbidden tech threatened to get out of control...Jules even said it endangered all space-time. Joan wasn't sure about that but was sufficiently frightened by the experience to be relieved when they returned to their friends aboard ship. After their return, she filed her report with the Survey and thought that would be the end of it. She'd almost forgotten that Jules retired from Military Intelligence and old habits die hard. As it turned out, he'd filed his own report to former colleagues and whatever he wrote must have set off alarm bells because the next thing they knew, the *E.R. Burroughs* had been ordered to cancel the remainder of its tour and return to Mars immediately.

"What's our ETA, Pris?" asked Jules, appearing in the control room hatchway.

"Just under two point forty hours," replied Pris. "Have to admit, you guys can be pretty efficient when you want to be."

"I only need five minutes, it's Joan who takes up all the time," said Jules with a wink.

"I could cut that time in half if I didn't have to constantly fight off your advances," said Joan, punching Jules in the stomach with her fist.

"Ouch," laughed Finley from where he was scaling down the boosters.

"That message we received to turn back sounded serious," said Pris without turning her attention from the instruments. The approach to Mars with its two moons was tricky even for the best navigators.

Jules recognized the note of curiosity in the statement and was genuinely sorry he couldn't fill in she and Finley more than what they already knew...which was not much. He'd warned Joan to say as little as possible about what happened on Cygnus Alpha 12. Knowing they'd have to tell their partners something, they told them about the downed ship and the attack by the troopers, including their escape from them. Nothing about the black hole tech or the near catastrophe that had faced the entire galaxy that he'd barely averted.

"Military Intelligence takes everything seriously," replied Jules cautiously. "We did find a Coalition ship after all. You can't blame them for wanting to know all about it."

"Think they'll be sending a salvage operation to recover the wreck?" asked Finley.

"Possibly...or a demo team."

"Wonder how it ended up way out there in the first place?"

"Your guess is as good as mine. Up to no good, that's for sure."

The Terran Consortium had been at war with the Outer Arm Coalition off and on for over fifty Earth years, having come in contact with it when a survey vehicle similar to the *E.R. Burroughs* encountered an advanced colony of a subject people deep in the newly discovered Atullun Nexus. It was fired upon without any warning and managed to limp back to Altair IV with the story. After that, the Consortium dispatched a task force to the Nexus to chastise the colony but ended up tangling with a Coalition battle fleet instead. Luckily, the enemy had no idea of the power of Mark IX photon pulse cannons and had the worst of the fight. It was not to be the last anyone heard of them. The war was one marked by a number of deep space skirmishes and full-scale battles numbering over a dozen in the decades since with neither side getting the upper hand. And though Consortium strategists had no doubt that they would end up the ultimate victor, it was not going to be a cake walk.

Time passed all too quickly until finally the *E.R. Burroughs* received clearance from Marsport and Pris calculated a course that would take the ship in by Deimos before slinging around to the planet's equator. From there, it was a simple affair for the experienced Finley to cut the boosters and allow the ship to slowly descend, using Mars' thin atmosphere as a brake.

"What it amounts to is a controlled fall," explained Finley as atmospheric condensation streaked the forward view ports. Suddenly, the wispy cloud formations gave way and the red and pink soil of the dusty planet loomed ahead of them.

As the ship continued to slacken speed by use of its belly thrusters, the green of cultivated areas, irrigated by waters located beneath the poles, came into view. In another few minutes they came within sight of Marsport, its multiple bubble domes gleaming in the weak sunlight.

Finley pulled back on the cyclical and the *E.R. Burroughs* pulled up, coming to a hovering stop over a scorched landing pad. In a matter of seconds, he had the survey ship on solid ground and cut the whine of the thrusters.

"Welcome to Marsport," he said.

**VISIT OUR WEBSITE
FOR THE FULL INVENTORY
OF QUALITY BOOKS:**

*http://www.roguephoenixpress.com*

*Rogue Phoenix Press*

Representing Excellence in Publishing

*Quality trade paperbacks and downloads
in multiple formats,
in genres ranging from historical to contemporary romance,
mystery and science fiction.
Visit the website then bookmark it.
We add new titles each month!*

www.ingramcontent.com/pod-product-compliance
Lightning Source LLC
Chambersburg PA
CBHW060149130626
46556CB00006B/2567